I0731167

REFRAIN

BEAUTIFUL MONSTERS BOOK #2

LANA SKY

CADENCE

A BEAUTIFUL MONSTERS NOVELLA

LOVE AND
REVENGE GO
HAND IN HAND

CADENCE

A Beautiful Monsters NOVELLA

LANA SKY

Cover Design by Cover Couture
Editing by Erica Russikoff
Formatting by Charity Chimni
Proofreading by Charity Chimni and Mickey Reed Editing

A BEAUTIFUL MONSTERS NOVELLA
DANNY

My parents claimed that heaven is beautiful. Peaceful. Divine. But, unlike them, I don't put much stock in antiquated notions anymore. I've learned my lesson the hard way. Places, no matter how sacred, can always burn to the ground.

People are far more resilient, collecting damage over their battered souls like trophies. Put two such creatures together, and they become like magnets. Clinging. Inseparable. Here and now, with this man inside me, I'm unreachable. For a second. Maybe two. The real world can't touch us until we decide to let it.

Settling onto his back, he groans in that unsettling way that makes my toes curl into the sheets. It's partly sated, partly pissed. He's frowning, even as I face him and run my fingers over his chest, delicately tracing the swath of tattoos adorning it. The caress doesn't soften his expression. No, apparently sex can't erase the darkness in his mind for long. Darkness I carved there with desperate, selfish strokes.

"You sure about this?" he grunts without looking at me, denying me that contact I crave. His gaze stubbornly fixates on the ceiling as I lower my head and press my lips to his chest. My Lucifer. He's warm. Like fire. Like hell.

I can't resist swiping my tongue against him, and I wind up tasting salt.

Rather than answer his question, I slide my thigh over his hip and mount him completely. He hisses when I do, automatically palming my waist as I straddle his hips. His crudely bitten lip conveys a statement he doesn't voice out loud. *No fair.* He's semi-hard already, stirring against my lower back. One swipe of my fingers along the tip has him shuddering beneath me, and my sly grin offers a nonverbal rebuttal. *All is fair in war.*

It's cruel to tease, but desperate times call for desperate measures. I seek out his gaze—ruthlessly. Shamelessly. I watch the pleasure unfold across both indigo irises as I palm him, forming a fist in a series of quick, sure strokes. His eyes narrow, but rather than protest, he tilts his head back and braces his hands against the mattress. Resigned. Emboldened.

Think you can break me? Do it, then.

Dare accepted. My hair falls forward, across my face, as I lean down, bringing my lips as close to his as I dare. My right arm contorts against my back, my fingers still wrapped around him. Each stroke elicits a reaction he can't hide, even as his gaze eyes me defiantly.

My Lucifer. He'll never ever let me watch him fall. He prefers to drag me down with him. When I least expect it, one of his hands captures my hip, the callused fingers biting deep. Painfully. I do my best to bite back the moan building in my throat as his thumb begins a dangerous path toward my inner thigh. He chuckles at what he finds there—slick wetness. My body betrays me almost as eagerly as his does —not that either of us surrenders.

We fight fire with fire. Months of exploring him have armed me with ample knowledge to exploit. His neck is his sweet spot, a rare weakness. One swipe of my tongue and he tightens his grip on me in retaliation. A nip of his jugular between my teeth draws out a growl.

But as well as I've come to know him, he knows me better. Always. His fingers find that secret, sweet place inside me that makes every thought…

Disintegrate.

The next second, I'm on my back. He's on top of me, marking his ownership by seizing my lips. He's already staked his claim over my soul. My body.

But there is one part of me we both know he'll never be able to claim. No matter how much I wish he could.

My mind is a corroded, warped lock box and no one has the key.

Not even I do.

"I could go alone?" I croak out against his mouth the moment his cock teases my entrance.

His eyes are blue fire as he braces his weight over one hand while the other guides the head of himself inside me. One thrust doesn't sheath him the entire way, and the aching fullness draws out a cry I can't suppress.

Oops. These walls are paper-thin, and I suspect that the manager is already close to kicking us out after one damn night. Still…

He starts to thrust in earnest, and the pathetic whimpers deepen into full-throated moans. I can't help it. He plays me like an instrument, manipulating the remaining shreds of my sanity. Our melody is a beautiful sound—wet skin rasping over skin mixed with intermittent gasps. But my tainted thoughts form a chorus, impossible to smother.

Through gritted teeth, I add, "I'll go alone."

He says nothing, thrusting a slow, steady rhythm until I can't say a damn thing. My body copies his pace, hips arching into each thrust. Hard. Harsher. Harshest.

God, he feels so good—I'll never get over that. Good the way salt does when ground into a wound. Painful. Burning. Sinful.

All I can do is savor. His skin. His mouth on my throat. His teeth delivering a searing tit-for-tat along my neckline, avenging my earlier assault. He's vicious. I'm vengeful.

The next minute, I'm on top of him again, raking my nails down his chest, feeling the skin relent in their wake. "I'll go alone," I tell him, panting out the words as my body continues to rock on him. Back. Forth. Slow. Fast.

A curse revs up in his throat, ripping from him seconds before I feel him buck against me and grind out his release. Then his head falls back, his eyes drifting shut in bliss. My appreciative sigh disrupts loose strands of my hair. I rarely get to savor him like this. It's surprisingly overwhelming, watching my devil revel in the feel of me.

It doesn't last long though. Without warning, he shifts his weight, throwing me off. Instinct spurs my body into motion, and I wind up on my knees, clutching the end of the mattress for balance.

"Like hell you are."

The bed creaks on its flimsy frame, and I turn my head just in time to see him climb to his feet. Another sigh escapes me. Light plays off the gold in his skin, enhancing the shadowy lines of each tattoo. He's shaking, still riding the high of me. Without looking back, he pads to the corner of the dingy suite and fishes his jeans from the floor. After he gets them fastened, he stoops for another article of clothing and tosses it back to me.

"Let's go."

The abrupt change of heart isn't worth challenging. Instead, I savor the victory and snatch up the shirt he threw to me. It's one of his—my wardrobe staple lately. The gray cotton reeks of him—sweat, cologne, and that rare spice his skin emanates. It's potent enough to distract me from the fact that, once again, I've manipulated him into doing my bidding. Not that he'll ever call me out on it.

And he should.

Vinny always told me that I was selfish in the rare moments I felt brave enough to challenge him. *"You only care about yourself, Daniela."* But that's the irony my old tormentor didn't live long enough to realize. The more I care about someone, the tighter I cling to them. The more I suffocate them. Even the devil isn't immune. Dark circles haunt the skin around his eyes as he pulls another shirt on and heads for the door.

"Wait…"

He stiffens at the sound of my voice. It's funny how we can communicate so well in frantic touches and hushed groans —but not like this. Out loud, spoken into the air with no sheets to smother the truth into.

"Have you talked to Espi?"

Guilt eats through the delicious aftermath of Dante. His brother is a sore topic we both avoid, like an open wound. Espi—sweet, kind Espi. I stole his brother away without a word of explanation. Does he hate me?

I would.

"No," Dante says. His guttural tone draws an invisible line in the sand I instinctively heed. *Not now.*

Letting the topic go, I climb off the bed, and we pack up what little we've brought between the two of us. After five years spent trapped in one place, I'm awed by this newfound sense of wanderlust. The devil doesn't seem to mind it though. He snatches up the ratty duffel we've been sharing and crams our meager belongings inside it. A toothbrush, a handful of clothes, and a wad of cash fished from underneath the mattress.

Along with something else. It's small and misshapen. A trash bag? He withdraws something from it, and it's black, slinky...

A dress?

Something glaringly out of place in a motel room that smells like piss and rotting garbage. He must have hidden it when I wasn't watching. The price tag is still on it, and I suspect, even before he holds it up, that it's my size. Small, cut modestly, with a dangerously low neckline.

I can't escape the comparison that flits across my skull —*Vinny never would have picked out something so daring*. To him, I was an object to be jealously guarded, but the devil seems to think the opposite.

"If you want to do this, then you need to look the fucking part." His expression is stern as he holds the dress out to me, but I know him too well. He watches avidly as I curl my fingers around the surprisingly soft fabric.

It's expensive, and given how little money we have between us, he must have scrounged the amount up on his own.

Does that alarm me? Maybe. Secrets never bode well. At the same time...

We're both selfish creatures at heart, still learning how to share. His eyes narrow as I take a step toward him and raise both hands above my head.

"Help me put it on."

He muscles in closer, snagging the hem of my shirt in his fists. The background noise of sirens and traffic fades to a hum as he strips me bare right here in front of the window, for any passerby to see. Not that I care if we are being watched.

His endless gaze swallows me whole. His nearness alone is a prison more confining than any Vinny could have ever devised. Maybe because I don't want to escape it... I could stay here for an eternity, just watching him watch me. Those cold eyes reveal nothing. I have to feel what he's thinking; even his touch holds a predatory efficiency. Without a care for the waste, he bunches his old shirt up and tosses it toward the small wastebasket. My new dress slides easily over my head, falling down to my knees. I move to take the shorts off myself, but he beats me to it, hiking the hem up to wrap his fingers around the waistband. One tug. Two. He doesn't shy away from grinding his callused fingertips into my skin with every inch he frees from the confines. When the garment finally strikes the floor, I step out of it.

"Thank you," I say, smoothing my hands along the soft fabric.

He frowns, insulted by my gratitude. I don't think he's used to it yet. Luckily, there is one language he appreciates beyond simple words.

Coiled, tense muscle ripples beneath my fingers as I run my hand along the length of his arm. The motion draws him in closer, his eyes drifting down to admire the skin bared beneath the neckline of his gift. When our gazes reconnect, he leans in, and our lips meet. Soft. Gently. Violently. We can never play nicely for very long.

Sure enough, teeth come out to play seconds into the kiss. He nips my lower lip, hard enough to sting, as one of his hands fists in my hair, holding me steady. His tongue grinds against mine, erasing all traces of my thanks. Just when I start to push back, he pulls away, swiping at his mouth with the back of his hand.

"Let's go," he tells me, jerking his chin toward the door.

I follow him, running my hand along my hip to smooth the dress. He's right. I catch sight of myself in the bathroom mirror and have to admit—I look the part. The dress hugs my body. *Obscene,* Vinny would have said. My hair hangs wildly around my shoulders, barely grazing my chin. I noticed the dark circles around Dante's eyes, but mine sport the same. Together, we both look the part—fallen demons scrounging around hell.

Ready to conquer the whole damn thing.

"Come on." He tugs on my wrist, pulling me along once again.

Together, we enter the hallway and leave the motel. The shadow of the massive buildings that tower around us blocks out most of the daylight. He picked this spot for its close proximity to the heart of the city. A hellish mecca where criminals lord over their subjects.

For all of his hesitation before, he doesn't falter a single step as he turns down an alley, dragging me behind him by my wrist. In a dizzying rush, we skirt the bustling traffic of the main street in favor of the shadows. He seems to dwell within them, my Lucifer. Darkness enhances the ebony in his hair as it fans across his face, obscuring those searing eyes.

I fall into step behind him, eyeing his broad shoulders, which are straining against the cotton of his shirt. His grip tightens, keeping me tethered to his side without my having to say a word. The action reassures me more than I'd like. What feels like an eternity ago, music was my refuge—not a person. Not someone so unreachable that, at times, it really does feel like he's not human. Someone who knows me better than I'd like. We cling to each other, using our limbs like a leash. Which one of us really owns the other?

Who knows?

All that matters is the danger awaiting both of us at the end of the short trip to the heart of this rundown district. It's deserted here. At the same time, the hair on the back of my neck rises on end with every step we take. It's the same feeling I stomached during the years spent in Vinny's suite.

Someone is watching me.

"From the left," Dante mutters. He stiffens at the hint of danger in the air.

The danger I willingly led us into.

My steps quicken, which draws me to his side. I cock my head just enough for my voice to reach him. "Do you have…"

He doesn't even have to answer. His right hand goes to his hip, brushing the bulge of a gun. Of course, he's armed.

So am I, admittedly in a very different way than he is. We guard our respective weapons closely, waiting until the last possible second before…

It happens fast. Two men appear from an alley up ahead. They're dressed simply, shrouded in black hoodies and jeans. But I know the look in their eyes. I see it every day in the mirror—hunger. Hunger for power. Hunger for revenge.

"You're late." The speaker lingers beyond the mouth of the warehouse, just beyond sight. His voice is gruff. Familiar, though I've only heard it once before. A face comes to mind regardless. Dark, beady eyes. Short, graying black hair. His name is something long and Italian in origin. Vinny used to just call him Fitz.

He's low-level. Someone Vinny used to call a "pusher." A common thug who worked the streets, clearing the route for whatever drugs or women Vinny wanted to sell. They used to call him a mutt, a term that might be fitting, all things considered.

Where else does a mutt belong but a junkyard?

The air here reeks. Not even the breeze blowing off the wharf can dispel it. The closer I stand to Dante, the less the stink can reach me. But not even the devil can shield me from the worst of his realm.

"Are you ready for this, princess?" Fitz asks, his tone mocking but cautious. His posture straddles the thin line between wary and eager. "Once you fuck with the Russians, there is no going back. They'll be out for blood."

The Russians. A syndicate with an iron-like grip on the sex trade—and other illegal operations flooding the city with vice. Vinny considered them cherished business partners once.

Now? They're the first on my list.

"I'm more than ready," I say, surprised by how fiercely my voice comes out. "Are you?"

The men gathered around me share guarded looks and then nod.

"Good." I hold my hand out, empowered by my new dress and the creature standing beside me. "Then give me a gun."

After all, if I'm to destroy my old captor's world, I have to enter the flames.

REFRAIN

BEAUTIFUL MONSTERS BOOK #2

REFRAIN

A BEAUTIFUL MONSTERS NOVEL

LANA SKY

Editing by Erica Russikoff
Formatting by Charity Chimni
Proofreading by Charity Chimni and Mickey Reed Editing

CHAPTER ONE
ESPI

TWO HUNDRED DOLLARS. WHO WOULD HAVE THOUGHT you could put a price on one's soul? But, the four crumpled bills lying at the bottom of my med kit are proof enough of the bargain basement price of mine.

Was it worth it? Maybe not. So much for buying a plane ticket out of here any time soon—Hell, I'll be lucky to afford my rent next month. I just hope my landlord accepts blood money. Literally. Red drops splatter across everything in my kit as I toss a pair of tweezers onto the top rack and slam the lid down.

"Here." The punk beside me shoves another wad of cash into my hand, which I don't bother counting. Tattoos streak his fingers, marking him as a gangbanger, though I'm not sure where from. That's probably a good thing. "Man, thanks. You don't even—"

"Don't mention it," I say over him, rising to my feet. "Seriously." The way I cut my gaze in his direction makes him back up a step. "Don't."

I sidestep the only other person in the room—a man moaning on a cot set up at the back of a narrow apartment. The place is a mess. Old takeout everywhere and lines of coke in plain view on the plastic card table that serves as one of the few pieces of furniture. It's a stash house, picked more for its obscure location by the docks than anything pretty.

"The stitches need to come out in ten days," I tell the man beside me on my way to the door.

Whether he listens or not doesn't really matter. My payment only extends so far. For some reason, I find myself pausing near the door anyway to fish my cell phone from my pocket. A message waits for me, floating on the screen. It's from Arno.

Don't forget. Moe's tonight. Keep him guessing. I'll pay double.

Great.

I swipe the text aside and rattle my number off to the punk watching me. "Give me a call," I say. "The price is the same."

"Thanks, man."

That word haunts me as I leave the apartment building and step out onto the street. *Thanks.* A small consolation considering that the guy on the cot has a gunshot wound the size of a nickel. Chances are he didn't get that injury from a harmless accident, and the remaining possibilities aren't that innocent. An ambush by a rival gang? The police? Maybe he was one of the punks featured on the news last week who held a family captive or robbed that liquor store. He probably got what was coming to him.

I didn't ask.

I never do.

I never dwell, either. Instead, I smother the guilt with a lit cigarette and inhale so hard that my throat hitches and I wind up coughing. Not many people crowd the streets this time of night, but those who do shoot me sideways glances. It's the med kit drawing their attention, mainly the blood glittering on the side of it.

I wipe off what I can on the sleeve of my sweatshirt and then toss the clothing into the trash, walking the rest of the way wearing only a shirt. I stick to the alleys, weaving in and out of the puddles of light cast by street lamps. This part of the city has a gritty atmosphere that is impossible to ignore. You're in hell without having to glance at a street sign to know it. Half-naked women huddle on the corners, showcasing gaunt limbs for the cars that cruise by. One of them, in particular, leans against a dumpster just beyond the next block I cross.

Her eyes meet mine for a split second, and then she sinks into the shadows, crooking her finger for me to follow. The moment I draw even with her, she blows out a breath tainted with vodka and only god knows what else.

"You're late," she says. Her words run together, exaggerating her Russian accent, as blue eyes accusingly meet mine. "They don't like that, you know. It makes them nervous."

"I got held up," I say, lifting my med kit. "I'm here now. Tell me what's up. But first things first." I take a few bills from my pocket and press them against her palm.

Instantly, the tense line of her jaw relaxes a little. She almost looks her age—too damn young to be wearing the skimpy, black dress displaying a swath of pale skin. Ratty, brown hair brushes her shoulders but doesn't offer much cover on its own.

After a wary glance behind her, she leans in. "Piotr's gone. You'll meet with Vlad tonight. He thinks you're an easy mark, so he'll try to win you over with dances, maybe a girl or two." She shrugs like it's normal to equate people with currency. "But there's something else. I don't know why, but the guards have been edgier than usual tonight. Like they're expecting something. I'll keep my eyes open and let you know if I notice anything strange. Though I did see a truck circle this way a little bit ago. The cops think we don't notice when they drive normal cars."

"Huh." I pocket the information for later. Antsy Russians are a bad sign. So are the police, but for the moment, they're the least of my problems. "Hide this for me, will ya?" I hand over my med kit.

"Still playing doctor?" Her tone is more amused than judgmental as she accepts the plastic case and tucks it behind the dumpster. "One of these days, you'll be the one who needs stitches." Her smile fades. "Especially if you keep coming here."

I muster a half smile of my own. "How else am I going to save up enough to get you out of here?"

She scoffs and rolls her eyes. "Right now, I need to get back before they come looking for me. There are four guards tonight, all armed," she adds. "They shouldn't bother you, but just in case."

I accept the information with a nod. "I'll keep my eye on the exit. Stay safe tonight. And, Domi?"

She pauses on her way to the street.

"You know I'm not joking about getting you out of this place, right?"

She shrugs. "You're insane. Though, if you weren't, I would have ratted you out a long time ago."

She's gone before I can laugh at the joke. Alone, however, it doesn't sound so funny. In a world where someone can virtually own another, few things are.

I'm definitely not laughing as I return to the main street and head for my destination—a club named Moe's. It lurks in a brick building a few blocks up. Two bouncers guard the door while scores of women walk the strip. Domi's one of them, lurking out of sight. The money I gave her is enough to help her make her quota tonight. Helping her tomorrow solely depends on if another gangbanger can get himself shot—and happens to be desperate enough to seek out someone like me to patch him up. Funny. I used to consider myself an artist, finding refuge in colors and paint. Now, my art extends to the medical jargon I read in a book, and a whole lot of trial and error.

Admittedly, that's the most dignified of the ways I make my money. Another? It's not so pretty. Some might call it downright shady.

Setting my sights on the wooden door leading into the club, I pick my way through the women posted on the street and approach one of the bouncers. He frowns as he looks me over and then jerks his chin to the door.

"He's waiting for you," he grunts, making the statement sound more like a warning. "Go on in." He shoves the door open, and I step through it.

My soul may have a price tag, but at least I still have one. In a place like this, that's a rare thing to find.

Cold eyes greet me as I enter the front of the club—a narrow office where another bouncer guards a second door. I'm already dreading what waits beyond. Chaos, for one. Piotr, the man who runs this branch of the syndicate, keeps his club brimming with drugs, sex, and booze. Enough vice so the twisted fucks who come here forget that the girls prancing around in risqué costumes aren't here by choice.

Domi's lucky to be outside tonight. At least she can hide. That isn't the case in here. Piotr's trained thugs don't miss so much as a trembling shot glass. Any girl who doesn't play her part is given a shove and a pointed look. The smart ones don't screw up twice.

"He's waiting for you."

I smother any reaction as a hulking bodyguard appears at my side, his voice deeper than the pulsing music. He inclines his head and starts toward the center of the club, where a balding man in a black suit is watching a parade of women strip naked on the stage that spans the length of the room.

"My friend!" The man rises to his feet as I approach and offers a meaty hand for me to shake.

The gesture is for show—a way for him to draw attention to his scarred knuckles should I forget the danger he represents. Not that I can. Even the dumbest gangbanger knows who Vladimir Olshenkov is. There is a reason his nickname is The Butcher.

"You're late," he says, narrowing his beady eyes over my face. "I hope I didn't interrupt some other business."

I shrug off the subtle threat lurking in his tone and plaster on an expression that I hope passes for a smile. "Nothing important."

Satisfied, Vlad lowers himself back onto a leather couch positioned near the stage and pats the space beside him. "Sit."

I do, angling my face toward him—not that it helps much. In my peripheral vision, a girl takes off the thin strip of fabric serving as her top and my jaw clenches. "Arno's sorry he couldn't make it," I say. Not that he ever planned to come anyway.

"Do this for me," he begged. "Act like I want to make an offer—not that I ever would go into business with those fucks. I just need eyes on the inside."

For what? He never told me.

I never asked.

"Arno," Vlad says, nodding. "He is busy. I understand. You are busy yourself." He nods to my hands as if they convey more than I realize. Maybe they do. The left sports five fingers, like most people's do. The right...doesn't. "It's why I don't mind that your boss sends you in his place," Vlad adds, laughing deeply. "He must depend on you a lot, what with your brother being gone."

I swallow hard, keeping every muscle in my face as still as I can. I've met with him three times this month alone, but this is the first meeting that he's brought up Dante.

"We manage," I say tightly.

Vlad's smile doesn't reach his eyes. "I would hope you do. Here." A girl slinks past, carrying a tray of shot glasses. He grabs two and offers one to me. Vodka, probably. "A toast. To new business."

Not if I have any say in it. But there's the rub—a truth that stings even as I contort my hand to slam my glass against Vlad's. Arno does business with whoever he wants.

Like always, I'm just along for the fucking ride.

CHAPTER TWO

CHLOE

The real Devil sets up shop in a brick building downtown, where a flashing neon sign above the door reads *Moe's*. He doesn't require fire or brimstone to keep his captured souls in line, either.

Just money. A lot of it.

Workers and patrons alike congregate near the entrance to the club, and I squint to tally up what little features I can decipher. Dark hair, not red. Thin, but not petite. One question lingers no matter how many details I hunt for. After all this time, will I even recognize her?

The engine of the truck cuts off with a death rattle–like hiss, mercifully drowning out the thought. "Take it all in," my partner, Grey, warns as he rolls down his window and spits onto the pavement. "*This* is what you volunteered for rather than taking that nice, cushy desk job."

"Very funny," I counter, making my voice snappy on purpose. After less than a month of working with him, I've learned that he doesn't tolerate fear from anyone. "Are you going to suggest I wear kid gloves, too?"

"Fair enough," he says. "But this isn't like our usual beat. And it certainly isn't like that Podunk town in Montana you transferred from. Welcome to the goddamn strip."

He doesn't know of my past. The horror unfolding in my gaze could be a result of my so-called innocence as far as he's concerned.

Not painful recognition.

Seven years later, the rundown block looks untouched, as if the past few years only affected me.

"Parker?" Grey snaps his fingers beneath my nose.

"Huh? Oh." *Parker*. That's right. I'm not Ksenia anymore, the urchin who escaped to the west. It's *Chloe Parker* now, someone supposedly stronger. Harder. Braver?

"Don't tell me you're chickening out," Grey adds. "Though I wouldn't blame you." With twenty years of experience on the force, he doesn't miss my nervous swallow. His eyes narrow. "Remember, it's straightforward, but let's go over the basics. You are here because…"

"Because I'm the only one who could fit into a size two."

"Smart ass," Grey mutters. "For real, kid. Why are you here?"

Because I'm stupid. Because I'm an idiot for returning to this damn city. Because I'm desperate enough to chase a ghost.

"Because I spent two years in special victims," I say out loud, "even if it was in a 'Podunk' town in Montana. I'm trained to carry a weapon, as well as consult on sex crimes, and I transferred here to make a difference—"

"And you're our cover if any of the press find out about this fucking suicide mission and whine about how we're taking advantage of a bunch of hookers."

"Or that," I say. He always did have a way of getting to the heart of the matter.

"Let's cut to the chase. You mingle. You see if you hear anything interesting. Piotr's been busy these days. Word on the street is that he's cutting a deal with Arno Mackenzie, the gun runner. Not to mention his dealings with the Cartel. See what you can learn, but then you leave. Don't speak to anyone for too long. They may seem like harmless little girls, but don't buy the act. They'd sell your ass out in a heartbeat."

He's referring to the women gathered along the sidewalk with even less patience than me and my so-called humble roots. So many haunted, battered faces. Hope and dread mingle into a painful mixture that lumps in my throat. No red hair or blue eyes. Maybe I don't want to find her after all. Not like this.

"I'll let you off here," Grey announces. "And for god's sake, stop fidgeting. You never wear a dress before? *I* could blend in better than you." He scoffs at the black fabric clinging to me like a second skin, and I let my hand fall from the plunging neckline. "Don't forget. You're the one who volunteered for this. Though, if you've changed your mind, I could get us another assignment before the end of the shift—"

"No." I push the door on my end open and climb out without giving him the chance to reach for his radio. "I can do this."

I adjust the red wig shielding my natural hair and spot my destination. Memories taint the air, as tangible as the cigarette smoke and polka music seeping through the walls of the nearby club—a repulsive enough combination to deter even the drunkest local. If not, the burly bouncers stationed on either side of the entrance do the trick.

They stare right through me as I pick my way across the street. Either luck is on my side, or something else consumes their attention. Keeping my head down, I don't question. In and out. Information. That's all I need.

Red hair. Blue eyes. Petite.

"The fuck are you?" Someone nudges my hip the moment I mount the curb. Not a redhead, but a lanky brunette with a thick Russian accent. The remnants of a healing bruise circle her left eye, and she hasn't even bothered to hide her mark —the indigo tattoo at the nape of her neck that proclaims her name and her number. 23.

I ignore her, pushing through the thick of the crowd, but her breath remains hot on the back of my neck.

"This street is *Piotr's* territory," she hisses. "He doesn't like competition."

I stop cold. That name shouldn't affect me the way it does. Not now.

"I've never seen you before," the girl adds, continuing to follow me the moment I remember how to move. "Most girls usually don't look so…clean."

She's right. Everyone here is sporting some bruise or another. Each injury serves as a painful incentive to fight for the next car that slows before the curb. A panting blonde wins this round and claims the passenger's seat of some creep's Volvo, slamming the door behind her.

I stare long after the car has turned the corner. Once upon a time, I was that girl.

Not anymore. The night air sinks into my lungs, acting as an anchor against the memories, and I blink, focusing on the club once again. The bouncers guarding the doors are alert tonight, but it's not the girls they're watching. The road has their sole attention. They don't even trade a joke like they would have in the old days. It's as if they're waiting for someone.

Or some*thing.*

"They'll beat your ass if they know you don't belong here," my newfound shadow snarls into my ear, following my gaze. "I suggest you leave, or—"

"Have you seen this girl?"

The change of subject throws her off, and she steps back.

"She's fifteen. Red hair. Her name..." I reach into my bra and withdraw a crumpled photograph I printed from a police database what feels like a lifetime ago. The edges flutter in the wind as I shove it beneath the girl's nose without looking at it myself. "Her name is Anna."

The girl raises an eyebrow, cutting her gaze to the photo and then away. "No."

Disappointment claws through my chest, but I swallow hard and return the picture to its place nestled against my rib cage. This could be a blessing in disguise. After all, there's a reason Grey wanted to focus his operation here. More girls than usual have been washing up in rivers or winding up dead in alleyways. All of them sport the same infamous indigo tattoo.

The syndicate is getting sloppy.

Or fearless.

"You said Piotr owns this block?" Somehow, I don't choke on the name.

"Yes, Piotr. He runs the entire strip. And you don't *want* him to see you," the girl whispers. "You're pretty. He likes that."

"Is he here?" My voice shakes this time. But I'm here for Anna, not him. I'm here for Anna...

"No, he isn't," the girl says.

"What?" My confusion is genuine. Piotr's absence is a new development. An alarming one.

The brunette blinks, her gaze a fraction sharper as she hones in on my ill-fitting wig and then my thigh as if sensing the holster strapped to it.

"I need to work." Her gaze flickers away, and she's already backing out of my reach. "I'm not sleeping in the alley again, and Vlad said he'd break my jaw next time I—"

"Vlad's in charge now?" Old fear seeps into my tone, impossible to smother.

Suddenly, the microphone hidden against my chest weighs a ton. I don't even have to picture Grey's reaction to know I've gone too far. *Focus, girl,* he'd snarl. *If you can't keep your shit together, then cut and run.*

"Thanks," I croak, turning on my heel. "I'll take my chances on another corner—"

"Wait." The girl grabs my wrist, stopping me mid-step. "Oleg," she calls to one of the bouncers. "New girl feels sick. I'll show her where to wash up."

Oleg, a beefy man with a bald head and a beer gut, grunts. "Five minutes."

The girl pulls me along, and I do my best to stagger, keeping up the act.

"Where are we going?" I ask when we reach the back of the club.

A bony hand slams into my lower back, shoving me forward. *Shit!* I stagger into the wall, helpless as my wig is yanked from behind. Not off, but *up*, revealing the nape of my neck.

"Let go!" I twist, swatting her hand away, but it's too fucking late.

Without resistance, the brunette takes two steps back, a smug smile tugging at her mouth. "Everyone's heard of Piotr," she says. "*Everyone—*"

"So what if I have?" I can't stop myself from rubbing the back of my neck, where my own tattoo lurks.

"Listen." With a wary glance at the mouth of the alley, the girl steps closer. "I've been here six months, and I've seen six number tens come and go since then. It's like he hates the number more than the girl who wears it—wait!" She looks back as a fire door opens from the inside of the club.

A man is standing behind it. He's tall, with a buzz cut, a tailored suit, and a cold expression. A bouncer. "You two," he snarls in Russian. "Get back to the fucking road—" He breaks off, cocking his head as someone shouts something from within. "Wait. Come. You dance tonight."

The girl beside me doesn't hesitate. She hastens to the door, her eyes downcast.

"Did you fucking hear me?" The man whistles to me as if beckoning an animal. "Come."

My feet drag me forward. The moment I reach the doorway, I'm shoved inside and transported seven years in the past. The hall even looks the same—peeling linoleum and gray walls. Up ahead, the faint pulse of music—different than the polka blaring in the front office—seeps out.

We're herded down the hall, into the main club. At least a hundred men crowd a barroom, all facing a raised platform in the center of the darkened space. For their entertainment, a handful of topless girls barely out of puberty prance around to the beat of pounding bass.

Dancing, they call it.

My only consolation is that none of them have red hair.

None of them are Anna.

"Hey! You there!"

A man in a leather jacket barrels in our direction. I don't recognize him. Built like a bear, he's the epitome of the bouncer Piotr liked to employ. Every nerve in my body hums with awareness. Just how many marks in my file might I earn if I blow my cover now?

My fingers flutter to my hip, but someone pushes past me, knocking me off-balance.

"We have to change," the dark-haired girl says, raising her voice above the music. She snatches my wrist, tugging me along the outskirts of the club and down another hallway. With no one in sight, she leans in close. "No sudden moves," she mutters into my ear. "Trust me."

She turns, leading me inside a cramped room lined with shelves. It's one of the "dressing rooms," stocked with enough tacky lingerie to supply a pornography studio. Bustiers. Thongs.

"You have to get dressed," the girl warns. She shimmies out of her dress and pulls an even more risqué outfit from a hanger—a black thong and bra. "You might be able to sneak out if you can make it to the front. But not like that." She frowns disapprovingly at my body. "Here." She fishes something from a shelf, and a shudder runs through me at the sight of a white bustier and a matching pair of shorts. It can't be the same pair. It *can't.*

My fingers shake as I accept the garments anyway. She's right. Swallowing hard, I pull my dress off, and the microphone clatters as it hits the floor.

"You're a cop." The girl eyes the device while tugging on her thong. "Thought so—"

"What are you doing?" Not running to tell, for one. Why?

"I don't want to get killed tonight." Already dressed, she points to the bundle of fabric in my hands. "Hurry, before they come back."

I pull the bra on first before trading my underwear for a pair of white shorts. They're not nearly long enough to hide the gun.

"You have to leave it," the girl whispers.

I shouldn't, but my fingers are already unfastening the straps of the holster. With my free hand, I rip the wig off and shove the gun inside it before hiding everything on the lowest rung of the nearest shelf. The last item I tuck away is a discolored picture on printer paper. A haunted girl stares at me from the surface of it, almost as if accusing me of leaving her a second time.

"Wait." The brunette bites her lower lip, eyeing my back and the second tattoo etched there. "You'll need to hide that too. Here." She strains on her tiptoes and grabs something from a higher shelf. "Put these on—"

"No." I cringe into the wall and trip over my heels. "I'll wear something else."

"There's no time!" She presses the gaudy prop into my hands.

An ivory harness makes up the bulk of the costume piece. Two enormous white wings large enough to obscure my lower back spring from it. My throat tightens as I woodenly insert my arms through the frame.

"Better." Still chewing on her lip, the girl nods in approval. "Let's hope you remember how to blend in."

That sounds like something Grey would say. He's probably pitching a bitch fit by now. If I'm lucky, the least he'll do is ensure I'm fired. Though maybe not. Snippets of conversation might get him a warrant. But if I could get him Vlad…

"Hey!" A knock rattles the door. "Hurry the fuck up!"

I square my shoulders as the door is thrown open.

The bouncer appraises us and gives the dark-haired girl a scoff. "Go get a tray," he says, sending her off. Then he fingers my hair and frowns. "Who said you could switch the wig? Whatever. Come with me." He inclines his chin for me to follow but continues to speak over his shoulder. "You dance. If you prove your worth, Vlad may not dump your skinny ass in the river tonight."

How many of the girls juggling trays of vodka or dancing on stage hope to avoid that grisly outcome? With Vladimir Olshenkov's name thrown into the mix, there is no boast too brutal to be proven correct. If I ever felt fear in my days as Ksenia, Vlad is one of the few bastards I might have ever harbored it for.

I find him holding court from a leather couch positioned at the farthest end of the stage. He's cleanly shaved tonight. His girth has tripled since I saw him last, his jowls jiggling with every word he speaks. He isn't scowling though; the bastard must be on his best behavior. Following the line of his gaze, I see why. A man is sitting across from him—a guest of honor? This far back, I can only make out his silhouette.

"Go!" The bouncer beside me slaps my ass, shoving me forward. "And be sure to fucking smile."

My lips contort on command as I mount the stage. It's one of the few things that has changed in my absence. Added length makes it long enough to serve nearly the entire expanse of the club, holding several girls at once.

Before tonight, I was sure I would never be able to dance the way I used to, stringing my body along like a puppet on a wire. Surprise, surprise, my old routine is still ingrained—the fallen angel with the fake wings.

I'm the only woman on stage with a prop—a fact the men in the audience don't miss, a few whistling their amusement—but my attention is focused solely on the man seated at the head of the stage. The "throne," we used to call it.

Vladimir Olshenkov barely looks up from the swill in his shot glass as he trades a few words with the dark-haired man beside him. A well-known criminal? I hope so. The identity of some thug doing business with Piotr would be the perfect leverage to cover my ass with Grey. But no... He turns, and I don't recognize him.

A chiseled jaw anchors Romanesque features and intense blue eyes. Eyes that fixate on the right breast pocket where Vlad likes to keep his gun rather than ogle the dancers vying for his attention. The club itself holds his interest more than the dancers. He scans the room while brushing a mop of black curls from his face. Something's off about his right hand. The ring and middle fingers are normal, but the remaining three are formed of black material and metal joints. Prosthetics.

There are no identifying tattoos on his arms to symbolize whatever cartel he's loyal to. His black shirt and jeans can't be traced to any one gang.

"My associate apologizes for his unexpected absence," Vlad murmurs to him, his accent thick. "Please, enjoy yourself."

The younger man says nothing—or, if he does, I don't hear him. Desperate, I shuffle closer, dragging my hands along my hips while my heart hammers out a staccato rhythm.

All I need is a name. A location. Something worth the mounting risk. Something to leverage.

"Hey!"

I look down and find Vlad snapping his fingers.

"Drinks for my friend," he commands a startled girl holding a tray a few feet away.

The brunette I came in with. She hurries closer and offers her selection of drinks. The stranger takes a shot of vodka, while Vlad amuses himself by pinching the girl on her ass. She trips, landing across the stranger's lap, and spills booze onto the leather couch. I physically stop myself from lurching forward as the stranger grabs her arm. He should throw her off him. Hit her, even. Instead, his touch provides enough stability for her to lean against him, her mouth near his ear. The subtle motion of her lips could be a trick of the light. Either that, or she tells him something. Something that makes his gaze flicker toward me.

"Silly bitch," Vlad snaps, shoving her to her feet. She mutters apologies and scurries off while the two men shift away from the spreading puddle of alcohol.

Oh, Vlad. I would give anything to shove my heel through his eye socket. Twist. Stomp. Grind. This bastard deserves more than a simple bullet to the brain. He deserves to be cut, burned, tortured. Rage sears through my veins, goading my movements. It's his throat my groping fingers clench, not my breasts. Every sharp twist of my hips grinds the life out of him, bit by goddamn bit.

"You call this a fucking show?"

From my peripheral vision, I see Vlad gesture toward the women in front of him, myself included.

"Get me someone new."

My pulse skips. One of the bouncers rushes toward the stage, and I reach back to unhook my bra. With a flick of my wrist, I toss the garment at Vlad's feet.

"Wait." He holds his hand up as the bouncer nears my position. Then he sinks back against the cushions of the couch, rubbing his chin. "She can stay."

Air floods my lungs in a dizzying rush. He always did prefer the slow, vulgar shows. The kind where the girl pretended to fuck the stage, salivating for any man to give her a fix. He liked breaking those girls even more.

But a striptease can only buy me so much time. *Focus!* The girl told me that making it to the front is my only way out. Taking my eyes off Vlad, I scan the far wall, spotting the exit, which is guarded by another bouncer. Slipping past him should be easy enough. Gradually, I inch backward, still flexing my hips. One step. Two…

"You."

Every ounce of air leaves my lungs as Vladimir sits forward, eyeing my body with a frown. This is it. I wait for his beady pupils to narrow in recognition or for his hands to curl into fists.

One of them slashes through the air, gesturing toward the couch. "He wants you to give him a dance."

He didn't notice. My heart starts beating again only to sputter to a stop as my brain processes the full command. *Give him a dance.* Slowly, my attention returns to the other man.

He's watching me. Dark stubble covers his chin, but his smooth, porcelain features remind me of something from a cathedral fresco. Like a cherub. Or a demon.

I dismount the stage on trembling legs, and another morbid memory flashes. I hated being singled out for these impromptu lap dances. They, more than anything, were the source of the beatings Vlad or Piotr would dish out every night.

"We have better girls," Vlad says as I approach. "But if you like...you get to know her a little better, no?"

The other man mulls over the prospect of owning me. "All right."

"Excellent!" Vlad claps and lets out a hearty chuckle. "You" —he snaps his fingers—"take him in the back."

Those five words teleport me into the past. *Take him in the back. Suffer for twenty minutes. Earn your keep. Do it again. Back. Fuck. Money.*

Anything to avoid a beating.

"Are you deaf?" Vlad slaps me on my ass, snapping me into action.

I woodenly reach for the blue-eyed man's hand. The wrong hand. He draws back, clutching his arm to his chest. He extends the opposite hand, however. When he finally stands, he towers over me. And he smells. Like vinegar. Or something more chemical in nature. Ammonia?

His shoulder collides with mine, jarring my precarious balance and cutting the thought off. He's impatient.

Taking his lead, I start forward, pulling him after me.

"Enjoy," Vlad tells the stranger, his voice conveying a warning to me at the same time.

Don't screw up.

The threat chases me down the long, winding hallway, where faint moans and grunts come from behind a row of doors, many closed. A lone bouncer inclines his head toward the only open doorway.

I know, even before I freeze over the threshold, which room will be free. An agonizing pinch of nostalgia strikes again, ripping through my rib cage. *Home sweet home.*

My old prison has seen some renovations. Piotr's opted for a darker decor nowadays. The dark-gray walls reflect the glow cast by silver sconces affixed above the bed. It takes up the most space—a custom size that allows him to "entertain" more than one girl at a time. Two oak nightstands bookend either side, and one holds another infamous artifact from my past. Round. Silver. It's a basin probably meant to adorn some fancy dinner table. Piotr used it as an ashtray— usually. Some nights, it became his makeshift weapon. Vlad must want to impress this guest if he's letting him have his tryst in here.

It's cold. My teeth slam together as goosebumps rise over my arms. I left the bustier somewhere on the barroom floor. Along with my pride. My sanity. My career.

No more detours down memory lane. I have to get out. Find Anna. Flee. My thoughts race to form a plan as I turn to face the man following in my wake. My eyes go to his waist, searching… *Bingo.* I sigh in relief. He's wearing a belt —black leather with a silver buckle. I reach for it, forcing my lips into a charming smile.

"Let me help you with this," I purr.

Then I'll strangle him with it. Not kill him. Maybe. Just stun. Buy more time. Get to Vlad and *make* him tell me where Anna is…

"Wait." He closes the door and cuts those piercing eyes in my direction.

I don't find an angel in them now, and my feet propel me back against the wall without requiring any input from my nerves. It's instinct, one my brain can't reconcile. Fear of *him?*

"Let's just cut to the chase," he says, his voice alarmingly soft, reinforcing my unease. "I know you're a cop."

CHAPTER THREE
CHLOE

Think. THE NEED HAMMERS AGAINST MY SKULL. IF HE really is one of Vlad's lackeys, then he'll call for help at any moment. I can't let that happen. Desperate, I scan the room for a lamp or another item I could use as a weapon. *There.* Piotr's prized ashtray is within my reach, a poetic sort of irony. I shift toward it, clinging to the wall. Just my fucking luck, the man follows.

"I'm no cop," I lie. Miracle of miracles, my voice doesn't shake. How in the hell *did* he know? "I'm not—"

"You came here *with* a cop. Don't tell me that's just a coincidence."

"What?" Dread knots my stomach. He has to be lying. Grey doesn't make dumb mistakes. His truck was unmarked. He wasn't even in uniform. "I don't know what you're talking about—"

"Cut the shit." His hand strikes the wall near my head, and the resulting bang snaps my nerves to attention. "Let's say I know a little birdy who warned me that a woman was headed my way. Average height. Thin. Red wig. You ditched the wig for some reason, but I know you're her."

My lungs are on fire. I've been holding my breath. "How?"

"You don't have a mark on you. At least…"

I flinch as the rough pad of his thumb grazes my forehead.

"Except for *that*. My little birdy mentioned this female cop would have a scar like that."

Breathe. I do as he withdraws, feeling my chest expand and contract.

"You're crazy—"

"Am I?" The shadow that falls over his face could be a trick of the ghoulish light, but he looks older. Harder. More demon than angel. "Tell me who your target is," he demands. "Or I go back out there and let good ol' Vlad know that he has a mole in his club. Are you after the girls? I know sometimes you cops like to use them as collateral to get to the big boys. That won't work."

"You could tell Vlad," I admit. "But he…he won't believe you." Only because he might already know. I feel it in my gut. Despite the few hiccups, this has been way too easy. "I'm not a cop—"

"Then who are you?"

I have just a second to compose a good lie. "I work for them. The police said, if I come and get them information, they won't charge me for prostitution, and I can be safe."

Blue Eyes tilts his head, unconvinced. I'll have to dig deep to fool him.

"Think about it. Could a cop just prance in here undetected? Without backup? Without a weapon? Look." I run a hand down the side of my tiny, white shorts. "I can't even hide a gun. Who would be that stupid—"

"So, who are you, then?" He advances another step, and I'm trapped. "Tell me the truth or I'm going to Vlad."

"I'm no one," I insist.

"Oh, really?" An alarming expression contorts his mouth. A breathtaking smile. A terrible grimace. "Then what *business* do you have with Olshenkov?"

I blink, unguarded for a split second. What business do I have with Vlad? Nothing. Everything.

"That's my business—"

"And your cop friend. Don't tell me he's just here to hold your hand?"

"His…business is about Piotr Petrov," I stammer, risking a kernel of the truth. "That's it."

"Petrov?"

I avoid his suspicious glance in favor of hunting for a way out. I could shove him into the bathroom and barricade the door. Incapacitate him somehow. I could…

"What's your name?"

"Why does it matter?" I glance at him sharply.

"I guess it doesn't," he admits. "Still want to know though." He angles his body toward mine—a stance that makes it ten times harder to sneak past him.

"Ksei," I spit.

He cuts his gaze to the doorway before I can tell if he believes me or not. "Well…what do you say we both get the hell out of here, then, *Ksei*?"

Go? My mind latches onto that word. I should fucking run.

Something about this room renders me helpless. The walls of my old prison are familiar yet different at the same time. Even the paint seems to be a slightly different shade of gray. There's a tinge of red now. Wait… That "speck" of red starts to flash. It doesn't come from the wall itself, either, but a small, black box mounted near the ceiling.

Shit. Recognition hits me like a punch to the stomach.

"The camera…" How could I have been so stupid as to forget it? "He's watching us."

Someone has to be in that little room at the back of the club, making the lens refocus to trigger the light. Vlad?

It doesn't matter.

"Wait."

A firm grip seizes my arm, but I'm already halfway to the door, my fingers pawing for the knob.

"Hey! Listen to me."

Listen. I'm years in the past, going through the motions with a client while Piotr coaches me—sometimes symbolically through the pulsing camera's lens. Sometimes he booked a bird's-eye view right beside the bed if the customer was into that sort of thing.

"Give the man his money's worth," he'd growl into my ear. "Make him beg for more…"

"Hey."

The gruff tone doesn't drag me back to the present as much as the gentle touch trailing down the length of my arm does. I wrench the limb back only to lose my balance and trip forward. A startled grunt bastes my skin, and I feel rather than see an unfamiliar hand slide down to my waist.

"Don't move," the man warns the moment I resist his grip. "Unless you want all of them out there to realize who you are."

Ksei, back from the dead?

No. A cop—that's what he thinks, anyway.

"Give me a dance," he suggests, his breath warm against my ear. "Something quick and easy. Then I'll leave, and you can slip out—"

"Why?" I draw back enough to see his face. "Why help me?"

"To be fair, I don't think we have a lot of time to waste on *talking*."

I swallow hard. He's right.

"Get on the bed," he says, following the same train of thought. Letting me go, the stranger backs up a step, tilting his head so that his expression is hidden from the camera's view. He sinks onto the mattress, watching me during the entire descent.

He's on my level now, and thoughts of escape come more easily, more tempting than before. I could hit him and make a break for the exit before Vlad could even rise from his chair.

My legs spur into action, bringing me forward, and his scent floods my nostrils. Sharp. Acrid—like smoke. The camera's still watching from the corner, its steady, red light blaring a silent warning.

"Lie down," I whisper.

A shadow descends across his face, hardening his features with every ounce of space I gain on him. I'm almost taken aback at how easily my body reacts to the role I have to play. My hands slowly slide across my bare torso, and the motion catches his attention. His eyes flicker down to my exposed breasts and a flash of heat jolts through my body— but that statuesque expression never wavers, even as I brace one knee on the side of his left hip.

Our postures now mirror each other's. Both tense, both untrusting. There is a stiff chill that shrouds the heat emanating from him.

I blame it for the shiver racing down my spine.

"Let's get you a bit more comfortable," I murmur as if Vlad is listening outside the door. "Maybe take your shirt off?" I run my fingers down to his chest, using the act as a cover to feel for a weapon. I find only coiled muscle that twitches, ready to spring into action, as I hook my hand beneath his shirt and lift.

I can only pray that Vlad doesn't see what they're really doing from his position. They're clenching. They're shaking.

Memories flood my brain one after the other, riding the telltale stench that lingers in the sheets. Piotr only ever wore one brand of cologne. *Krov'Volka.* Wolf Blood. I smell it even now with every frantic breath I take. He's inside me, whether I want him there or not. Just like old times.

No. You're here for Anna, I mentally chant. *Anna, Anna, Anna.*

"Wait." Suddenly, the man beneath me rears up, knocking me against his chest. His nearness triggers a million uncomfortable sensations. Unfamiliar body heat. Raw skin on coarse fabric. I almost miss what he says next. "What's that?"

I scramble back. "W-what?"

Faint thuds come from behind the closed door. Shouting. Glass breaking.

Vlad is throwing quite the party tonight.

"Shit." Blue Eyes lunges to his feet. It's the prime position for the dingy, artificial light to glance off the planes of his back revealed by his displaced shirt. Scars. The grouping of welts rises from his skin, more striking than any tattoo.

A revolting mixture of horror and pity floods my veins. I know those marks. How the wounds sting and burn as they heal. How the resulting scars swell against the skin like snakes. My fingertips run over my inner thighs without permission, sensing the uneven ridges of flesh.

I must have made a sound, because he turns, his eyes darkening when he realizes what I've seen. Before he can adjust his shirt, the door opens and Vlad storms in.

"We need to reschedule," he says brusquely. "Here. So that your friend doesn't forget our generosity." He reaches into his pocket and withdraws a roll of cash he shoves against the other man's palm.

"Why?" Blue Eyes accepts the money, but his feet drift apart, opening his stance. "Something wrong?"

"Change of plans," Vlad says. "Just some fucking pigs causing trouble. Didier will discuss your...*friend's* future business before seeing you out."

The stranger doesn't even glance back at me before leaving. I follow him, keeping my head down, my eyes averted from Vlad. *Focus,* Grey would warn. *Don't break your cover, no matter what.* My foot breaches the threshold the moment a hand seizes my shoulder and yanks me back.

"Oh, no, you don't. Not you."

The door slams, and I'm wrenched around, forced to bear the full brunt of Vlad's scrutiny. His gaze skims over my shoulder, and a chilling grin shapes his mouth.

"Number ten. It *is* you. What? You thought I wouldn't notice? You can change your hair or fix your face, but you can't take the whore out of the bitch, can you?" He sounds smugger in Russian than he ever could in English. "Couldn't get enough of Piotr's cock, could you, Ksei?"

My pulse hammers in my ears. The bed is the only barrier big enough to scramble behind and put between us. *Fight,* Grey would hiss. My hand slaps my thigh, registering the absence of my gun. Shit. Something glimmers from the corner of my eye, so I grab it. The ashtray. My fingers tighten over the awkward shape as I raise it between Vlad and me.

He's already snatching his butcher's knife from his back pocket. With one hand, he tears off the leather sheath covering the blade. "What I really want to know is—Who helped you?" He bares his teeth in a vicious snarl the moment I flinch. "You think I'm stupid? You couldn't have survived this long on your own. So, who?"

"Maybe you're not as untouchable as you think?" I counter, but he's right. I didn't survive Piotr on my own—and I'd rather die than betray my benefactor.

"Is that so? Speaking of *touching*, Piotr's missed you," he tells me, hefting the blade so that the edge catches the light. "I called him—"

"What?" I step back. Air won't go into my throat. The room caves in, the walls looming closer. *Focus…*

"I refreshed his memory," Vlad says, his voice distorted, coming from a million directions at once. "There's only one bitch I remember with a face like that. I thought he killed you, Piotr. I spent a week scrubbing your brains from my shoes, after all. You were always his favorite, sneaky little Ksei. But I don't think he'd mind if we have some fun, no?"

He lunges. Lightning fast, Vlad aims lower, and I lash out, nails drawn, in a vain attempt to block the blow. I strike flesh, but so does he. *Pain.* I double over. Fire sears my every nerve ending as something wet and warm dribbles down my arm, coating my fingers and threatening my grip on the ashtray.

"Just as feisty as always," Vlad admits. He swipes at his forehead with a meaty hand and hisses to discover that I've drawn blood. "You always did cause more trouble than you were worth—"

"Like Anna?"

He chuckles at the name, shaking his head. "A friend of yours?"

"Don't play dumb." I swallow hard, eyeing the blade. Pain disrupts my focus, consuming every nerve in its path. I blink, and one sneering monster splits into four, cackling from every corner of the room. "Where is she? I know you remember her. I *know* she's here—"

"Anna…" He contorts the name around his tongue and then spits onto the floor at my feet. "I think I recall one girl with that name. Small. Pretty little girl. If I remember correctly, Piotr threw her out, along with the rest of the trash you called family."

Red. It's all I see, swallowing Vlad as he swings at me again. But my arm flies out as well. A sickening thud warns me that one of us struck true this time. Him? No. Groaning, he stiffens. Staggers. Falls.

I'm over him in an instant, adjusting my grip over the ashtray as he clutches his head. "Where is she?"

"You little—"

"Where?" I hit him again, startling him mid-curse.

He merely laughs, focusing his gaze on me. "Dead. She's fucking dead—"

I hit him again. My movements devolve into a frantic motion of my hands rising and lowering over and over. No matter how many times I strike, he's still laughing at me. Taunting me.

"You'll never find her," he sneers. "She's dead. A ghost. All this time, you were chasing a ghost—"

Vibrations ricochet through my body. Footsteps. I heft the ashtray, ready to strike. But the figure staring at me is all wrong. His face is too pretty. His eyes are too blue, widening at the sight of me.

I look down and discover why. My fingers are slippery, caked in warmth. They loosen their grip on the ashtray, and it falls only to bounce against a shapeless lump smeared in red.

If good ol' Vlad isn't already in hell, he's well on his way there.

"We've gotta get the fuck out of here," the blue-eyed man says.

We? My tongue feels too heavy to question. I'm too heavy. My body reacts solely on autopilot to take the hand he's extending toward me. One yank has me on my feet, and he rips something from my back—the wings—and drops them onto the floor. Behind him, the door swings on its hinges. Chaos issues from the hallway. Shouting. Vlad's name echoes in different voices. Far away. Closer. Then closer...

"Hey!" Someone snaps his fingers.

My brain sputters back to life. I focus on his face and notice the pink lips moving in tandem. Saying something. Shouting something.

"Come on!"

We're in a hallway now. Or more like Blue Eyes is, dragging me along after him. It smells. Acrid. Sharp. Like smoke. It's darker as well. The pounding bass has cut off, revealing a cacophony of shouting in its place. Screaming.

"Fuck!"

A metallic clang draws my attention over Blue Eyes' shoulder. He's standing before a fire exit, slamming his hand against the door. It's locked and chained from the other side to thwart any brave girl who might get the idea in her head to escape.

"I know a way." My voice sounds too thick. I blink again, and the world drifts in and out of focus.

"Where?" He hooks his palm beneath my chin when I don't answer quickly enough. "Come on. Think! Where?"

I blink again. Twice. Three times. Shadows flicker beyond him. Vlad's men.

"This way." I turn back toward Piotr's room, my old cage.

I used to study every inch of the four enclosed walls. I bet I could still find every trace of old blood, every stain I left behind. He's here, weighing me down even now as I stagger toward his private bathroom. My foot strikes something I didn't expect, and I nearly trip over it. Something heavy. Human.

"This way?"

Blue Eyes is too fast. He muscles me forward, already catching on to our only chance for escape—the window placed right above the Jacuzzi-style bathtub. Apart from the ventilation, I think Piotr enjoyed the power that came with dangling what appeared to be an easy escape before his victims.

"You have to break the glass." The words trickle out of me.

I don't know if Blue Eyes heard them or if he's already come to that conclusion himself. He lunges across the tiled flooring, and the next second, a waist-height vase meets the glass's frosted surface.

Then I'm aware of fresh air and chaos. Sirens wail above the general clamor of traffic, and an icy wind nips at every inch of bare skin—though I'm not anywhere near as cold as I should be. A glance down reveals why. Someone dressed me in a black button-down shirt long enough to reach the tops of my knees. When? I can't remember.

"Hey."

A firm shake on my shoulder drags my attention to the man standing beside me. His torso is bare; it's his shirt I'm wearing. Lean muscle flexes with tension, betraying the strength his lanky frame disguises. That's not all. A tattoo spans the width of his chest. It's new, the skin still peeling around the edges. Eight letters mark his flesh, etched there in black ink. Something so odd that I have to read it twice.

MURDERER

"We need to move," he says.

We must be in an alley. It reeks of trash. Slick wetness crushes underneath my bare feet, but I don't even have the strength to shiver in disgust. It's like Vlad took a piece of me with him to hell. I laugh, the harsh sound clashing with the gruff voice cutting over me.

"Stay with me."

How? I'm not Chloe anymore. She's lost…

It's only when I glance at my body in an effort to find traces of her again that I realize that the blood covering me isn't Vladimir's. Not all of it. It drips, forming a morbid symphony that echoes off the brick walls of two nearby buildings. *You're in shock,* a part of me declares. I'll bleed out soon enough. Minutes maybe.

"Hey!" He shakes me again.

But I don't have the resistance to withstand the motion. My head goes back and forth.

"Shit!"

Suddenly, the world shifts. My feet aren't on the ground anymore, and I'm staring up at the impassive indigo sky. Air rushes by, clawing at my hair and flinging it in every which direction. We're moving faster.

But not fast enough. Footsteps gain on us too quickly to outrun.

"Espi," a woman exclaims, panting. "What's going on—"

"Nothing good," the man holding me says. "Get as far from here as you can. Call me when you're safe. Got that?"

"Okay."

The footsteps trail off again, swallowed by a rushing sound that drowns out everything else but the roar of police sirens and one last piece of Grey's advice.

If you're ever stupid enough to blow your cover, know this…

It only gets worse from there.

CHAPTER FOUR
ESPI

I DON'T STOP RUNNING UNTIL THE WAIL OF SIRENS fades to a distant hum. Though it could just be that the woman moaning in my ear drowns the sound out.

She's in bad shape. I'm drenched in her blood, and it splatters the sidewalk with every step I take like someone painted our trail in ruby red. We won't escape notice for long. I feel eyes on the back of my neck already, hunting my every move as I weave through an alley and cut onto a back street. All the stealth does no good.

Someone is on my tail.

He's good, staying in the shadows. From what I glimpse out of the corner of my eye, he's tall and wearing a hoodie with the hood drawn low to disguise his face.

But I'd know that shape anywhere.

My footsteps slow as guilt wars with the part of me I've smothered for the past six months. The Espi who wants some goddamn answers. The Espi who's pissed. The Espi who doesn't care that some woman is about to bleed out on his watch.

He wants to say his fucking piece.

Gritting my teeth, I look over my shoulder and make my voice loud enough to carry to the entrance of the alley I'm in. I know he's there. "You've picked the perfect time for a reunion," I tell him.

The figure lingers just beyond the corner of the nearest building for a second. Then he steps forward, and I see his face. "You want to tell me what the hell you were doing there?" he wonders.

Typical Dante. Five seconds and he's already waltzed right back into the role of big brother.

"You want to tell me where *you've* been since you skipped out on me?" With nothing more than a crummy note and a few thousand dollars, I might add. That's all I'm good for, apparently. Always pity, never the truth.

"Did Arno put you up to this?" He cuts his gaze to my chest, coldly taking in the new tattoo there. Then he looks down at my feet, and his eyes widen.

I glance in the same direction and wince. "It's not my blood," I blurt out. But it's a lot. And I'm just wasting time.

"Is that so?" He finally seems to notice the woman I'm carrying. "Trust me, this isn't something you want to stick your nose into—"

"What were *you* doing there?" I ask, cutting him off. Sure enough, the line of his jaw tightens. Once again, I'm not good enough for a solid answer. "Whatever. Tell Danny I say hi."

Damn. I don't know where the venom came from. Jealousy? No. Not really. You have to want something in order to be jealous of whoever has it. After all this time, I'm not really sure I need someone who sticks around out of pity.

"Espi..." Dante sighs in that heavy, exhausted way only he can. Like the weight of the world is on his shoulders and he's the sole person who can hold it. Fuck asking for help. It simply isn't his style. "You know I wouldn't do this if it weren't to protect you. Right?"

"I..." The unmistakable tone of a police siren snags my attention. "Shit." I readjust my grip on the blonde while juggling my med kit. It's only as I bounce on the heels of my feet that I realize I'm hesitating. For the first time, I register how fucking naked I feel without my shirt. Show and tell through old scars is a game I don't want to play right now.

In the end, he's the one who leaves first, fading into the dreary landscape. "I'll draw them away," he calls back.

I take my out and run.

The farther I go, the easier it is to refocus. When I reach my house, I'm already counting how many stitches it will take to sew the woman up. Twenty, maybe. She'll need to be numbed too, and I just pray that she still has a pulse.

I enter through the back door, hoping my neighbors aren't watching at this time of night. My place is a mess. I have to flick a light on and carefully pick my way through stacks of blank canvas just to reach my bedroom.

Hopefully, Domi got away, because I won't have much cash left to help her after this. I'll need new sheets. There's no time to strip the mattress, and the blonde leaves a vivid splotch of red the moment I set her down. She's pale as shit. It's an ominous sign paired with the state of her arm. I have to roll the sleeve of my shirt up just to get a good look at the wound. Vlad fucked her up good.

Forget stitches. If I don't stop the bleeding soon, she's dead anyway.

I leave her there against my better judgment and race into the bathroom. I only have one clean towel. When I return to the room, I use it to apply pressure to her arm. Within seconds, the material is already damp and colored scarlet.

But that's the least of my problems.

She's awake, her eyes glazed and unfocused. They stare beyond my head as her mouth contorts, but she never forms a single word. Just a piercing scream that cuts me to the core. The kind of bloodcurdling sound that would make anyone within a mile radius immediately call the cops.

"Shit. It's okay," I say, trying to make my voice soothing.

Either she doesn't hear me, or she doesn't care. Her limbs flail, the injured one spraying blood across the wall in a violent arc. My first instinct is to cover her mouth beneath my palm, but her teeth sink in deep. She's strong—I'll give her that much credit. Her fingers clutch at my shoulder, the nails slicing through my skin. I'm panting with the effort it takes to shrug her off.

My med kit is at my feet, and I kick it open without thinking. In ten seconds, I have a syringe drawn and stuck within a vial of sedative. The last of it fills the barrel just as the blonde gets her feet on the floor and tries to stand.

I clench my teeth at the sound she makes. It's pained and wild, like a trapped animal. With one hand, I pin her down while the other stabs the needle into the crook of her uninjured arm.

The drug won't work immediately. After rummaging through my kit, I find two objects I've only had to use a few times—a pair of handcuffs. She kicks me as I get one set around her right wrist and secure it to the bed. Her fist weakly slams into my shoulder as I capture her other wrist and slap a cuff onto it as well.

Jesus, she's loud. Hysterical. I briefly consider using a pillow to shut her up, but she finally dies down, her eyes sliding shut.

Thank god I invest in the good narcotics.

Not that I have much time for relief. Someone's at my front door. Pounding on it.

The cops?

I grab a new shirt from my closet and wipe off as much blood as I can on the sheets. As much good as that does. Now, I just resemble a serial killer rather than the survivor of a bloodbath.

"Give me a minute!" I shout on my way into the kitchen. I risk making Officer Do-Gooder suspicious just long enough to wash my hands. Breathless, I dart down the hall and throw the front door open.

"It's about fucking time!"

I nearly barrel over in relief at the sound of that voice. The man standing on my porch is no police officer. Hell, Arno would probably take offense to the comparison. I bet he came straight from the bar. His eyes are bloodshot, nearly the same shade as his hair.

"What the fuck happened? I tried calling your cell, but you never answered." He pushes his way past me and strides into my kitchen as though he owns the place. Facing me, he crosses his arms over his chest. "The Russians' territory is swarming with fucking pigs. What the hell happened?"

Despite everything, I shrug. "I thought you could tell me."

Though maybe the blonde woman can. She knew that place. Something tells me she knew Vlad too, considering the greeting she gave him.

"So much for doing business with the Syndicate," I tell Arno. I can't keep the relief out of my tone.

"No shit," he says and braces his hands against my kitchen table. "Now, tell me. What happened?"

After taking a deep breath, I start from the beginning—but for some reason, I don't mention the blonde or Vlad's happy ending.

Maybe it's out of selfishness, one of the few traits Dante and I seem to share. I want to hear her story myself, before anyone else can drag it out of her.

Maybe she'll spill what she knows if I ask nicely?

Though, with Domi's life on the line, I'm not sure if I can afford to wait.

CHAPTER FIVE
CHLOE

There're three of them. They're playing cards in the larger room, while the rest of us huddle together, two to a cot, our arms strapped down. One of them comes in, brandishing a syringe. Spotting me, he smiles. "This one is ready to make us some money…"

I jolt awake. Or did I? Pieces of my nightmare chase me into the present. It's too dark. A metallic stench taints the air, and my inner elbow throbs. Terror claws through my belly as my thoughts dissolve and collide—and that's not the worst part. My arms are positioned on either side of me, weighed down by my wrists. Bound.

Don't panic. I suck in air to avoid just that. One breath. Two. It's cleaner than I'm used to. My new prison isn't quite a cellar. Something above ground but still enclosed. A closet?

Either Grey has a funny concept of punishment, or someone else grabbed me in the aftermath of whatever happened at the club.

"Get off my case, Arno," a man snaps, his voice sounding muffled but close. In another room? Deciphering his location takes a back seat to the name he said. Arno. It rings a bell. An alarming one. "I told you I don't fucking know what happened. Someone tipped their hand, but it wasn't me—"

"You don't think I fucking know that?" a deeper voice cuts in. "But that's it. Six fucking months down the damn drain—"

"You think it was the Cartel?"

"Fuck no!" Unstable laughter echoes off the walls. "Those fuckers couldn't get in the door without shooting themselves in the foot. No. That shit was too clean. I'm just glad you got out okay. If I had known there was any risk, I fucking swear I would have never let you—"

"I know. I know." A tired sigh follows. "Don't sweat it. The Ruskies must have pissed off someone else. You'll find out who. You always do."

"You're damn fucking right I will," the other man agrees.

They sound closer now, as if they've been walking while chatting, nearing my darkened prison. The lack of urgency unsettles my stomach. They're comfortable.

"Lie low for a while until I figure out what the fuck is going on. If anything happened to you, Dante would—" The man cuts off with a sharp intake of air.

"You can stop worrying now, Mom," the other voice finally pipes up. "I did get a few boo-boos though. Want to kiss them better for me?"

"Knock it off, you little shit." Another gruff laugh echoes off the walls, followed by a few more minutes of unnatural silence. "Take it easy, Espi. I fucking mean it. Come to the bar once you've gotten some rest, okay?"

"Okay."

A door opens and closes. I think... My eyelids feel heavier by the second. To conserve energy, I rely only on what little clues my senses can gather. Judging from the muffled sound, a solid wall separates me from the room where a lone figure starts to pace. One of Vlad's men? No. They aren't built like a typical guard. Their footsteps barely make a sound, their path aimless, bringing them closer. Then farther away. Closer. Away. Closer.

On their next trip in my direction, the doorknob jiggles, and my nerves prickle to life. *Get ready...* I flex my wrists, testing the give of the manacles. One is loose enough to slip it off—if I can move, that is. My muscles react sluggishly to my brain's commands.

Wake up! A few of my fingers twitch in response to the plea. Good enough. I even manage to peel one eye open as a rush of air alludes to a door opening. The entering figure must switch a light on nearby. Suddenly, everything is bright.

"Shit. You're awake." His surprise is a bad sign. In my experience, captors were only that confident if their victims were drugged. "Try not to move," he warns, his tone gruff. "You'll bleed through the—"

Move! The word triggers every instinct I have. My loose arm twists and I pull, ignoring the burning, icy scrape of my flesh against metal. Two agonizing tugs free it, but a smattering of rushing footsteps warns me that I'm too late.

"Shit—"

I kick my feet out only to feel air. Taking a risk, I throw my weight toward the empty space.

It's a mistake. My head explodes, my thoughts splintering. As if the agony surging down my spine jumpstarts my vision, it clears. I'm in a room. The floor beneath me is smooth tile, and the lone window across from me isn't barred. An ebony sky serves as a fitting backdrop for the figure standing in the center of the room, watching me.

I blink rapidly to register his features. Glinting, blue eyes. Black hair slicked back away from a painfully innocent face. He switched the other shirt for a gray one, pairing it with ratty jeans.

"Take it easy." He warily holds his hands out in front of him.

His voice. I recognize it from the earlier conversation. *Espi.* Is that his name?

Not that it matters. If he works for the Syndicate, I'm as good as dead.

"Get these handcuffs off me—now!"

He winces.

I'm shouting. I'm screaming. "Get them off! Get them off—"

"Calm down." He's closer.

I smell him now. Mint and cigarettes. Did he pick the habit up from Piotr?

"Look!" He pulls a key from his pocket and holds it up to the light. "You lost a lot of blood. I didn't want you to reopen the… *Shit.*"

I follow the direction of his gaze, wincing with every shift of muscle. My other arm is still attached to the edge of a narrow cot. Unlike the naked, industrial setup I'm used to, someone draped this mattress in red sheets—sheets that used to be white.

Vlad delivered his parting gift well. Rent flesh forms a gash from my shoulder down to my forearm—or so I gauge from the blood trail seeping through a white towel someone wadded around the limb. Had he a larger knife, good ol' Vlad would have lived up to the little nickname Piotr bestowed upon him—The Butcher.

"There."

The pressure on my wrist loosens, but the loss of support throws me forward. I hit the floor hard, my vision blinking in and out of focus.

"Okay? Just take it easy."

I have to brace one hand flat against the floor to hoist myself onto my knees.

"Are you fucking listening to me? You want to bleed out all over the fucking floor?" He's shouting, the baby-faced angel.

That's not what leaves me reeling. His voice breaks with an emotion I'm not used to hearing in another person. Not genuinely, at least. Worry.

The same emotion makes my heart hammer against my rib cage as my knees buckle, and his arm encircles my shoulders to keep me upright.

"If you don't let me help you, you're going to bleed to death. You want that? Huh?"

I don't like how he phrased the question. Coldly. Definitively. As if he'd really leave me to my fate.

I should say yes...

"Lean on me." The surprising note of authority springs my body into action. "Can you stand up?"

With his shoulder for support, I manage to. Once on my feet, I scan the room. It's smaller than I thought. There's a tiny closet near the back corner, its door opened to reveal the meager contents within. A small array of T-shirts and a few ratty pairs of jeans hang from hooks. So this isn't a dungeon, but a bedroom. His?

"Can you walk?" The gritted tone drags my attention back to him. He's eyeing the arm sandwiched between us, held at an awkward angle. "Try to move. Come on. One foot in front of the other."

I try. He winds up supporting most of my weight, but we eventually make it into a larger room. He must live here. Though what would serve as a living room in any conventional residence acts as storage for large, white squares. My brain sluggishly tries to put a name to them. Canvas. Some are blank, while others sport splotches of paint. Reds. Yellows. Oranges.

An inferno of color.

"All right, here we go…" He lowers me onto a gray couch that's seen better days, and he has to nudge a stack of canvases out of the way to clear enough space for me. "Fuck." Muttering under his breath, he darts to another corner of the room.

There's a kitchen there—a small one, anyway—composed of a dingy fridge, a sink, and a single row of cabinets. He snatches something from the top of the fridge and then turns to the sink. Water runs. His shoulders move. He's assembling something. Another syringe? I wince; the throbbing in my inner arm is too distracting to focus for long.

"You injected me with something… Didn't you?"

Guilt laces his tension, stiffening his shoulders. He doesn't answer, and by the time he returns to my side, I can't remember why the question even matters.

"Let's sit you up." His voice deepens as he crouches in front of me.

He has a boxy object tucked under his arm and a wad of wet rags in his fist. He sets the rags aside and lifts the lid of the box. It's plastic, with compartments inside that separate what appears to be a makeshift first aid kit—gauze, scissors, and vials of liquid.

Liquid potentially potent enough to cause the disorientation disrupting my senses.

"What did you give me?" I muster up enough strength to grab his shoulder. "What did you inject me with?"

He shrugs me off in order to hunt through the case. "A tetanus shot," he finally grumbles.

"What else?"

He meets my gaze, appearing as if he's trying to decide how much he can get away with hiding from me. In the end, he shrugs. "A sedative."

Shock doesn't have time to finish racing through my system before he rears back on his knees, his expression grim.

"Look, I don't know if you remember or not, but you weren't exactly jumping at the chance to have me help you."

He tugs on his collar, revealing a jagged scratch stretching toward his shoulder, and my nails throb as if in guilt. "You were going to either scream loudly enough that someone called the cops or bleed out. I couldn't let that happen—"

"So you drugged me?"

"Yeah. I did." He holds my gaze without flinching.

There's no gray with him. Just black and white. *Either I inject you with an unknown substance, or you die.*

"I need to stitch you up." He rummages within his case and withdraws a black satchel, scissors, and a packet of surgical thread. The sort of stuff the average gangster wouldn't keep above their freezer.

"Stitch me?" My words run together, thick and garbled. "You do this often?"

"It's going to hurt," he says rather than answering my question. "It's going to hurt *bad*. I don't have any lidocaine. I used the last bit of my narcs on you too, not that it seems to be helping with the pain."

Only now do I realize how heavily I'm breathing. Sweat coats my skin. I blink, and there's suddenly two of him.

"I could get you some whiskey…"

"No." I shake my head. That was Ksenia's old vice. These days, I barely think about the bottle anymore. "Just…just do it."

He rises to his feet, and I can't help the way I stiffen when he lowers himself beside me. Up close, I'm assaulted by his conflicting smell. He's darkness. Smoke. Unknown. Clean. Too many different scents to pinpoint.

Then he touches the makeshift bandage and deciphering him takes a back seat to breathing. He wasn't lying. With every sickening tug on the damp towel, blinding agony descends in full force. Gritted teeth can't silence my cry.

"Jesus Christ—"

"Whiskey it is." Without hesitating, he heads for the fridge.

I watch through blurred vision as he fishes a bottle from inside it and pours a small amount into a shot glass snatched from a nearby counter. He brings both back over to the couch and sets the bottle on the floor between my feet.

"Here."

My fingers tremble as they accept the glass he's shoved into my hand. I take a sip as the bastard uses the distraction to pour some of the liquid from the bottle directly onto my wound.

Liquid sprays from my mouth, along with a stream of curses I can't even make out, though he calmly acknowledges each one.

"I know. I know." With a suspicious sense of practice, he lays his tools out beside us while the alcohol sears its way through torn flesh and muscle. "All right," he grunts out by way of warning. "Here we go."

I can't watch, so I stare at the wall and count the millions of ways my body succumbs to the whiskey along with whatever else he injected me with. Whether it's due to delirium or the alcohol, I don't feel a damn thing. Just the sickening push and pull of rent skin being sewn back together, stitch by stitch by stitch.

"It doesn't hurt as much if you don't focus on it. My brother taught me that. Once I busted my knee open jumping off the monkey bars, and he had to rush me to the ER, carrying me on his back the whole damn time." He laughs.

The sound chimes through the dulled mush of my brain. It's beautiful. Men shouldn't sound beautiful.

"I had to get ten stitches," he says grimly. "Before they even got the needles, I started to wail like a fucking baby, but Dante… He tried to tell me a story to take my mind off it all. He was fucking terrible at telling stories. I think this one was about a duck or something?" He trails off as he racks his mind for the memory. "I can't remember, but it barely made any sense, and he finished it off with, 'Fuck, that's it. The end.'" He laughs—more softly this time, but I don't miss the broken edge to the sound. It's pained, shattering the beauty. "I was too busy laughing that I barely even noticed when the doctor finished up."

He worked the entire time he spoke, gently manipulating the wound despite the prosthetics.

"You've done this before." The words cling to my tongue as I blink more rapidly, fighting to maintain my view of a dingy, beige ceiling.

Focus. Don't go under...

I think he'll ignore me, but after four more tugs, he sighs.

"You're going to need a lot more than ten stitches."

I'm not sure how many it takes to seal me up by the time he finally swipes at the wound with more alcohol and wraps the whole thing in gauze fished from his kit. No answer comes as he carries his bloodied tools over to the sink. I watch him as my eyelids flutter, memorizing the careful way he scrubs each tool before neatly laying them out on a dishtowel. The ease alone gives me the answer to the question he wouldn't acknowledge.

He's done this *a lot*.

"I'll put you up on the couch," he declares while cutting the faucet off.

I suspect he leaves the prospect of the cot out on purpose. Out of respect or a simple desire not to have his sheets bloodstained some more? I can't tell.

It's too hard to focus. It's too hard to care. But his eyes hold me captive, the sole feature of his I can make out clearly. They're electric, outlasting the darkness calling my name.

"Don't die," he tells me sternly. If his voice weren't so soft, the words could be mistaken for a command. Not a plea. "I used my last bit of nylon thread on you."

CHAPTER SIX
ESPI

YELLOW IS THE COLOR OF CRAZY. SOME ART PROFESSOR claimed that once during a lecture on additive color theory. Eight hundred dollars for those credits and it's the only advice I remember. *What do you get when you mix something as volatile as red with something as vibrant as green? You get yellow.*

This woman—she's the definition of the color yellow. Vibrant. Volatile. Her hair. Her skin. Even her eyes seem yellow in the right lighting—not to mention crazy. She has to be insane to have gone into that club alone.

Vlad sure knew how to pick his girls. He even gave me a rundown of what he looked for. Vlad liked them meek. Pretty. "A bitch who knows how to give good head." Ironically for him, this one gave him very good *head*. The cops won't have much of his left to identify him by.

He tried his best to take her with him though. At least she's still breathing, her chest rising and falling at a steady rate. I attempted to drape a sweater over her, but she shrugged it off. My brother was like that. Too fucking proud to accept so much as a Band-Aid if he hadn't earned it himself.

He'd know what to do if he were in my shoes right now. He'd do the smart thing and pass the buck. Or cut and run.

I grit my teeth at the thought and fish a pack of cigarettes from my pocket. I slip two cigs in on either side of my mouth and flick a lighter, burning both ends. One drag clears my head.

And Little Miss Yellow must take my sigh as her cue to wake up. "Where am I?" The brave Russian stripper's been replaced by a tired, weary American.

"Your accent's gone," I tell her. So Domi was right—She *was* undercover. Though as a cop? I'm still not sure.

"Where am I?" she wonders, her voice hoarse.

I kick back from the table, flipping my sketchbook closed. With one hand, I snatch the cigarettes from my mouth. "My place. It's safe," I add as her teeth skewer her lower lip. "Look, do you have some family I could call or something? I'll admit it—I looked for ID, but you've got nothing."

Just like that, her expression falls flat. She feels along her chest as if searching for something. Her fingers shake as they pull away empty. "I guess I don't," she says. "But why help me?" Her gaze darts to the front door. Even though she's sewn up, I doubt she can stand on her own yet.

"I don't know." I take another drag on both cigs and then put one out on the surface of the table, observing the trail of ash left behind. "I think it's a good idea if you stick around for a while though. You can crash here as long as you need to."

"Thank you." With her good arm, she feels around for the edge of the discarded sweater and drags it over her, blocking my view of any clues that might give her away. Like the scars on her legs. Or how the blood on her hands doesn't seem to bother her as much as my doubt does. "But I should get going."

"You should take this." I reach into my pocket and withdraw a wad of cash. She merely stares when I toss it onto the table. "I got that from…our little friend. It's yours—"

"Keep it," she says. "Consider it a gift."

I exhale, and the smoke distorts my view of her, Little Miss Yellow. Even so, her emotions are as easy to decipher as paint on a blank canvas. She's in pain. She's tired. Scared.

Don't I know the feeling.

"Let me get you something to eat." I stand and head for the fridge. "Do you want eggs? Or…" I yank on the fridge door and scan the contents inside it. So much for being generous. I don't even have milk. "Or eggs."

"I'm not hungry."

I glance over my shoulder and find her still on the couch, her head braced against the cushions. The act doesn't fool me. Her fingers keep fidgeting with the sleeves of the sweater. She's antsy.

"I know this isn't the ideal hotel, but again, I think you should stay here for a while, if that's all right with you," I suggest as I close the door.

"Or you'll handcuff me again?"

"I apologize for that." Going off her strained frown, I don't think she accepts it.

"What's your name?" she asks. This time, she doesn't even try to aim for tact in steering the conversation.

"Ksei. Is that your *real* name?" I dare her to tell me it is.

Her mouth opens and her pink tongue darts around the rim of her bottom lip. "It's Ksenia."

It's the truth. It's a lie. She's red and green, wavering between two sides of the same color. I don't challenge her though.

"Espisido," I say. "Everyone calls me Espi for short."

"Espisido." She draws it out like she's memorizing each letter, and I find myself gripping the fridge handle tighter. "That's an unusual name."

"So is Ksenia." When she doesn't run off, I decide to push my luck. "So, if you're not a cop, then what were you *really* doing at Piotr Petrov's little playground, Ksenia?"

"These will have to come out, won't they?" She innocently runs her good hand down the arm wrapped in gauze as if counting the stitches underneath.

"Five days," I tell her. "Ten tops. Don't go over that."

"Will it scar?" She's stalling. No. On second thought, she's trying to distract me from my original question.

"Yes." Only god knows why I play along. "It's gonna be a nasty one. If you like wearing tank tops, don't. Keep it out of the sun. Unless you want a nice, dark—"

"Thank you." She purses her lips as if she's not used to saying the words.

"Don't," I say. "I didn't disinfect it well enough. If that sucker turns gangrene and falls off, you can't sue me. *Khorosho*?"

"*Da*… You know Russian?"

"Enough to get by. I'm not a part of the Syndicate though. If that's what you're worried about."

"Fair enough." She extends one of her legs along the length of the couch, still anxious.

If she's not stupid, she won't try to stand. Though the smart thing to do would be to let her leave. All I need is to get mixed up with another Russian.

"So, you're not a part of the Syndicate," she says carefully. "Then who are you? Part of some other gang? Or is that tattoo on your chest just for show?"

Touché. "I prefer the term artist."

She raises an eyebrow, silently demanding more. An explanation. Something concrete.

I hate to disappoint the lady. "That's it. Espi, the artist. Not a part of the syndicate or any other gang. I do commissions at request."

"An artist." She eyes her arm with renewed interest. "You do your *commissions* often?"

"Only for the people I like."

"And for those you don't?"

I have to laugh even as I look away, hoping I smother the disgust that claws through my skin. "I prefer to make friends."

"Friends," she says carefully. "Who you like to keep captive?"

There's no way to skirt the loaded question, so I say nothing.

"I...I want to try to stand up," she says.

"I don't think it's a good idea."

She moves anyway, placing her feet onto the floor. To my surprise, she manages to stand on her own. One step and her knees buckle, pitching her forward.

"Hold on." I'm across the room in an instant, and I reach for her arm.

But she pivots, suddenly steady. Air rushes past my ears as her right arm swings out, brandishing something she must have been hiding beneath the sweater. Glass. Cylindrical. The whiskey bottle. I dodge the blow, ducking against the couch, only to open myself up to the kick she delivers right between my legs.

"Fuck!" I limp back, gritting my teeth at the pain.

She's out of the room by the time my vision clears. The moment I make it to my feet, the front door slams shut.

Shit. I could go after her so that she can't bring her Russian friends back to pay me a visit later. I could. But, in the chaos, I lost my last cigarettes. I need a new pack. I need a shower. The mounting excuses never address the real issue—I'm tired of chasing after people.

CHAPTER SEVEN
CHLOE

I'D ALMOST FORGOTTEN HOW POISONOUS GUILT IS. After all, Piotr taught me just one simple rule to live by —*Survive. Endure. Trust no one.* He wouldn't appreciate the newest addition to his mantra. *Don't die. I used my last bit of nylon thread on you.*

Going off how badly my arm's throbbing, I've probably undone his hard work already—not that it matters. The blood dripping down my fingertips might as well be invisible. I don't catch notice here, even barefoot. Sluggish movements propel my body forward without requiring too much input from my brain, and it isn't long before I spot my destination up ahead—Chloe Parker's home, a flat in an apartment complex on the outskirts of the Syndicate's reach.

The hallway is empty when I stagger through the doorway and past the main stairwell. Tears burn behind my eyes, impossible to fight back. If Anna were here, her captors would have her on the move after last night, along with the rest of the girls. Disappearing is my only hope to lie low and catch up. Find her.

The plan forming in my head is a simple one. Considering how badly I screwed up the op, Grey would sooner kill me than help cover my ass. Leaving is my only option.

I don't have much to pack. One bag should be enough. Some clothes. Some money from the stash in my mattress…

Every plan falls apart when I spot my door—namely what's on the generic welcome mat in front of it.

There *shouldn't* be a package lying there. This apartment isn't even listed under my information stored with the department, but I can't seem to halt my approach toward the box. Maybe I know all along who it's from, even before I notice the neatly penned script gracing the box's white lid, legible from yards away—*For my Ksei.*

No. I shake my head and force myself to blink. *It's not him.* Hope, the pathetic thing it is, forms a pitiful mantra that plays over and over with every step I take. *It's not him. It's not him. It isn't him.*

I come to a stop inches from the box. On autopilot, I stoop for the lid, running my finger along its crisp edge. It doesn't disappear. The words don't meld into something else. I know that script. The heavy-handed placement of the ink and the telltale dash above the I in my name. No one could fake that detail.

My fingers find the end of the lid, and I lift it free. There's a small, black device inside. A tablet. A note rests on top of it, but I ignore it and turn the device on. The screen lights up, already displaying the still from a single video. A white symbol dares me to strike it. Play.

My fingers shake. I reach out, intending to flip the damn thing over. Somehow, I wind up pressing on the screen instead. A grainy, black-and-white frame begins. Surveillance footage? This snippet stars two figures—a man —hulking, fat, with a balding head. Vlad. He towers over a woman. Blonde. Skinny. Half-naked, with wings sprouting from her back. She has something in her hand.

Something shiny…

I'm a disembodied specter watching my past self. Someone who looks like me, anyway. She's determined to bash a man's skull in. Determined to shut him up, even though I can tell from the bird's-eye view that he didn't even get the chance to speak before his brains splattered the walls.

It's messy. It's sloppy.

Watching it all…I feel nothing. I *smell*. My nostrils flare to catch a scent they shouldn't—spicy, dangerous. Wolf Blood cologne. The tablet falls from my hands and tumbles to the ground, bouncing against my closed door. The hallway is empty, but the scent is even stronger. It's the fucking note. It reeks of him. I don't even have to bend down in order to read it.

The three lines of text haunt me as I race from the building:

My beautiful little angel

I'll come for you soon

Moya lyubov—My love

CHAPTER EIGHT
ESPI

"You almost get yourself blown up, and all you can do is fucking pout." Arno means well—usually. Most days, he's just full of shit. "You need to get laid," he tells me on his way to the bar counter, a woman draped on either arm.

Beer is his poison of choice tonight. One of the women is holding an open can against his mouth, ready to pour on command.

"I need to get *paid*," I counter. God knows I need the money—anything to salvage the shitfest this day turned into. Domi will need every penny I can spare if she isn't already back under the Syndicate's thumb. It's nearing twenty-four hours without a call, and each passing minute diminishes the chances that she got away.

If she didn't, it's my fault. I should have taken her with me and left the blonde behind.

"Pour," Arno grunts to the brunette, who obediently tips

her can. He drains the entire thing before wiping his mouth with the back of his hand and then slapping her ass with it.

"You don't seem to mind that your business partner's taken a hit," I say. "Or did you change your mind about working with the Syndicate?"

God, I hope so.

"I'm drunk, Espi," Arno says as if that explains everything. "Tomorrow, I'll worry about that shit. For now, how about I pay you double? Francisco!" He gestures to the man behind the bar. "Pay up. Our little Espi's going to party tonight."

"Is he now?" Chuckling, Francisco wrenches the register drawer open and counts out double the amount Arno initially promised. Combined with what I found on good old Vlad, it's...it's enough to get by.

"Thanks." I pocket the bills and rise from my stool.

The bar's packed tonight. Naked girls gyrate on the stage for cash. Fighters cast bets in the back before slugging it out in the basement. Arno's done his best to make the place "bigger and better than the old piece of shit" by letting nearly every vice under the sun fly. When asked why, he claims that doing it all for the money—but that's only part of it. He's trying to forget every fucked-up thing that happened this past year. Dante's leaving. His sister's death. Somehow, the chaos helps.

"Leaving already?" he slurs in my direction when I start past him.

"Yeah. See you tomorrow—"

"Tomorrow? You should have some fun now." He shoves one of the women clinging to him toward me. "This kid," he slurs into her ear. "This kid is the fucking best. He's happy, that's what he is. Happy all the fucking time—"

"Bye, Arno." I slip past him, and he's too wasted already to follow me to the door.

It's dark out. Druggies perch on the corners, dishing out whatever their clients are willing to pay for. The man I pass knows what I want. I don't even have to ask before slipping a fifty into his hand in exchange for a vial I tuck into my pocket.

I take the long way home, cutting through alleys while wishing I had a can of paint. Some things are better left scrawled onto the sides of buildings rather than said out loud. Or drawn. Like the fact that an entire branch of the Russian Syndicate went up in smoke without a fucking trace as to who set the first match. Or that Dante seems to think my life is a revolving door. Not to mention my cell phone hasn't rung yet, and a certain woman with yellow, catlike eyes keeps popping into my head.

She's probably bled out by now...

I cut the thought off by fishing three new cigs from the new pack in my pocket and lighting them up one after the other. I drag on them all at once, and three puffs later, she's locked away behind a nicotine buzz. The rest of the whiskey in the fridge might drown her out for good.

If not, I could always head back to the bar and take Arno up on his offer. Have some "fun." Get wasted. Be happy. Try to forget the shit in my head—it's so easy for him. Though *everything* must seem easy when you choose to battle your demons with a shot glass and a bullet. Maybe he has the right idea, considering I don't know how I'll deal with my own.

And they just keep multiplying.

I round the corner and find the front door to my place swinging loose on the frame and glass all over the fucking walkway. The pieces glitter in the dark as if to taunt me. Shit. There goes most of my goddamn money.

I cross the street and shove all three cigs between my lips as I reach into the rusted mailbox hanging near the door. I withdraw the knife I keep there, testing the edge over the thumb of my left hand. It's sharp, but I'll still have to call Arno for backup, cutting his own fun short.

Or maybe not. Fresh blood paints a vibrant trail across the entryway, leading down the hall. I follow it, expecting a druggie or, at worst, some punk who might flee at the sight of the knife. The weapon turns out to be just for show, as my intruder can barely hold themselves upright. *Her*self.

"Damn it." She staggers against the table, swiping at my sketchbook, hunting for something. Her spine stiffens when I come closer. "The money Vlad gave you. Where is it?" Her accent's returned in full force, mangling her English. Her hands leave blood over the pages of my sketchbook as she flips through them. Red... Her face is green when she glances over her shoulder at me, her eyes bloodshot. "Where? I need it. Where is it?"

"I spent most of it," I admit. I have to juggle all three cigs in one hand while I reach into my pocket and withdraw the new vial, holding it up to the light. "I had to replenish my stock. I used the last bit on you."

She stares right through me, her eyes unfocused. Like how Arno looks when he's more upset than simply drunk. Old pain makes him reckless. Senseless. Dangerous. She moves the same disjointed way as she turns to the table and flicks through the shit piled in the center—empty cig packs, loose pages, and pens. "I need that money—"

"Why?" I toss two cigs onto the table, freeing my hands. From experience, I know they won't burn through the surface. "You want to get high?"

She doesn't look like a druggie—not that there really is a look. A hooker might shoot up heroin in an alley, while some doctor's wife snorts cocaine in her fancy boudoir. To each his own.

"No." She shakes her head. "I need the money. I *need* it."

Her hands, braced against the table, are the only things keeping her upright. Her legs quit that job a long time ago. I start to drop the knife. Then I slide it onto the table instead, far enough out of her reach but still within mine.

"You need more stitches," I tell her, eyeing her hands. "And let's just hope you didn't open the ones on your arm."

For fuck's sake, I hope she didn't. The only thread I have left is silk.

"I need…"

"You need rest." I risk taking another step so that her arm is within my reach. "I hate repeating myself, but hemorrhaging to death isn't a pleasant way to go. Trust me on that. And, if you fall, you'll bang yourself up even more."

She looks up at me with unfocused, yellow eyes. The blood loss will cause her body lasting damage. But the agony… That will drive her crazy.

I lift the vial in my hand and give it a shake. "How about this? I'll give you something to take the pain away. You stay here for the night. You *don't* hit me over the head with a whiskey bottle, and I'll give you the money in the morning. *Khorosho?*"

She eyes me warily—red and green on the same pale canvas. When she finally opens her mouth, I'm not sure if she'll speak or throw up. "Yes," she croaks in Russian, along with something I have to guess the general gist of—*Make it go away.*

Can do. The lit cigarette is still hanging from my lips as I cross over to the fridge and grab my kit from the top of it. I fish a needle out, crack the top off the vial, and draw up just enough to take the edge off.

When I turn around, she's watching me, part of her face pressed against the table. She clings to the surface, one of her hands braced against my open sketchbook, but she hasn't gone for the knife, at least. When I approach her with the needle, she holds her arm out. I strip off the sweater she's still wearing and roll her sleeve up. Thank god for small miracles; she's pale enough that I don't have to hunt for a vein. Once the needle goes in, I push on the plunger and watch her face change.

When her pupils dilate, I toss the empty syringe aside and grab her by the arm to lead her to the couch. She collapses on top of it, her head lolling back against the cushions, her glazed-over eyes finding mine.

"Why are you so beautiful?" She shakes her head and sighs. "It's not fair. You shouldn't be beautiful."

I don't know whether or not to take the word as a compliment. Beautiful. Going off her tortured frown, I'll assume it's an insult.

If only she knew. The worst forms of art tend to be the most eye-catching. The most dangerous. Like yellow eyes glaring through a haze of pain, disguising secrets the average observer would be too distracted to see.

If I'm beautiful, then she's mesmerizing. A fire, consuming anyone stupid enough to stop and stare for too long.

———

I WAIT UNTIL I'M SURE THE DRUG'S KICKED IN BEFORE I stitch her hand up and wrap the worst of it in gauze. She's hiding more secrets than just the accent; she's been stitched up before. In fact, someone went through a lot of trouble to make sure her pretty face stayed that way. The only anomaly is the sloppy scar along her hairline. My guess is that the goal in treating it was making sure she didn't die.

Tearing my gaze from her, I feel through the dark for one of my cigarettes. A glance out the window doesn't help me guess the time.

Morning in this neighborhood is usually marked by the sound of a car backfiring as the single mom across the street gets in from her nightshift. She'll dart into her house for about twenty minutes before rushing to her day job. Sure enough, I hear the mechanical pop as pink light spreads along the horizon.

The growing daylight colors Yellow in shades of gray. She's knocked her covering off again, though not on purpose this time. Even from across the room, I can see the sweat beading on her skin. She's fighting something in her nightmares.

She's losing.

It's a strange thing to witness from the observing end. She claws at the air while gritting out broken bits of Russian. "Anna…Anna!"

Someone she knows? The dream swallows her back up without any clarification, and she goes limp.

I don't know how long I watch her. An hour maybe? Longer? I'm not sure if I intend to sketch her when my hand drifts toward a nearby pen. The shriek of a ringtone takes precedence, and I can't smother a sigh as I grab my cell phone.

"It's about fucking time," I answer gruffly on purpose, disguising the sound of my voice. Not that I need to. There's only one person with this number.

"You know that help you promised me?" a woman wonders, her words distorted by a thick accent. "I need it now."

"Domi." I sigh. Relief and dread battle for supremacy, though I'm not sure which one my body decides to feel in the end. "Where are you?"

The options aren't many. If she escaped the Syndicate long enough to call, she couldn't have gotten far.

"The downtown precinct," she says, confirming the second-worst scenario. "For questioning. I don't like questions. You need to get me out. Now."

"How am I supposed to do that?" I wonder tiredly. The brush-off is just for show. I already have a plan forming. It's not a very good one, but it's all I've fucking got.

"Our…friend," Domi says as if reading my mind. "Did you get her out? She's okay?"

"She's *alive*," I admit, watching the woman in question stir in her sleep.

"Good," Domi says, a yawn in her voice. They must have kept her in a holding cell overnight. Though, ironically, even a cot in a precinct was a step up for her. "Then get her down here. Make her flash her badge and get me the hell out of here before they find me first."

There is no use in telling her that her "cop" turned out to be merely an informant right now. Instead, I glance at the clock above the stove and sigh. "Give me an hour."

I get an earful of Russian in return.

"I'll assume that all means 'please and thank you,'" I tell her. "Sit tight. I'm on my way."

She hangs up, and I use the resulting silence to inhale the rest of my second-to-last cig.

The damn thing's barely gone cold when I sense Yellow watching me. I can't tell how much of the phone call she heard, if any of it. She scans the wall behind my head while she attempts to regain control of her body.

She doesn't look so green, at least. The sleep did her some good on that front. Not so much for her suspicion though.

"I see that you did more of your…*art* while I was out," she says warily.

I find her gazing at her bandaged hand.

She inspects the sloppy job, flexing her fingers. "Thank you—"

"Don't," I say. "At least not until you see the nasty scar you're gonna have." A result that couldn't have been helped given the state of my kit. I need new thread. New needles. Details I'll just have to worry about later. I shake my head to clear it and run my free hand through my hair. "How do you feel?"

She takes her time before answering. The tilt to her mouth could almost be described as thoughtful. Or maybe it's a grimace. "Like shit."

"Good," I say, flicking a wad of ash onto a blank page in my sketchbook. It doesn't catch fire. The paper just smokes, and the ivory is swallowed up by ebony. "Last night, you could barely say the word *shit*."

"I'm sorry." She doesn't even seem to know why she's apologizing. Her mouth curls into a frown, her brow furrowing. "I didn't mean…"

"Don't worry about it." I can't resist the urge to physically shrug her guilt off. "Think of it this way—You were just part of a self-fulfilling prophecy."

She cocks an eyebrow. It's several shades darker than her hair. Either she fills them in, or she's not a natural blonde, a suspicion I file away for later.

"A what?" she asks.

I shake my head, turning my attention back to her face. She may know English well enough to suppress her accent, but she doesn't seem to have picked up many phrases. I take it she doesn't socialize much.

"Nothing. Just a friend of mine told me to have fun last night. What's more *fun* than stitching up a pretty girl?"

It's only when she flinches that I infer that "pretty" isn't a compliment where she's from.

"I didn't mean it like that—"

"It's fine," she says, but she draws her knees defensively to her chest. One of her hands feels down along her hip. She still isn't wearing much, other than my shirt paired with that bloodstained pair of white shorts, and she bites her lip at the realization.

"Change of subject." I clear the middle of the table with a sweep of my hand, as if the lack of clutter can reduce the tension. "Last night, you said something about money."

"I don't remember." Her gaze hardens up.

"Look, I'll give you every bit of what dear old Vlad left behind." I mean it, despite the fact that I could certainly use every dime. "But, first, I need you to do something for me."

She crosses her arms over her chest. So much for putting her at ease.

"Like what?" she asks.

I pinch my lower lip beneath my teeth and bite down hard. I don't like revealing the cards in my deck so soon. But a good rat needs his birdy friends, and this one won't keep singing if she's locked up.

"Remember that little flying friend I told you about?"

She stirs, renewed interest washing some of the wariness away.

"Well, she went and found herself a new cage," I continue. "I need your help to spring her. Do that, and I'll give you double what Vlad gave me."

"*Her*." The woman's quicker than I gave her credit for. Recognition swells in her eyes, and she sits upright. "Her. The girl—"

"Domi," I interject. I couldn't hide the annoyance in my tone even if I tried. So much for protecting my birdy's identity.

"Is she *your* informant?"

"She's my friend," I admit. "And, to be honest, she's the one who told me to request that dance from you—"

"Oh." She sighs, eyeing her hands. "And here I was, assuming you really were a pervert."

"That explains the whiskey bottle," I say. "You willing to help me or not?"

"I don't see how." She chews over the words, carefully spitting them out. "I told you—I'm not a cop."

"You don't have to be. Even an informant can get in the door. All you have to do is whisper into the right cop's ear. Your handler would be a good start."

Her face pales. "It's not that simple."

"Nothing ever is."

"I guess so." She sizes me up with those yellow eyes and turns away. "Do you have a bathroom?"

I point to the left, and she starts in that direction.

"Down the hall," I tell her. "Last door. Though, if you plan on climbing out of the window, don't."

Her steps falter just beyond the door.

"You'll just rip your stitches open. It's nowhere near as dramatic, but the good old-fashioned front door is the place to leave from if you want to bail. You should at least change first so that my neighbors don't think I make a habit out of having bloodied woman enter and leave my house. You can help yourself to anything in my closet."

When the sound of her footsteps starts again, they head for my bedroom. Not long after, the bathroom door closes and then the water runs, drowning out whatever she's doing inside it.

I eye the used-up butts of my last few cigs and wait. Ten minutes later, the door finally opens.

She took my good jeans, I see. One of my gray shirts hangs loosely on her, and she paired it with a black hoodie. She did what she could with her tangled hair and scrubbed the blood away, but she definitely doesn't look like a cop.

"Let's go." I push back from the table, slamming my sketchbook shut. I make a pit stop near the fridge for a bottle of water, which I toss in her direction. While she drinks, I grab a clean hoodie from the hook by the door and then lead the way out onto the street.

The single mom's rushing from the house across the way, scrambling to get into her car and drive over to the diner across town. Two scrawny kids peek out from behind the screen door, expressionless, as she warns them to get to school on time.

She's already driven off as Yellow and I clear the next block. It takes twenty minutes to walk to the precinct. Usually, it's fifteen, but she's walking slowly. Not out of pain, either. She's dragging her feet, looking more and more like a deer in headlights the closer we get to the station. Just as the building comes into view, she pulls ahead of me.

"Wait here," she says, her face hidden by the fringe of my hood, which casts a shadow all the way down to her jaw.

"Don't think that's such a good idea," I tell her, remaining right on her heels.

"Do you have a better idea?"

Fair enough. I fall back and watch her. From a distance, she almost blends into the riffraff of students and homeless crawling around this part of town. Almost.

But none of them look half as haunted as she does.

CHAPTER NINE
CHLOE

I SHOULD HAVE RUN WHEN I HAD THE CHANCE. BACK to Montana, or farther. Anywhere but here. Vlad's money is a tempting distraction, but maybe that's all it ever was. An excuse to stay a little longer. Search longer. Hope longer.

But if Anna was here, then I've already screwed up my slim chances of finding her.

My failure encircles my neck like a noose as I enter the precinct with the hood of Espisido's jacket drawn low over my face and no semblance of a logical plan. A receptionist guards the desk situated behind bulletproof glass at the center of the lobby, but she doesn't look my way.

I don't find Grey in his office. So I keep moving, slipping through a side entrance and into the alley where some of the senior officers park for a smoke. Sure enough, I spot his patrol car—his official one this time. He's sitting back in the driver's seat, a cigarette in one hand and a bottle in the other. Something tells me that's not coffee.

He has to see me coming from a mile away, but it's almost a full minute before he disengages the locks.

"Well, you're alive after all." He tilts the bottle in a mock salute as I scramble into the cruiser.

"You might as well let it all out," I tell him, bracing for the inevitable lecture.

Some unknown country song plays on the radio, and he's already adjusted my usual seat. The masculine vibe is a blunt reminder that Grey never wanted to take me on as his partner in the first place. He didn't "babysit," in his exact words.

"You look like shit, kid," he tells me, the likely start of a massive tirade. In the end, he just shakes his head. "I was prepared to cover my own ass. I had it all written up that you never showed. That job wasn't on the books…"

"But?" I sense a big one coming.

"*But.*" He scoffs and takes a drag on his cigarette. "That didn't exactly sit too well—the thought of you being dead because you couldn't keep your fucking head on straight. I spent all night looking for you. Only ten minutes ago did I finally rationalize that you were ashes in that fucking club."

Dark circles line his eyes. One good inhale, and I realize he hasn't showered.

"I called out," he tells me. "But I had to come here, just in case your scrawny ass would show. I'm still not convinced you aren't a figment of the rum though." He starts to take another sip, but I grab the bottle before he can.

"You shouldn't drink and drive—"

"You want to tell me what the hell happened, Parker? They found bodies in that place, you know. They think one of them is Vladimir Olshenkov."

Do I *want* to tell him what happened? No. Yes. Maybe.

"I will. But not right now. I..." I suck in air and swallow my pride. "I need a favor."

"Of course you do." Laughing, Grey takes another drag on his cigarette.

The acrid smell floods my nostrils, and I can't silence a cough. It reminds me of *him*, the "angel" who followed me to spy from the mouth of the alley. I can't see him—he's good, but nothing can erase his smell, and it haunted me during the entire walk here.

"First, you help me," Grey tells me, commanding my attention again. "When I go in there and tell the brass that you never showed, what the fuck should I say, huh? I'm guessing you aren't going in yourself, dressed like you crawled out of a dumpster."

"Nice one."

He has a point. As far as today is concerned, Chloe Parker is as good as dead. I could always go back to Montana, but not any time soon. If Piotr found my home, he found my accounts. Ironically, Vlad's money is my only option. The moment I get it, I'm on the next train out. Then the next boat. Plane. No route will outrun Piotr for long.

But I'll follow any path leading to Anna.

"Just tell them…"

"We'll say you're undercover," Grey says over me. "We knew that it would be breaking the rules, but the lead was just too damn big to lose. I need a name. A good one. You had to rub shoulders with someone before you got out of that death trap. I need a rat to pin this on. You owe me this."

A good name. Espisido is a terrible one. I don't recognize it from any of the databases, but I do recognize one.

"Arno," I say, recalling the man I heard speaking to Espisido the night he saved my life. "That's a dealer's name, isn't it? The one he goes by."

Grey sits straighter, the gears in his head already turning.

"Runs guns too," I continue. "Has a gang. What is his name? *Mackenzie—*"

"Arnold Mackenzie," Grey corrects, rubbing his chin. "That's a good fucking name. Very good. I guess he was working with Petrov after all, huh?"

I nod. "My turn. They picked up a girl last night—"

"A girl?" Grey rolls his eyes. "Fucking hell. I told you— Women like that bring nothing but trouble."

"She's young," I insist. "Brunette. Thick accent. Probably didn't give you her name. They think if they hold her long enough she'll spill something on the Russians, but she won't." I wouldn't. "Get them to let her go—"

"And *you* get me something on Mackenzie," he counters before snatching his bottle back. "Something solid that I can use to get us both out of this mess without a fucking scratch. You got that, Parker? Even if you do, I can only buy us a few days."

Days I don't have. The clock is ticking, and in the end, Grey will be left holding the short end of the stick.

"Look, I know I screwed up—"

"You think I don't know the risk I was taking, letting you go into that place alone? And I'm not just talking about the fucking danger of Vladimir Olshenkov and his buddy Petrov." Grey sizes me up and sighs. "You lost someone to violence. I knew the look in your eye the moment I saw you. Who was it, huh? Your mom? Dad?" He shakes his head. "That kind of evil… It leaves a mark on you—"

"I'm just a rookie from Podunk, Montana, remember?" I can't stop picking at the gauze on my injured hand. "Don't get soft on me."

"Whatever. I just need *something*." His neglected cigarette's grown quite the tail of ash. If he doesn't flick it soon, it'll fall off on its own, possibly splattering the leg of his dark-brown pants. "Something to nail even one of those bastards to the wall. A Russian. Mackenzie. I don't fucking care. Just something to prove that this all fucking means something." He gestures to the decrepit city landscape around us. He wants it all to matter. He did spend most of his life fighting for it, after all.

"Let the girl go, and I'll do my best." It could be a lie—the part of me itching to run wants it to be—but deep down...

Who knows?

"Give me an hour," Grey says while switching the car's engine off. "I'll see what I can do. But I'll say this again, Parker—This will only buy us time. And after this...maybe it's better for everyone if you go back to Montana."

If only he knew.

"Thank you. I mean it," I say.

Judging from the wary tilt to his mouth, he might believe me. "Just get out of here," he says. "Before one of those overachieving rookies sees you."

I reach for the door on my end. My fingers brush the handle, but I don't pull it just yet. "Were there any other girls who came in the other night?" I ask. "Young. Red hair?"

Grey shrugs. "Not anyone sober."

I swallow hard and accept the information with a nod. Averting my face from his, I leave the cruiser and face the street, ignoring the burning sting creeping behind my eyes.

Then I start walking, and I don't look back.

My shadow turns out to be quick. I find him where I left him last, leaning against the wall as if he never moved. Maybe he'd already caught on that I sensed him in my wake. It could be that he *let* me sense him all along.

"So?" he asks.

"Your birdy should be free within the hour."

"Then I guess we're done here." He withdraws a wad of cash from his pocket. "Here. It's yours, as promised."

It's enough money to outlast Piotr for a little while…

But it's nowhere near *enough*. My excuse has run out, but some deep-seated itch in my skin won't let me leave. Maybe it's Anna, calling to me. If I leave now, I might not find her again.

"Not comfortable with receiving payment upfront?" Espisido returns the money to his pocket. "Professionalism. I can respect that."

"Was your friend a plant?" I ask, changing the subject. "That's a stupid risk to take if she was—playing around with the Syndicate's toys. Though it would be even more foolish if she weren't."

"That's me. Foolish." He confirms the worst by shaking his head. "No… She's in deep. I've been trying for months to get her out. This is the only shot she has. If I'm lucky, those friends of hers aren't already watching the station."

"I see." There's a reason why he's willing to pay so much for my help now.

As he said, it's her only chance.

And, of course, he'll fail.

"How did you meet her?"

Evasive, for once, he stares beyond my head. "In an alley. Vlad made her sleep near the dumpsters as punishment one night. I gave her some food. She gave me a hell of a lot more. After that, she made a habit of pissing them off in order to sleep on the street. I did what I could to help her out."

"For *information*," I clarify. Someone risking their life to help another for their own gain is a lot easier to stomach than the alternative.

"Yep." He breaks the tension by fishing a cell phone from his pocket to check the time. "An hour, you said? The pigs always seem to be overachievers. Let's go now."

I wind up following him out of simple, burning curiosity. A lone man plans to grab a girl from Piotr Petrov's watch. I hope he isn't that stupid. I'm amused enough to ask.

"Do you have a plan?"

He shakes his head, but when he glances back at me, he's smiling. The slight quirk to his mouth ignites burning sparks beneath my skin. Once again, the only adjective I can use to describe one of his expressions is *beautiful*. It's not a compliment. I know firsthand what beauty means against a man like Piotr.

It's weakness.

"Think if I ask nicely they'll let her walk away?" He poses the question to the sky as he tucks his hands into his pockets, his stroll leisurely.

I'm almost fooled. Almost. But he's scanning the road, hunting the face of every pedestrian who rushes past.

"I think you're going to get yourself killed," I tell him truthfully. *What a waste.* That angelic face will be mutilated by the blow from some thug's fist—if he's not lucky enough to get a bullet to the head.

"Oh, I already know that." He stares me down head on, and a slight tilt renders his pretty smile a little less innocent. "That doesn't mean it has to happen *today* though."

"W-wait—"

I'm left reeling as he picks up speed before slowing down as we near the precinct. He decides to cross the street toward a bodega. Then he cuts through an alley, and we linger near the mouth of it, assaulted by the stench of rotting garbage wafting from a row of trash cans a few yards down.

He surveys the front of the police station, and I copy him. Vagrants and detectives alike go in and out. I recognize some of them, though distantly. It's like I'm viewing a slideshow of someone else's life. Maybe I read the summary somewhere, but I forgot the context. Wholesome rookie cop transfers from a Podunk town in Montana—only she's not so wholesome, and Newtown was never her home.

"There she is," Espisido whispers.

A woman exits the front of the station, her dark hair a ratty mess, her blue eyes bloodshot. The man beside me tenses up, but he doesn't start forward. He merely whistles.

I don't know how the sharp sound manages to cut over the bustle of early morning traffic, but the woman flinches, her gaze flitting in our direction. Another whistle and she takes off, descending the curb and cutting through traffic. She's fast, but when a man climbs out of a dark van parked a block away, my heart lurches ominously.

"Shit." Espisido hisses through his teeth. This must have been his plan after all—hope that he could beat them to her. "Get back."

We move deeper into the alley, but he doesn't take his gaze off the girl once. The brute on her tail is all muscle. He cracks his knuckles with every step he takes, his eyes narrowed over his prey.

A terrifying realization hits me like a punch to the stomach —She won't be fast enough. Maybe Espisido knows that too, because he's inching backward until we're out of sight, tucked around where the alley turns.

The girl falters just beyond the bodega. Another low whistle draws her closer. By then, it's already too fucking late.

"No." A hand descends over my shoulder before I even register moving. Espisido. "It's okay," he says.

But all he does is whistle again.

The sound lures the girl a few steps closer. She's nearly halfway into the alley by the time the thug catches up. His size alone blocks the entrance, rendering our direction as her only exit—not that she makes it that far. With the ease of a hand swatting a fly, the man snatches her wrist and hauls her backward. I'm close enough to make out the words he snarls to her in Russian.

"*Where the hell were you going? Get to the van!*"

"*No!*" She tries in vain to push him off, but the bastard's already forming a fist, aiming it at her chest.

"Wait here," Espisido speaks directly into my ear this time.

The next moment, I'm staring at the back of his head. He's drawn his hood low, his gait unsteady. One of his hands pulls something from his pocket. It's small, cylindrical. A syringe? If I didn't know any better, I'd assume he was a druggie, too damn high to even notice the scene unfolding in front of him.

The bastard has Domi by the waist now. She's flailing, struggling to keep her feet on the ground.

"Excuse me." An almost comical scene interrupts the horror —a stoned druggie stumbling into the thug's side. He draws away with an apology, continuing his listless walk toward the mouth of the alley. He's only a few feet away when the Russian starts with a grunt. One of his meaty hands loses its grip on Domi and swipes at his neck.

"What the hell?"

The lanky figure turns, blue eyes gleaming through shadow. "Domi, run!"

It all happens too fast. The girl takes off in my direction while the thug whirls on Espisido. He found a rock from somewhere. Like a ballerina on lithe feet, he dodges the punch the man throws at him and aims a blow of his own. One sickening thud and the bastard staggers into the wall, groaning out curses. The blow alone won't down him, but something tells me that whatever Espisido injected into his veins will.

But the brief advantage won't last in the long run. It could take minutes before the drug takes effect—and Piotr's men never go out alone.

Espisido meets my gaze as Domi races between us. "Go!"

He nods to where the alley extends, and my hand flies out, seizing a bony wrist. I use it like a leash to tug her after me, around the corner. Grunts echo behind us. Another thud. A groan...

Not *his*. I feed myself that lie even though it's stupid to care. Luckily, Domi doesn't need much persuasion to run.

We cut through alleys, sidestepping curious shop owners taking the trash out and yawning workers starting their commutes. My heart won't stop pounding. Few people are wandering the streets, but I scan their faces one by one. Hunting. Searching. The lanky man a block down isn't wearing a hoodie. Neither is the figure exiting a building up ahead.

But their eyes follow us. Every road for at least a mile, runs straight through the heart of the Syndicate. We're walking targets for any snitch looking to win favor with Piotr—at this rate, we won't make it another block, let alone to safety.

Unless…

I don't think. Instead, I steer Domi down a side street and grit my teeth at the sight appearing up ahead—an auto mechanic shop notorious even to the police. Some days, the man who runs it restores vintage cars for wealthy clients. Others, he smuggles cocaine into trucks that are towed across state lines. It's all in a day's work for the main distribution branch of the Syndicate.

A shudder racks my spine as I cross the road and approach the building from the front with Domi in tow. Near the side entrance, hidden from the street, I turn her face me. "Wait here."

"What about him?" Wide-eyed, she gazes back the way we came. "We need to—"

"Trust me." I don't give her the chance to argue, and I slip around the front of the building just as a familiar van turns the corner. Shit.

I enter the building without thinking through the consequences. A raised garage door reveals the car being restored here now—a vintage Volvo. With no worker in sight, it looks like an unexpected windfall for any thief worth their salt, but none of them venture here for a reason —only a fool would steal from Ivan Ivanov.

I find him in the main shop when I finally gather the nerve to tug the glass door open and step inside. It's like walking back in time. The small, square room even smells the same, though some of the furniture is new—a black leather couch in the lobby and a flat-screen television mounted on the wall. Living under the protection of the Petrovs, he's done well for himself, it seems. When I spot him, his back is to me as he swipes at the counter with a wet rag.

An infamous tattoo spans the back of his neck as a warning to anyone who isn't aware of his identity—a hawk in midflight, the symbol of the Syndicate. His plain, black shirt and pants are less expensive than Vlad's tailored suits but just as impressive. It's a fitting ensemble for a lieutenant of the *Volki*.

"What is it?" He snaps, glancing over his shoulder. The moment he spots me, his stern frown goes slack. "Ksei...Ksenia?"

"Hello, Ivan." My throat goes dry, and I have to swallow hard to moisten it. "You also told me I could always trust you." I display my hands to show I'm unarmed. "I hope I still can. I-I need your help."

He sighs, my old friend. The past years have taken a toll on him. Most of his dark hair is streaked with gray. He's grown his beard out, but his blue eyes have retained that same disarming gleam.

"My help? Does it have anything to do with this?" He reaches behind him and snatches something from the counter.

Shit. My heart sinks as I recognize the shape even though it's been burned, the outer casing singed and melted—a ruined service weapon typical of a police officer.

"Did you think I didn't know you were in town?" Ivan asks before holding the remains of my gun out to me. "Though after last night, I was sure you were dead. I had my men scour the ruins of the club for any trace of you. I was just about to call in a favor to have you scrubbed from the database." He sizes me up with a sweep of his eyes, and with every inch, they narrow. "You did a very, *very* stupid thing. I didn't even know you'd let yourself get transferred to this shithole until last night. After everything I've done for you —" He forms a fist and slams it against the countertop. "What the hell were you thinking?"

Rather than defend myself, I take the gun. My nostrils wrinkle with the acrid stench of smoke, but I'll write off the feeling twisting through my stomach as relief anyway. This is one less mess Grey will have to explain on my behalf.

I don't dare ask Ivan how he managed to infiltrate what was sure to be a hive of police activity by now. Ivan Ivanov knows *everything*.

"So, who did it?" I croak once I've gathered up the nerve. "Who attacked the club?"

I steel myself for the answer. Another gang? The police would never be so reckless.

"I don't know," Ivan says. His expression is carefully blank. "I thought *you* would."

So much for his omniscient reputation.

"Well, I don't," I admit. "Someone...someone got me out before I saw much."

"Oh?" His eyes narrow in a silent demand for more.

"A man," I add. "I don't know who he is or who he works for."

"His name?"

My mouth opens, but this time, the words stick in my throat. A baby-faced angel may run with street thugs like Vlad, but he's no match for a man like Ivan Ivanov.

Neither am I.

"Did you hear me?" His voice lowers in warning. "Ksenia..."

After a sharp intake of air, I spill the rest. "He said his name was Espi. Espisido."

Ivan frowns, mulling the name over. I don't realize I'm holding my breath until he sighs and my lungs contract in response.

"Never heard of him."

Is that more relief flooding my veins? Whatever it is drains the energy I have left. My hand flies out against the wall for balance, but my outstretched fingers miss the frame of a hanging photograph by inches—a much younger Ivan grinning beside an even younger Vlad. I flinch at the reminder and tear my gaze away. In the process, I find myself staring down at my arm. Only a few tiny stitches are visible beneath the sleeve of my borrowed shirt and sweater. The artist wasn't exaggerating his talents, considering they've held this far, at least.

"Whoever he is, I don't think he's part of the Syndicate." It feels important to say that, conveying an underlying message I'm not brave enough to say directly—*He's no one. Leave him alone.*

"Hmph. I'll look into it."

"I didn't tell him much," I add. "Just enough to keep him from asking too many questions."

"Too many questions." Ivan laughs.

He's in front of me in an instant, and I don't even see the slap coming. It's sharp, stinging, but he hooks his meaty palm beneath my chin and forces my gaze up to meet his as my eyes water. The concern I see there is more painful to endure. I don't deserve it.

"You need to *focus*, little girl," he insists, his accent thickening over each word. "I promised your father I'd look after you. After everything… I've done what I could. I even humored your little bid to join the pigs." He spits the word out and releases me to sway on my feet. "All you had to do was stay away from here. Especially from Vladimir and Piotr. I risked my fucking neck enough helping you the first time—"

"I think I saw Anna."

He recoils. A part of me wants to take his reaction as a good sign, but it's a hollow comfort. His alarm quickly gives way to a terrible expression that takes the form of a frown. Pity.

"Ksenia." He sighs heavily, shaking his head. "So *that* is why you came back—"

"I saw her," I insist. My fingers fly to my chest, but my proof is gone, burned to ash along with Vlad. "I *did*. In the international database. A girl who had been detained here a few weeks ago. She had her eyes." That beautiful, haunting navy.

"So that's why you joined the pigs," he says, seeing through my lies in advance. "To keep looking? Tell me you're not that stupid."

"It's her," I say. "I know it's her—"

"She's dead," Ivan says. Not brutally or harshly. Just firmly —as if he's told himself the same two words enough times to believe them. I can stomach his anger, not his pain. "You know if she weren't I would be the first to get her out."

But he couldn't. Only I can. With my newfound strength, my resources with the police, and *my* instincts. That is how I've rationalized it all this time. Anna is still out there, somewhere. Waiting for me.

"She's gone," Ivan says softly. "She's gone, Ksei, and you were reckless to come here. Especially after Vlad."

Does he know the fate of his friend? His frown reveals little, and I can't bring myself to ask. He has a good point, drawing my attention to my current dilemma.

"I said I needed your help," I start, swallowing hard. "There's a van, looking for a girl. I need you to call it off—"

"Call it off?" Ivan raises an eyebrow, and I cringe in anticipation of another slap. One doesn't come, however, just a heavy sigh. "What the hell have you gotten yourself into now? If anyone saw you come here," he adds, "it will be my ass on the line."

"I…" Deep down, maybe I knew all along that coming here would be a waste of time. A dead end.

But, for the second time today, perhaps Ivan doesn't know everything.

"I will give you one last piece of advice," he tells me, jabbing a single finger in my direction. "Leave town. Forget your name. *Forget* the Petrovs."

"You think I haven't tried?"

"Maybe you haven't," he says. "Not hard enough, anyway."

I'm halfway to the door when Ivan calls out.

"Wait." He lumbers closer and takes the gun from me, tossing it back onto the counter. "I'll have my men get rid of that. And as for your name…forget what I said. For your father's sake, never forget who you are. You are *Olenova*."

He raises his fist, and I contort my fingers to form one in return. Our knuckles meet for one brief moment.

"Go," he says, drawing back. "I'll make a phone call. Just stay the hell out of sight, understood?"

"Thank you!" I push the door open and scramble out, but Domi's not where I left her. *Damn.* Whirling around, I spot a dark-haired blur disappearing around a nearby building, and I race to catch up.

"What are you doing?" I snarl the moment I draw even with her in a narrow alley. My hand snags her shoulder, yanking her to a stop. "I told you to stay there—"

"Yeah," she hisses, wrenching out of my grip. "So that you can deliver me to them on a platter? I know whose place that was. You're one of them!"

"Wait. Just slow down." I direct the plea more to my body than to her. I need my pulse to slow. My thoughts to stop spinning. I need to forget his fucking face.

A face that won't look so pretty once Piotr's men are through with him. Ivan may call off the thugs for now, but the reprieve may come too late.

"Forget it. Keep moving." I release Domi's wrist and shove her forward. "I'll catch up."

There's only one shortcut back to the precinct. How many blocks have we covered already? Ten? Twenty?

He's already dead. If I'm lucky, they left his body on the road at least. Something for the rats to savor.

"No!" Bony fingers clutch at my shoulder. "They'll—"

A sudden sound draws both of our attention. Footsteps. I watch in a frozen, morbid fascination as a body unfurls itself from the top of a fire escape clinging to a decrepit building up ahead.

With the fluidity of a gymnast, the figure jumps and lands mere feet away from us, one hand pressed against the pavement to steady their landing.

It's a man. Tall. Slim. Familiar. I exhale as blue eyes meet mine through a fringe of dark hair.

"Miss me?" He's smiling. Of all things, it's the strangest occurrence of today. Unlike his amused smirks, this grin looks…

Real.

"Let's go." Domi's still tugging on my arm, though she slows for Espisido to catch up. She must be used to this little trick of his. "Go! *Go.*"

I don't know why I submit to being pulled along by the wrist as Espisido takes the lead, drawing his hood low once again. Maybe I'm still delirious.

Watching him, I swear the dark sleeves of his jacket flutter out beside him as he moves. Almost like wings. But even angels aren't invincible. He's limping, favoring his right leg, though his expression never wavers.

And he never stops smiling.

CHAPTER TEN

ESPI

Yellow follows us into a diner. She stands guard as I shove Domi into a booth but doesn't take a seat for herself. Too many heads swivel in our direction, so I shift farther down, opening a space beside me.

There's no time to warm her up. "Have a seat."

She does reluctantly, squeezing in beside Domi. As for the brunette beside her... With a sigh, I strip my hoodie, wishing I'd had the foresight to bring one for her.

"Domi, remember that new hairstyle you wanted to try?" I tell her out loud. "The pixie cut? And you wanted to get it bleached too. Red. That'll look cute. We can do it today before you go on your trip."

I keep the tone light and casual for the benefit of anyone listening in. Including staff, there are only about ten people in the place, but Domi's bloodshot, kohl-caked eyes draw their attention. The bad kind. An old woman a few tables over keeps sneaking glances at our corner and palming her cell phone.

"My trip?" Domi does her best to play along. She shimmies into the hoodie but isn't stupid enough to draw the hood with all eyes watching. Good. She tries running her fingers through her ratted hair and gives up halfway. "A haircut. Good. Good. I'd like that."

"Good. Your grandparents will be happy to see you again."

The lady across from us returns to sipping her coffee and reading the paper—but one skeptic isn't fooled.

"Her...grandparents?" Yellow's gone back to laying on the thick accent. Her gaze darts from me to Domi as if to say, *Don't ask*. She doesn't want to remove all of her masks just yet. "Where do they live?"

"Upstate," I say. As far north as she can fucking get on a one-way bus. I'll give her enough money to buy a plane ticket after. Somewhere far from here.

"That close?" Yellow raises an eyebrow. "You think her...*friends* won't be able to find her there?"

I shrug. "It doesn't matter if she's fast enough."

Yellow laughs, but amusement never reaches her eyes. "Fast enough. You think that matters? You think she's the first girl to run away to her *grandparents*?" The flat of her hand strikes the table. Hard. "They know the likely routes we take. They tip off the bus drivers for intel. They have plants on the airlines. They know the clues to look for. By the time you realize that they have her, she'll already be gone. To another club. Another city."

Her voice is too loud. The little old lady at the next table over is staring again.

"Fine, then." I fold my hands on the table. "What do you suggest?"

"I…" She trails off, her gaze on Domi.

The girl's been watching us the entire time, her head bouncing between us like a ping-pong ball in a match of table tennis. Smart little Domi. She's keeping her mouth shut.

"She should stay here," Yellow says finally. "They wouldn't expect it."

Here, as in the city, right under the bastards' noses. It's a good enough plan in theory, but there's an obvious hole.

"Where?" I ask.

There is one place I could stash her though… Somewhere where she'd be safer than anywhere else. But I'd have to get a certain someone's permission for that—and that might require a truckload of goddamn alcohol and more of my savings down the drain.

But it's not like I have any better ideas.

"I know a place," I grit out finally.

Yellow settles back in her seat. Not the way a normal person might. Just enough so that she no longer looks like she's about to lunge across the table and punch me in my mouth. I can live with that.

"So, change of plans," Domi says.

I look at her for the first time in what feels like ages. Her black eye still looks like shit. Her clothes are no better. The cops must have given her the oversized orange flip-flops on her feet, but she'll need to change soon if we want to shake the Russians from her trail.

Even so, she musters up a smile. "Do I still get my hair cut?"

A corner of my mouth quirks up. "Damn right, you do. Whatever floats your boat. Hell, I might even join you and get one myself." I unlace my fingers and run them through my hair, knocking the worst of it back from my face. "Ouch." I hiss at the burning sting that flares in response.

"You're hurt." Yellow leans forward and swipes the pad of her thumb against my forehead.

"I must have banged it on something."

"Like a fist," Yellow says, her jaw tight.

"It's fine—"

"Here." She snatches up a wad of napkins without taking her hand from my face.

Her fingers are warm. Too warm. They shake as if it's taking all of her energy to extend the limb. She seems determined to wipe the blood away though, so I let her.

It's been a long time since someone else has tried to wipe away my boo-boos. Maybe not since Dante.

And he was never this gentle.

"I'm sure you have *your* tetanus shot up to date?"

So Yellow has jokes. She wads the used napkins into her fist, and when the waitress comes to our table, she quietly requests a glass of water, still eyeing my forehead.

I order stuff off the menu at random. Both Yellow and Domi look like they haven't had a good meal in a while. When the waitress scurries away to the kitchen, promising to bring a pot of coffee, we wait.

The two women take turns eyeing each other while I tally up all the many ways this little stunt will cost me. I'll need to refresh my kit sooner than I planned on, thanks to Yellow. That's at least a hundred. The drugs are easily another two or three. Taking care of Domi will cost me only god knows how much.

"Are you a gymnast?" Yellow doesn't like silence too much. She's itching to fill it. "Are you?"

I shake my head. "Unless studying at the school of 'badassery on the jungle gym' counts as proper training."

That cracks a smile out of her. I copy the expression, but her mouth falls flat.

"Doctor. Artist. Acrobat." She tiredly rattles off the list. "You're quite the one-man show."

"More like a shitshow." God, I need a cigarette. My fingers flex against the table, desperate to light one up.

"Here." Domi reaches down the front of her dress without giving a damn for whoever might be watching.

The moment I see what she has in her hand, I don't care if she brought the attention of the whole police department.

"I scored these from a cop on my way out," she tells me as she lets two limp cigarettes fall onto the table. "Told him that he had a cute face."

"You beautiful, beautiful girl." I snatch up one, ignoring the slight dampness, and reach into my pocket for a lighter.

This café's old school, thank fuck. They even have a complimentary ashtray beside the ketchup bottle. I light up quickly and take a hit.

Yellow's still watching me, her brow furrowed. With her beside Domi, the similarities between them add up. They both sit hunched over and sneak glances at the door as if waiting for the moment a Russian will come barging through. Strip away the different hair colors, and you'd have the same battered woman.

"How long are we going to stay here?" Domi's getting anxious, but the moment the question leaves her mouth, the first plate of food arrives. The next second, she's too busy stuffing eggs and pancakes down to care about leaving.

I let her have the lion's share. Even Yellow caves and samples a piece of toast. At least one of us can loosen up.

Two hard pulls on my cig don't ease the ache in the pit of my stomach. Half a cup of coffee doesn't chase it away, either. I'll need whiskey tonight. Maybe the rest of the damn bottle. It's like I'm turning into Arno.

I'm nearly finished with the cig when Domi sets her fork down, having cleared four plates. Yellow copies her, and I fish a fifty from my pocket to cover the meal. When we leave the diner, good old reality comes back with a vengeance. Somehow, I've got to get back to Arno's territory without arousing suspicion or being tailed. That's hard enough on a *good* day.

"You think you can keep her safe?" Yellow speaks against my ear. Her breath smells like blood.

I take another hit of the cig to drown out the stench. "Maybe," I say, eliciting a skeptical sigh from her. "Look." I turn around, yanking the rest of the cash from my pocket. I slap most of it into her hand without bothering to count the bills. "I'll take it from here. Here's your cut."

"And then what?" She withstands the contact of my palm against hers with the money in between, but she doesn't try to take it. She eyes me instead before turning to watch Domi over my shoulder. "Let's say you get her to wherever you plan to. Then what?"

"I'll cross that bridge when I get to it."

"You think it's really that easy?"

"I've gotten this far."

She frowns and tries to pull her hand away, but I don't let go until her fingers finally curl, snagging the bills.

"My place. You remember how to get there?"

She nods. "Why?"

"Stick around here for an hour at least. There's a convenience store on Fifth. Get some hair dye. Some scissors. Whatever else you think our friend needs. Meet me back at the house. Don't come in through the front—only the back. Got it?"

She's still holding the money. The wind tears at it, threatening to snatch the whole lot from her hands. "And if I don't?"

"Get those stitches out in ten days." I turn back to Domi and grab for her arm.

She's already swaying on her feet, and I feel something that might be pity—she's in for a rough trip. I'll have to take the long way back through the city. We're only a few steps away when Yellow's voice reaches me.

"You would really trust me?"

I stop walking. Trust? "This is the part where I threaten you to keep your mouth shut, I guess."

Arno would.

I sense rather than see her nod.

"Typically," she says.

My cigarette's almost out. I'll need another. "Buy me a pack of smokes while you're at it. If not…see ya around."

She should be able to find her way out of the Russians' reach on her own. If there's one thing Yellow seems to be an expert at, it's running.

CHAPTER ELEVEN
CHLOE

I should take the money and run. I keep telling myself that, even as my feet carry me farther from freedom. My arms ache, weighed down by several grocery bags. Juggling them takes most of my energy as I set my sights on my destination and choke down my doubt.

The house at the end of the block looks deserted, but when I circle around it, I find a rickety gate unlocked. A concrete stoop leads to the back door, nestled beneath a worn awning. I mount the steps and knock once. Not even a second later, it opens from the inside.

"I see you decided to join our little party after all." Espisido appears in the doorway, and I bite my lower lip at his expression. His narrowed eyes betray suspicion, and they probe the shadows at the edge of the property before he steps aside. "Come in."

They've eaten again. A box of pizza contains two remaining slices. There's no sign of Domi in the narrow kitchen, but a faucet is running deeper inside the house.

"I see someone went shopping," Espisido remarks, drawing my attention back to him.

I press the bags into his hands.

He rummages through each, one by one. When he spots a new pack of cigarettes, his lips split into a genuine grin. "You're a lifesaver."

I shrug the gratitude off. "Those things will give you cancer, you know."

If anything, his grin widens more. Pearly-white teeth serve as the basis for the breathtaking expression. I almost can't tell where it ends and the wariness he hides so well underneath begins.

"Cancer, maybe," he says. "But not an aneurysm any time soon, and that's all that matters to me."

He might be onto something. There are worse vices he could choose—if he hasn't already.

"Domi!" he calls, raising his voice. "Let's get you pretty."

A door opens down the hall—the one to the bathroom, I presume. A woman steps out, wearing only an oversized T-shirt, with a toothbrush sticking out of her mouth. She sizes me up in a single glance. "You came back."

"Fire Engine Red," Espisido reads from a box of hair dye before I can say anything in return. "What do you think?" He tosses the box to Domi as she pads closer.

"Pretty." She fights to keep her expression blank as she eyes the box—but I know that look. She's picturing a new life tucked inside next to the bottle of dye. Will it bring her better fortune than the last? She sighs, uncertain of the answer. "Let's get it over with."

After steering her to a chair near the table, Espisido cuts her hair first. Short. She's left with barely enough length to scrape into a ponytail. Her expression is stoic as she eyes the shorn, dark strands falling into a heap at her feet. When he starts to open the box of dye, however, she squeezes her eyes shut.

"Short hair I can work with, but just…just don't leave me bald."

Espisido chuckles. "I'll see what I can do."

I don't know what makes me creep closer to him. My fingers won't stop shaking until I snatch up the directions and listlessly flip through the pages. Somehow, I find myself wearing gloves and helping to smear the dye over every inch of the girl's head.

We work quickly, cleaning up the hair on the floor while the dye sets in. Afterward, Espisido makes her wash it out in the sink. Unsatisfied with the color, he opens another box of red and repeats the process before sending her off to shower with a bottle of shampoo fished from one of the shopping bags.

He waits until the bathroom door closes and the water starts to run before he turns to me. "Thanks. I don't think I could have gotten her here without your help."

It doesn't seem worth pointing out that, in this case, self-preservation and "help" are two very different things. To make use of the awkward silence, I move past him, positioning myself near the opposite end of the kitchen.

"I'm glad you got her away," he adds. "But it's funny." The lowered octave of his voice sets my body on edge even before he comes up behind me. "I know you haven't brought anyone with you. But I still can't help wondering why you would cut through Ivan Ivanov's territory, of all places. Especially given your feelings for dear old Vlad."

Alarm stiffens my spine. So he's not as unfamiliar with the map of hell as I'd hoped. "It's hard to plot a course when you're running for your life—"

"Uh-uh." He shakes his head and takes a step in my direction. The act moves him out of the path of the light, draping his face in shadow. "Don't play dumb with me. First, you know Vlad, and now, Ivan."

"Is that so?" I address the question to the wall. My palms are slick. Thoughts crash through my head in disjointed bits and pieces.

It was stupid to come here. Stupid to stay in this goddamn city. With Piotr looming overhead, trying to ignore him at all was just fucking stupid.

"What do they call it? *Pobratim.* Blood brother. That's what all the big-name Russians in the Syndicate refer to themselves as, isn't it? It's a little strange that you would run *toward* one after you just killed the other—"

"Milo Olenov. Ever heard of him?" My throat aches in the wake of that name, but I can't seem to lock the words back. "He was Ivan Ivanov's true *pobratim.* Before Vlad. After Vlad."

"Hmph." He's smart enough to process the words without saying anything in return. All he does, in the end, is reach for one of the shopping bags. "I'm guessing this shade is for you." He holds out another box of dye I only vaguely remember picking up.

I take it, but the motion draws his attention to my injured arm.

"Shit. Take the jacket off," he commands, hissing between his teeth. "Let's see what you've done."

"W-what?"

He grabs my wrist and steers me closer to him. I suck in a breath. His grip is loose—I could break away if I wanted to. But I don't, even as he takes the box from me and places it on the table.

"Let me see." He has my arm out of the jacket's sleeve in seconds. Warm fingers gently hold the limb out, displaying the row of gauze. His touch is electric, as if all of his nervous energy is eager to seep into my skin. "Just as I thought," he grouses, gazing at patches of red speckling the bandage. "You must have ripped some open. I should have added no heavy lifting to those care instructions." He meticulously peels the bandage back and sighs in relief.

None of the stitches are torn, though the area around the wound is bleeding and inflamed.

"I don't care what you do or where you go from here on out, Yellow. Just don't mess up my work." He wets a rag beneath the faucet and returns to carefully dab at the wound the way a painter might touch up his masterpiece with a brush. He's careful. Gentle.

I can't stop myself from flinching with every touch. Maybe it's the suspense. Or the next question lurking within his gaze. I'm waiting for it. My teeth sink into my lower lip as if imparting strength. I'm ready…

But, when Domi reappears from the bathroom with a damp mop of bright-red hair, either he's distracted, or he saves that question for later. "You look cute," he declares.

In a way, she does. She looks *cute,* for a battered, broken shell of a girl who can barely keep her eyes open and her guard up. I recognize the way she juts her chin into the air; she doesn't want to seem weak.

But the artist apparently has x-ray vision. "Go crash in my bed," he tells her. "It has fresh sheets. I'll check on you in a bit, and we'll go from there."

She doesn't argue. With one last searching glance in my direction, she enters the bedroom and then closes the door behind her.

"You're really going to keep her here?"

"Not here." He's seated himself at the table and withdraws the pack of cigarettes from his pocket. "I know a place where she'll be safe. In theory, at least."

"In theory."

"There's a friend I know," he adds after a moment's silence. "He has a bar where she can work for a few days. Lie low. It's not ideal, but then again…"

I finish the statement for him. "It's not being forced to work a street corner, either."

"That too." He lights the end of his cigarette with a jet-black lighter.

Hypnotized, I watch him inhale the first puff. He drags on it as though it's more vital than oxygen, his lips parted and glistening pink.

"What about you?" he wonders, exhaling a cloud of smoke. It obscures his face, making it impossible to read him. "What does an informant do as her day job?"

"Keep her mouth shut," I say, dodging the question. "How does an 'artist' come to rub shoulders with one of the main players in the Russian Syndicate?"

"Well, you don't mince words, do ya?" He takes another drag on his cigarette and then lets it dangle between two of his fingers. "You tell me something. I'll answer a question of yours in return. That's how this game will go. *Khorosho*?"

"Okay." I take a step closer to the table and meet his gaze directly. "I'll go first. How did you meet Vlad?"

"I think it might be better if *he* told you that story." He flicks the end of his cigarette into an ashtray. "My turn. Who are you running from? Really. Don't feed me some line about Vlad."

"Vlad's dead—"

"And you're even more spooked *now* than you were around him," he declares, so damn smug. With one flick of his gaze, he strips me naked, but it's not my body he wants. Just the pitiful soul shivering underneath. "Why?"

I can't help the tired laugh that trickles out of me. Hell, maybe it's genuine. He's unknowingly pointed out the utter depth of my stupidity, and I don't even have the energy to play pretend.

"If I told you, you wouldn't want me here. Believe me."

"Try me." He takes another puff.

Suddenly, it's impossible to maintain eye contact. I break it and stare down at the table. He has his other hand pressed flat against it. For all of his bravado, he's just as on edge as I am.

"You've stuck around for a reason," he suspects. "At first, I thought it was because you wanted something. Maybe you really cared about Domi. But, now, I know there's more to it—"

"Like what?" I look up, eyeing him through loose strands of my hair.

"You don't have anywhere else to go. Do you?"

The truth hurts, they say.

Rather than respond, I reach for the box of unused dye, scanning the name printed beneath a smiling model—buxom brown. "Can I use your bathroom?" I hear his sharp intake of air and rush to cut him off. "I'll play your game. I just need... I just need..."

I need to scrub. Erase. Drown my screams in the shower spray and try to fucking think. I need to *think*. I need to remember.

Piotr's coming for me, but that familiar mantra of escape is surprisingly absent. A foreboding whisper has replaced it, running through my mind on a morbid, incessant loop —*moya lyubov.*

Espisido stands as if the act alone gives me permission. He stoops for one of the grocery bags and unpacks the items. Some of the things I don't even remember buying. Toothpaste. Shampoo. Deodorant. Body wash.

He forms them all into a shapeless stack and holds them out to me. "Take this stuff while you're at it."

I obey, carrying the pile into the bathroom. It's small, decorated in simple, dark shades—a black shower curtain, a navy rug, and a gray curtain shielding the only window. I strip my borrowed clothing, shivering once I'm naked in the center of the cramped space.

It's like the smoke-laced cotton kept it all at bay—the pain, the fear, the guilt...

Not for Vlad. Oh, no. It's *him*. I can't get his fucking voice out of my head—*"You don't have anywhere else to go. Do you?"* Something tells me he wasn't talking about a home, either. He *knew*, peering deep beneath my skin without permission.

The most alarming part? He didn't need my permission.

Snap out of it. I shake my head in an effort to. When that doesn't work, I run the shower and assemble the dye kit. With every glob of black over gold, I breathe a little easier. It's like every fucking strand belongs to Piotr. I can still feel his fingers running through it. I can still hear his voice in my ear.

"My little Ksei..."

It won't take him long to find me. No matter where I go. Where I hide. I should be tracking another gun down. I should make a new plan. I *need* to be ready for him.

I have to find Anna.

But I'm so damn tired… It takes all I have to scrub my hair clean and rinse my body beneath the scalding shower spray. I wind up lingering in the stall until the water's gone ice cold and my teeth are chattering loudly enough to drown out the voices in my head. Far too soon, a louder sound cuts over the drone. Knocking.

"Hey. You all right in there?"

I jump and look at the window, gauging the passage of time. The sky looks a darker hue of indigo.

"You okay?"

The doorknob jiggles. I guess he left me alone for as long as he dared. Either I'd climbed out the window despite his advice, or I'd drowned myself—I can tell from his cautious tone that those are the two suspicions he's torn between. I'm tempted to let him barge in and see the truth for himself.

"I'm…I'm still here," I call out once it does really seem like he will open the door. "I'm still here."

"Okay." He retreats down the hall but returns a few minutes later. "I've got some clothes," he tells me. "I'll leave them right here."

I don't bother thanking him. I just give my hair one last rinse and then climb out onto a ratty, threadbare towel, ignoring the reflection in the mirror. A neatly folded stack of clothing waits for me just outside the door—a sweatshirt and oversized sweatpants. They smell like him. Smoke and mint.

I dress quickly, and when I leave the bathroom, I find him on the couch, taking in my damp, dripping frame.

He indicates his approval with a tilt of his chin. "I guess I can't call ya Yellow anymore."

"Huh?" I raise an eyebrow, but he doesn't elaborate. Rather than pursue the issue, I cross the kitchen and grab one of the empty shopping bags from the counter, shoving my soiled clothing inside it. "If you have a washing machine, I don't mind—"

"Don't worry about it." He points toward the corner. "You can set them there."

Once I do, there's nothing else to do with my hands. I'm forced to wring them together, wincing as my thumb jars the row of stitches on the injured one. He doesn't attempt to forge a conversation. It's like he knows I'm distracted by the thick, accented drawl crawling through my thoughts.

Moya lyubov...

"I should probably get out of your hair," I blurt out, suddenly desperate for him to say something. Even goodbye.

"Or not," he says, fulfilling my wish. "I take it that you'll be needing a job, too."

I flinch, shaking my head, but a fitting excuse won't come. "Think your friend would mind?"

"He will," Espisido admits. He's got another cigarette in his hand, inhaling more of it than the oxygen around us.

Between puffs, he adds, "But I'll take care of him. I'll admit that it doesn't hurt that you have a pretty face."

I must make a sound, because he looks up sharply, his gaze homing in on how my fingers curl into fists.

"Fuck, I don't mean it like that. Arno's just a pig. That's all."

"It's all right." It's not his fault that life in the club ruined that word for me, stripping all sense of compliment or affection from each syllable. *Pretty.* "D-don't apologize."

"Remember, you need to keep those dry," he scolds, eyeing my arm. He's by my side in an instant, frowning at what he sees up close.

I had to take the gauze off to shower, and residual soap bubbles dot the visible stitches.

"Clean and dry," he insists. "Say it for me at least one time so that I have a solid defense when you sue me for infection."

"You should worry about yourself."

He's still bleeding, just a faint reddish streak along his hairline. I don't realize I've touched him there until my fingertips register the clammy flesh of his forehead.

"I'll live," he says, shrugging me off—and not for the first time.

Whenever I touch him, he reacts the same way —defensively.

"I don't know about you, but I'm beat." He approaches the couch and plumps the pillows, arranging them in a more ideal position to sleep. Then he surprises me by stepping back. "You can crash here tonight. I'll take the floor."

"You don't have to," I protest, but he's already backing up against the wall.

His back hits the surface, and he uses it for support to slide down to his knees. "I'm good here. Go ahead." He closes his eyes before I can argue. In an instant, his expression relaxes, but the stern set to his shoulders gives him away. He's awake and alert, sensing my every move.

Maybe it's the noose of my own lies that finally draws me over to the couch. I smell him in the cushions, muddling my brain and combining with the dark, violent thoughts that threaten to descend. I don't know if he serves as an antidote or merely a more potent poison, but my mind clears a little.

Just as long as I breathe him in.

———

It feels like I've only had my eyes closed for a second before I'm peeling them open again. A melody of hushed voices is all that gives context to the darkness looming around me. My chest constricts. For a sharp, blistering moment, I'm not sure where I am...

"It's okay. You're safe."

Just like that, I'm rescued from the grip of the nightmare, even as my heartbeat quickens at the lie. *Safe?* When I finally turn my head and spot a pair of familiar blue eyes, they seem more serious than mocking. He might believe those words.

Standing in the center of the kitchen, he's wearing a pair of dark pants and another hoodie. Domi is beside him, wearing jeans and a shirt similar to his. A jacket is draped over her arm, and she found a pair of tennis shoes, too.

"You want that job I mentioned?" Espisido wonders, drawing my attention back to him. He has the hood of a sweatshirt pulled low over his face, and a lit cigarette held to his mouth—what I'm beginning to suspect is his signature look.

When I don't answer, he seems to take my silence as a yes.

"Come on, then," he says. "You ladies are late for your interviews."

The playful humor doesn't disguise what lurks underneath. Tension laces his posture as he drags on the cigarette for a second too long. For our destination being a supposedly "safe" place, he seems pretty reluctant to head there.

Rather than ask why, I stand and do my best to shake off any lingering exhaustion.

"Here." He already has a hoodie and a pair of sneakers that look slightly too big waiting for me.

I pull them on, and together, the three of us leave the house. I can't tell from the pitch-black sky above, or the silence encasing the streets, whether it's late at night or early in the morning. The time seems to be irrelevant anyway, as this part of the city lives well after the sun goes down. Poverty and grime form a beautiful monochromatic blend of shadow, perfumed by the stench wafting from overflowing dumpsters. Judging from the abundance of empty warehouses, I suspect we're on the farthest outskirts of the industrial district, well beyond Grey's and my beat. It's an infamous area, known to be controlled by one gang in particular.

My gaze flickers to the man walking steadily in front of me, this angel with cotton wings. First, he mingles with Russians. Who else?

The question has more weight to it when we turn the corner and approach a bar at the end of this block. I recognize the name instantly, if only from the rumors of who owns it. *Mulligan's.* On the battered sign above the door, someone crudely scribbled *II* in permanent marker beside the name. Taken in all of its ratty glory, the strip of wood shines like a beacon, christening the castle of this self-proclaimed king.

"Let me do the talking." Espisido pulls up beside me, his mouth near my ear, his breath fanning my throat. Too warm. Too real. I have to shift slightly out of his reach to avoid the crossfire. "I can't guarantee he'll say yes, but just… just trust me."

Trust him. A laugh trickles from my throat. It's *almost* possible to overlook the audacity of the request for one reason alone—He's anxious again, his jaw rigid as he pulls ahead. Feeding off his unease, Domi falls into step between us, and we march almost single-file through the wooden door marking the entrance.

What place might an angel deem safe? Well, hell, of course.

It's loud inside—louder than Moe's. A deafening rift of shouting melds with the heavy rock music hammering against my eardrums. There are people *everywhere,* a sea of flailing limbs and blurred faces crammed within a backdrop of dark walls and wooden floors. It's a sweaty, claustrophobic version of the fiery pit.

A bar counter resides along one wall, across from a row of pool tables. At the back of the space is a stage where a half-naked woman demonstrates just how many ways she can swing from a metal pole without falling off. In one of the corners, men openly count obscene stacks of money while bellowing out bets, apparently on "Who says Arno kills that fuck?"

The winning odds lean overwhelmingly toward "yes."

"This way." Espisido takes my wrist, guiding me down a narrow hallway where some of the intensity of the noise fades. "He's up here," he tosses back over Domi's head. I suspect that the commentary is for my benefit, reinforcing his previous warning. "Just follow my lead and take everything he says with a grain of salt."

It's a subtler way of phrasing *keep your mouth shut, no matter what.* As if to illustrate the urgency, he tenses as we approach a closed door.

A man is standing beside it, his arms crossed. "You might want to come back later, kid," he warns. "Arno's busy right now."

Espi opens the door despite the warning, revealing the chilling scene within.

Two men are sitting on either side of a table. One of them is holding a gun to his head, nestled in a sea of red hair, while a crowd of at least ten men watch on.

"You ready, you little shit fuck?" The man holding the gun flicks the trigger. Once. Twice. On the third attempt, he pulls it.

My hands rush to cover my ears, but the resulting sound is too soft. Just an impotent click quickly followed by raucous laughter.

So *this* is Arno. Cold, green eyes stare through his opponent as he offers the gun on the palm of his hand. "Your turn." A heavy accent shapes each word—distinctive of one of the city boroughs. "You feeling lucky, motherfucker? Or do you finally want to talk?"

I can't see the other man's face from my position as he chokes out a watery laugh that fails to convey any bravery.

"I'm not no fucking snitch, asshole—"

"You hear that?" Arno asks the group of men surrounding the morbid table setting. He throws his hands into the air and releases another chilling chuckle. "This motherfucker ain't no goddamn snitch." He turns the gun again, holding it out trigger-end first. It's a familiar gesture that makes my blood run cold. "Then prove it," Arno snarls. "Put your goddamn money where your mouth is."

The other man finally takes the gun and presses it to his temple. An eerie hum echoes throughout the room, building in intensity. At first, I almost believe that it's the man's heart beating that loudly—but no, a glance down reveals that the steady thump is being made by Arno as he taps his fingers.

"Tick fucking *tock*," he growls.

The man pulls the trigger. *Click!* The poor fool can barely smother a sigh of relief, though he can't hide his body's reaction—a small puddle is forming around his feet.

"My turn." Arno snatches the gun and brings it to his mouth, wrapping his lips around the opening. He shoots, and another blank shot rings out. "Bang," he says. "There are still three chances left. You want to keep playing or fucking talk? Though I will say that this is the part where the game starts getting *fun*…"

"Okay, okay." The man shakes his head. "I didn't see nothing—"

"Then what the fuck are we talking for?" Arno reaches into the pocket of his jacket and draws a gun that I suspect has every chamber loaded.

"Arno..." Suddenly, Espisido's closer, his shoulder jarring mine, as a ripple goes through the ragtag group of spectators.

They're watching with more than just amusement now, like a pack of dogs anxious for the first drop of blood to be spilled.

"And there he is." Arno hones his gaze in our direction, still aiming the gun.

It's like a million words pass between him and Espi— judgment, arrogance, assertion, guilt.

"Where the fuck are my manners?" Arno wonders gruffly. "Allow me to set the stage. *This* motherfucker sucks dick for the Cartel, and one of their warehouses went up in smoke less than two hours ago—"

Smoke. Fire. I struggle to piece the details together in context with what happened at the Russian club.

"Little Benny here was meant to be guarding the door— obviously, he fucked up. But he saw something." With little fanfare, Arno aims the barrel of the gun squarely over Little Benny's forehead and caresses the trigger. "I went out of my fucking way to invite him to my party, but he seems to think he's too good to talk. I might have to make it *easier* on him to keep his fucking mouth shut."

The man in the hot seat races to display his hands in a gesture of surrender. "Hey! Hey! I didn't see nothing, but I *heard*, okay!"

"Who?" The sound of the weapon cocking gives a finite backdrop to Arno's command.

"Some bitch. I don't know who, but she gave the orders—"

"Some bitch?" Arno raises an eyebrow. "A woman?"

Little Benny frantically nods. "Yeah. She kept to the back, but I heard her."

"You didn't see her?"

"N-no," Benny admits. "But she had an accent. Some kind of Spanish—"

"Spanish," Arno echoes. After a harsh moment of silence, he puts the loaded gun away. "What else?"

Benny shakes his head. "That's all I got before they started wiping people out. I barely got the fuck out of there with my head—"

"Story time's over," Arno interjects. "Boys. Take our friend here and show him what other games we like to play."

The command snaps two of the spectating thugs into action. They rush to the table and grab Benny by either arm before dragging him to his feet and past us, into the hall.

"Everyone else, get the fuck out," Arno bellows. "Except for *you*." He jabs a finger in Espi's direction before he can move. "We need to talk."

"Fuck," Espisido grunts under his breath. "Give me a second." Sighing, he spares a glance at Domi and then flags one of the passing men down with a wave of his hand. "Hey, Francisco!" He mutters something into the man's ear on his way into the room. Then he looks over his shoulder, meeting my gaze. "Stick around," he says. "I'll come find you when I'm done."

The door closes behind him as the other man advances toward Domi and me. Francisco, I presume. He's tall, with wiry, dark hair and chiseled, gaunt features that have seen better days.

"The kid said to show you around," he says rather than introduce himself properly. "So let's go."

With a wary glance shared between us, Domi and I follow him.

The music is just as deafening the second time in, but somehow, I manage to hear Francisco bellow above the noise.

"Espi said you two want jobs. I won't even ask your ages"—he tosses a pointed look at Domi—"and I don't have time to be a fucking babysitter. Pick a spot, and you learn the ropes as you go along. Consider this a working interview. So, what about you, little girl?"

Domi glances around the club, unperturbed by the noise. She's seen worse. Heard worse. Spotting the bar, she points to it, her chin set in determination.

"That's my domain," Francisco shouts back. "You better keep up. And what about *you*?"

What about me? *I* shouldn't even be here, but rather on a bus, or a plane, or a train. Piotr is in my head already. He's in my skin, lingering like an itch I can't scratch. A wound that won't heal.

"Hey!" A hand collides with my shoulder, jarring me back. "You wanna work or not?"

I'm tempted to refuse. Little Espi should learn to gather his demons from better stock—*good riddance*. I even start toward the exit, but I catch sight of a nearby man who is leering at the girl beside me. Already, Domi is catching more attention than she should. She's too *pretty*, as much as it disgusts me to use that word. Hungry eyes linger over her smooth skin and her shapely body.

Maybe life as Chloe Parker isn't as easy to suppress as I'd hoped—I won't leave her alone here. For now.

My gaze is already roving in the direction of the stage, where a woman in a glittery thong is in the process of taking it off while the men around her drool to the tune of music.

The performance would earn her a bullet to the brain at *Moe's*. Piotr prized his dancers for their "art form" over vulgarity.

Stop. I shake my head to resist the impending trip down memory lane. Too late. I can still feel him behind me. Beside me. *Inside* me.

"You want a job or not?" Francisco asks.

I hear myself sigh above the pulsing bass, though I'm not sure if anyone notices. "I've only ever had one...*job*."

"Oh?" Francisco ruins his hard-ass façade by sounding genuinely curious. "Let's see it, then."

I set my sights on the stage, swallowing down a bubble of unease. "But first, what's your policy on serving shots to your prospective employees?"

He laughs. "There wasn't one—until now."

He heads for the bar while I watch the current dancer finish her set. Anna should be my focus. Running. Hiding. Not what a certain angel might think if I let him see my horns.

Or just how far I've fallen from grace.

CHAPTER TWELVE
ESPI

"DID YOU HEAR WHAT THAT DUMBASS SAID?" ARNO hisses the moment we're alone. "*Spanish.*" He snatches up the bottle of rum and drinks right from the rim. After swallowing, he spits onto the floor and wipes his mouth with the back of his hand. "I bet the fucker's never heard of goddamn Portuguese."

"That's quite the leap to make from a woman with an accent—"

"A leap? Do *you* know of any bitch in the Cartel who gives orders?" He slams the bottle onto the table so hard that most of the booze sloshes out from the top. "Oh, what's that?" He tilts the bottle to me like a makeshift microphone. "I fucking thought so. It's her. You know, I saw her kill a man once. It was sloppy. Messy."

Messy...like the murdering of a club full of Russians on Petrov's payroll. Whoever she is, the lady certainly has a flair for the dramatic. And a death wish.

Could it be Danny, a woman who all but grew up in the heart of the mafia? I don't know. I don't want to. Here I was, holding out hope for a happy-ending motorcycle ride into the sunset for her and Dante after he got her out of that hellhole.

"What? That surprise you?" Arno chuckles to rub in my silence and takes another sip of liquor. Then another. A second later, he's finished off the whole damn bottle. "I'll tell you what would surprise me though." He slams the bottle down again, his eyes gleaming in the dim lighting. "If *you* heard from Dante or that little bitch and didn't think to enlighten me."

I grit out a sigh. "I haven't heard from either of them—"

"You wouldn't lie to me, now would you?" He's been drinking too much. The violet bruises beneath his eyes warn he hasn't slept, either—though that can't be completely blamed on paranoia or grief.

In six months, he's turned the Gardai from a laughingstock into a force even Piotr Petrov has to acknowledge. Surprise, surprise, revenge fuels most of that newfound ambition. The best of men could forgive someone for bailing on them once.

Never twice.

And I know better than to pour salt into his wounds now. Dante can do his own dirty work.

"You haven't heard anything?" he presses. "Not even a fucking postcard?"

"If I had, I would have told you." I sound like a hostage reading a script, though maybe I am. I've memorized what to say when he's like this. It's become a fucking mantra. "Look. Dante's my brother—"

"You think I don't fucking know that?"

"But so are you. You were always there for me. *Always.* I won't bail on you." Tonight, anyway. "You know that."

"Do I?" Arno hisses out a breath, his shoulders slumping as he braces one hand against the table. "I do—I fucking know that. I *know* that."

We both just needed to hear me say it, though for very different reasons.

"It's probably just a fucking coincidence," he adds, shaking his head. "Some new gang on the scene that wants a cut of the pie. Whoever they are can get in fucking line." He runs his hand down the side of his jeans, his palm resting over where he keeps his gun.

That little tea party didn't cure his itch for violence. Before the week's out, he's going to empty that chamber into someone. It's another addiction he's developed, in addition to booze.

"You said that guy worked for the Cartel, but he wasn't from south of the border, if you know what I mean," I say, changing the subject. "Jose isn't known for his inclusive employment policy."

"You're right. He didn't," Arno admits between clenched teeth. "He was one of the Jersey Devils. Those crack-dealing punks. Their whole den got wiped out two nights ago, courtesy of the so-called *Spanish* bitch, and he ran to Jose like a little pussy rather than remember who his gang owes their protection to. Word on the street is the arsonists are the same ones who ghosted the Russians, but no one seems to know where they hold base or just who they're after."

"Shit."

"You got that right." Arno hauls himself upright and runs a hand through his hair. The look on his face could be called a smile by some loose definition of the term. Nothing seems to reach him these days like the threat of a good fight. "But you didn't come here about that." He meets my gaze directly, and I almost think I see a hint of his old self. "You wanted something. What?"

It's not an ideal subject to tackle while he's still got Old Besty the revolver in his pocket, but rarely is he this lucid after downing a whole bottle.

"I have some friends who need jobs—and before you even ask, they both could bring trouble." I inhale sharply, wishing I had a cigarette to take the edge off. "*And...* they're Russians, both from Piotr's territory."

"Are you fucking kidding me?" Arno raises an eyebrow, his fingers twitching in and out of fists. "I assume you have a good reason for bringing that shit into my bar."

"No *good* reason," I admit. "They need protection—"

"What makes you think that *we* won't need protection if they decide to bring their little Ruskie friends in for a tour?"

"It's not like that. One of the girls was one of…one of theirs," I say for lack of a better word. "Newly freed this afternoon. She needs someplace to lie low before I can get her out of the city. *And* she's the one who fed me all that intel on Vlad and his operation. Information you can use now to take over some of the bastard's territory, if you haven't already."

Arno always was an opportunist.

"As for the other… She killed Vladimir Olshenkov that night at the club. With an ashtray. Use your imagination to figure out how."

"Damn," Arno grunts. Whether in amusement or appreciation, I can't tell. "So, Vlad's dead."

I nod. "I guess I never got to give you the full story of what happened."

"I figured as much on my own. The Ruskies are running around the fucking city like rats without a queen. Piotr must not be back in the country yet. I might as well make my mark while I can." He has that hungry look again. The one he typically wears before playing games of Russian roulette.

"So, can they stay?" I ask, bringing his attention back to the subject at hand.

He shrugs. "I got to meet them first. See for myself where their loyalties may lie."

"I had Francisco show them around. They just want to make some money. You'll barely even know they're here."

He scoffs. "I doubt that. You have a way of attracting trouble. Just like—" He shakes his head to cut the thought off. "Let's go. I need another drink."

He snatches up the empty bottle and carries it with him to the door. When we reach the main room, jeers and whistles rise up from the crowd, rivaling the intensity of whatever song's playing. True to form, Arno smiles fiercely before slapping the ass of the first woman to sidle up to him. He'll never let them see the worst the bottle brings out in him.

He'll never let them see the doubt.

"That one of them?" he grunts once he's finished putting on his show, having spotted Domi already.

I make out a flash of red hair behind the counter. "Yeah."

"Where's the other one?"

That's a damn good question.

The thought's barely finished crawling through my head when the music cuts off, and someone grabs a microphone near the front of the stage. "Get ready for a special show, you fucks," the emcee declares. "We've got a newbie to the spotlight. Put your hands together for Angel!"

The name alone draws laughs when paired with the appearance of the woman who climbs onto the stage. *Angel.* She definitely doesn't look like one. Maybe it's the dark, unholy gleam in her eye. Or maybe it's the dry, lifeless, dark hair and the oversized clothes she's wearing. In comparison to Darcy's skimpy, pink halter, it's not the type of attire these men are used to.

"The fuck?" Arno hisses.

The music starts up, drowning out any argument he makes. Only there's no beat to rile the crowd or pounding bass to dance to. Apparently, someone thought it would be funny to set Angel up for a humiliating little "audition." I can't put a name to what runs through my chest when I see her standing there, frozen solid, her head bowed.

I spot the DJ grinning behind the booth and start in that direction, curling my hands into fists. Once I get my hands on him, he'll be the one entertaining everyone.

No.

Flashing yellow eyes stop me in my tracks, and I nearly plow into some biker in front of me. Any protest dies in my throat. Her hips sway as if to spite me, forging her own sensual rhythm from the music. Slow. Fast. Slower. Brown hair drapes her shoulders as her head rears back, displaying her throat and stealing my fucking breath away.

At Moe's, I was too busy making sure not to blow my cover to watch her dance. A beautiful blonde was a dime a dozen in a place like that—it felt wrong to look.

But here…

The defiant tilt of her chin dares me to look away—*"And here I was, assuming you really were a pervert."*

Fuck it. I *am.* Her swaying limbs capture my attention and consume it. The longer I stare, the more disoriented I feel. It's like she's on another goddamn planet. The noise doesn't affect her. No one can touch her.

Especially not me.

With an easy shift of her weight, she grabs the pole with one hand and swings herself around it. Only a few words trickle across my brain to describe the movement—sloppy, wild…fucking beautiful.

She peels the sweatshirt off first, building tension with every slow raise of her fingers. It hits the floor as the stage lights reflect off the sweat on her skin like glitter. The smooth curve of her back is all I see. Then her hip. The top of her thigh…

Gritting my teeth, I turn away and find that Domi's watching me from the bar. When I take the stool across from her, she hands me a drink, but her eyes don't leave the stage.

The dance could last minutes. Seconds. I just know that I'm still staring at my hands when the emcee reclaims the microphone and shouts something to stir up the crowd.

A hand falls over my shoulder. Arno. "They can stay," he grunts as he pushes past me.

I should follow him. Anything but wait for the slim figure weaving through the crowd toward me. She's still topless, her unbound hair doing little to hide her body from every horny biker clambering for a glance. As she draws even with my stool, she leans in so that I can hear her above the music. Her smell affects me more than the booze does.

"Is something wrong? Did I rip any stitches?"

"What?" I look down, hunting for blood. My hands are shaking too badly to touch her. I have to knot them into fists. "They look fine to me."

She's trembling though, like a druggie during a wild high. For whatever reason, she seems to think I'm the unstable one. Her hand brushes my arm. "Are you okay?"

"You don't have to do this," I tell her, raising my voice over the music. "I mean, you don't have to dance if you don't want to." *Real smooth, Espi.* I don't even know what I'm trying to fucking say, but I can't stop talking. "We can find something else for you to do."

"Is there something wrong with dancing?" Her wary tone warns that I've stepped on a landmine.

"No. Of course not. Here." I shrug my hoodie off and offer it to her.

She accepts it without comment, draping it around herself and zipping it up to her chin.

"You got the job, by the way."

"Good." Her expression doesn't change as she claims the shot meant for me and drains it. Then she wipes her hand across her mouth and turns away. "But I won't stick around for long. I wouldn't want to make anyone *uncomfortable*."

Shit. She slips through the crowd before I can say anything. Going off the slight flush to her cheeks, I've pissed her off.

Way to go, Espi. I start after her, but in the end, I just order another drink. I've made enough of an ass of myself for one night.

God willing, it won't happen again. Maybe she should make good on her promise to skip town. I tell myself that's what I want.

But a part of me doesn't buy it, no matter how many shots I down.

Not one fucking bit.

CHAPTER THIRTEEN
CHLOE

A HALF-NAKED WOMAN GAPES AT ME FROM THE surface of a mirror. She's a wreck. God, I barely recognize her. Brown, bloodshot eyes flutter in a losing battle against exhaustion. Her pretty face is her saving grace. If I squint, and in the right lighting, I'd still call her attractive enough. She might even hold my attention during a dance.

But she couldn't hold his. How pathetic is that? I finger his sweatshirt, unable to forget his face or that tight, hollow expression. The more of my clothes I took off, the less he bothered to hide his thoughts. The confusion. The curiosity. The pity...

He *pitied* me.

"Think these will fit?"

"Huh?" Distracted, I turn my attention to the blonde beside me, who is presumably in the middle of finding me something "hotter" to wear than my current attire.

"You look like a size two." She holds up a pair of tiny denim shorts and a white bustier and tosses them both onto a rapidly growing stack compiled against the back of a metal folding chair.

We're in what I assume is the equivalent of Mulligan's dressing room. There are no brooding guards here to enforce a code of strict silence—just a burly man lurking outside the door, whom the blonde cheerfully referred to as Joe. His job seems to revolve more around keeping unwanted visitors *out* rather than anyone in.

"You looked good out there," the woman continues as she fishes through the wardrobe and surfaces with a bit of slinky, black material that I think is meant to be worn as a skirt. "You must have danced before. Where at? Murphy's? Sirens? Big Daddy's?"

"I don't think you'd know it," I tell her, fighting to keep my voice steady. "They…they didn't pay well."

"Oh." The blonde frowns and tugs yet another garment from the closet. "You can take these, too. The last girl to fit this stuff hasn't worked here in ages. I'm Darcy, by the way." She turns to me with her hands on her hips and extends one in my direction. "Welcome aboard. Our slots typically start at nine," she adds once I've shaken her hand. "Ten minutes a girl. We rotate every hour. You can take Molly's spot. She got herself knocked up a few months ago, so she's out on 'maternity leave' until next week." She makes air quotes around the words, her voice colored by double meaning. "It's nearly the end of the shift, so you'll meet the rest of the girls tomorrow night. The key players you really need to know are Arno—big guy, red hair, crazy as shit. He owns this place. As long as you don't piss him off, he'll have your back."

"Sounds fair enough."

"Right? Then there's Francisco, the bartender. Arno's right-hand guy. He can make you any fucking drink on the house —but he's always listening. If you want to talk shit about this place, don't do it while he's around. And then there's Espi…"

"What about him?" My lungs tense up as if they're fighting to inhale every trace of that name. Curiosity? Maybe that's it, explaining the way my pulse hammers even as I picture his face.

"He's Espi," Darcy declares. "He's a good kid, but don't underestimate him. A lot of people try to because of his age."

"How old is he?" I'm caught off guard by the way my stomach clenches in anticipation of the answer. Does it really matter? Maybe. That angelic face could leave even Grey guessing.

"Twenty, I think," Darcy says offhandedly. "He won't bother you, if that's what you're worried about. He usually keeps to himself."

I watch her flip through another series of hangers, desperate to suppress the relief I shouldn't feel.

She's pretty. Piotr would have put her on his stage as well, but not because of her looks. I saw the way she counted the stash kept inside her sparkly, pink bra.

This isn't a game to her. This is business.

"That's all I can tell you for now," she says as she shoves the remainder of the approved clothing into a duffel bag. "The rest, you just have to learn as you go along. I guess you can enjoy the rest of the show. Tomorrow, the fun begins. Anyway, I'm on in five."

She flashes a grin before running a hand through her loose hair and prancing down the hallway that leads to the stage. I hear the usher announcing her arrival from here. *Bunny.*

Left alone, I don't know whether or not to take her advice. Enjoy the show. From what little I've already seen, there isn't much *to* enjoy. The girls are pretty. They're shapely. They're harmless.

They've never learned to swing on a pole while Piotr watched from his throne and cracked each knuckle in warning. They've never had Vlad to contend with should they bore their audience.

They've never had to *crave* the safety of the stage.

Is this the life Anna's been forced to lead? I picture her swaying against a metal pole, and my throat becomes painfully tight.

Desperate to clear my head, I leave the dressing room with the bag of clothing and hunt for a familiar face.

The bar is packed nearly wall to wall, but I still don't have trouble differentiating one haunting scent from that of booze and vomit. I follow it over to the bar counter, where I find Espi watching Domi serve up liquor.

Noticing my approach, he lifts a bottle of beer in salute. At least he isn't holding a grudge for earlier. "How do you like the place so far?"

It's a rhetorical question. I think he's just hunting for anything to say at all. Despite the noise and our raucous surroundings, it's easy to sense the tension lying underneath. Arno may hide his emotions well when there isn't a gun to wave around, but at the heart, he's no better than Vlad. They emit their poison subconsciously, infecting everyone around them.

He's anxious. He's worried. Unsurprisingly, Espi seems to be of the same mind. He indicates for me to follow before stepping away from the bar and down a narrow hallway that opens up to a rickety stairwell.

"I got you a place," he announces, turning to face me directly. "If you wanted to stick around here. You and Domi can share it for now. It's above the club." He looks pointedly at the steps.

"Oh." I let the offer sink in, digesting what it really means without him having to explain it out loud—He'll get his house back, at least. "You think she'll be safe here?" I can't hide my skepticism if I tried.

As if to punctuate my words, the sound of shouting followed by glass breaking reaches our corner. A second later, we hear Arno bellow out, "Let 'em fight!"

"Trust me," Espi says. "This place may look rough, but it's safe. But just in case"—he reaches into his pocket and withdraws a small object—"there's always this…"

He slides something across my palm, and my hand instinctively cradles it. It's heavy. Familiar. I relish the weight as my forefinger seeks the trigger out. It's a gun. Espi's expression never wavers, and it takes my tongue three attempts to spit out any words at all.

"Why…why would you give me this?"

"If you don't want it, I can teach Domi to use it—"

"No. It's fine." It's better than fine. I didn't realize how much I've missed the familiarity of the weapon, but I do now that I'm holding one in my hands again.

The memory of Piotr feels a little further away. Not by much, but it helps.

Still, the bigger question springs to my lips. "You would trust me with this?"

He shrugs casually. "Why not?" He makes it seem so spur of the moment.

But it's not like that. I can see it in his eyes, which attempt to avoid mine for once. He's thought about this long and hard. He knows it's not his only option—but he also knows that I could kill a man with an ashtray or attack *him* with a whiskey bottle unprovoked. He's already seen the truth—I'm much safer with a gun.

"I've got some stuff to take care of tomorrow," he tells me, shifting his weight from side to side.

"Is something wrong?" Cotton and warmth tickle my fingertips. I've touched his shoulder without realizing it.

"I'm fine," he says, gingerly shrugging me off. "You and Domi can settle in. I'll be around tomorrow night to check in on you."

"And that's it?" I find myself asking. "You take in two women you barely know. You set them up in your 'friend's' bar—a man I just saw torture someone into a game of Russian roulette. Then you leave, and that's it?"

If he were attracted to me, that would be one thing—but he maintains a healthy distance between us and just offers up another halfhearted shrug. "That's it." He heads back toward the bar but hesitates over the threshold of the hallway. "You can head on up and check out the place if you're sick of hanging out around here. Francisco will watch over Domi. It's the last door on the left. Key's under the mat."

After another prolonged second, he leaves without waiting for an answer. Keeping the gun in one hand, I feel my face with the other. Maybe it's written there? Everything I'm thinking? Or is it just that damn easy to read me these days?

In contrast, his emotions are transcribed in an archaic language. One minute, I think I've deciphered the code.

The next, a new symbol comes into play, and I have to start all over again.

I find myself taking the stairs two at a time out of a need to do something else than wallow in self-pity. A short hallway is lined by a row of closed doors. I follow his instruction and approach the last one on the left, finding a key hidden underneath a black welcome mat when I arrive. Once I get the door open, I have a decent view of the entire apartment. It's small and cramped but clean. There's only one bedroom, however, right near the front door, two twin beds placed on either side of it. In addition are a gray couch in the middle of a small living room and a narrow kitchen.

It's not much, but it's definitely more than the average person would dish out to a stranger.

This suffocating sense of emotion weighs me down as I lock the door behind me and carry the bag of clothes into the bedroom. I toss it onto one of the beds and perch myself on the end of the mattress. Only now do I remember Grey, though maybe I've been unconsciously ignoring his request all along. *Get me something on Mackenzie.*

Well, he has a fondness for triple malt whiskey.

A million new secrets swirl inside my skull as I lie back against the wall, leaving my body slung horizontally across the mattress. I'll let my eyes close only for a second, or so I tell myself. I'm not stupid enough to stay here. I'm not stupid enough to pretend that Piotr isn't on the prowl or forget that Anna may still be out there.

I'm not *stupid* enough to trust.

————

I'M NOT SURE WHAT NOISE SNAPS ME FULLY AWAKE, BUT I open my eyes to a ghost. Bright-red hair is all that gives her contrast against the wall.

"An...Anna?" Hope wells up in my throat as I greedily seek out each childish feature.

It dies in vain, of course, swallowed down like vomit. This girl is too old, her nose too big, and I would pray to never see such darkness in the eyes of a child.

"No. It's me—Domi. Did I wake you?" She's already fully dressed, sitting on the opposite bed.

Apparently, she helped herself to the spare clothing but somehow managed to pick the most risqué items to wear. Her outfit of choice is a black lace bra she's paired with one of Espisido's hoodies, the only saving grace.

"No," I lie. "I was already awake."

"Good." She kicks her feet into the air while her wide eyes scan my face. "So, it really is you. Number ten. Piotr's *angel*."

She gives the word a nasty twist. How strange is it that such a name can have so many variants depending on how it's uttered? Reverently by some and reviled by others.

"I would have thought…" My throat is too dry, and I have to swallow hard to clear it. "I would have thought that he wouldn't talk of me much."

"He didn't," Domi admits. "But we still listened. We all knew of the girl he used to have. His prized little pet. The things he made her do…" She shudders and wraps her arms around her slender front. "She was our bedtime story. A reminder of all the ways that, no matter how fucking awful it was, it could always get worse."

I turn my face toward a threadbare pillow. It's hard to stomach this mythical version of myself—the girl who strayed too close to a monster and got eaten alive. If only that were where the story ended.

"And what impression do I make?"

Her gaze sweeps over me once she's given permission to truly stare. "You're pretty," she says carefully. "I thought you'd be prettier."

I shrug. "Fair enough."

"So… Did you really do it? You really killed Vlad?"

I don't answer. I don't have to. She's already heard the story from somewhere, and I can see the curiosity burning within her eyes. There's hunger too. Espisido's not the only one familiar with violence.

"What was it like?"

"Messy," I tell her. "Very, very messy."

"Oh." Her teeth click together noisily, as if they're trapping more questions behind them. Exuding nervous energy, she jumps to her feet. Her outfit seems even more garish when I take her in—an underage demon in a hooker's clothing, draped beneath the cloak of a fallen angel.

"How did you…" I trail off, unsure of how to phrase the question. *How did you wander into hell?*

"Family debt," she says simply, as though we're merely discussing the weather. "I was sold to pay it off. It was okay though." She glances back at me over her shoulder and shrugs. "I had three other sisters."

That awful ache in my gut—is that pity? I've spent so long suppressing it. Guilt, empathy, pain—they aren't emotions prized in either Piotr's slave or a cop.

"Can I ask you something?" She's looking at the floor, her expression unreadable.

"Yes?"

"Piotr. If you saw him again. If he came after you. Would you kill him?"

It's a dangerous question. The most alarming aspect is how quickly I come up with an answer. "Yes."

"Good." She meets my gaze again, her eyes blazing. For a split second, she seems eons older than she should. Someone who's experienced more suffering than most people do in a lifetime. "Anyway, Frank said we could come downstairs early," she says, effortlessly changing the subject.

"He said he'll give us some food and show us the ropes before the bar opens."

"Frank?"

"Francisco." She takes her time, pronouncing every syllable. "He got pissed with how I was butchering his name and told me to just call him that. He let me in last night too. You fell asleep with the door locked." She flashes a mischievous grin I don't have the energy to return.

"Sorry."

"It's all right," she says, shrugging. "But let's go now. Frank tends to yell."

Taking the hint, I pull myself upright, groaning as every ache and pain decide to make themselves known. My left arm is on fire. My hand feels no better. I need to eat something, preferably something other than bread and alcohol.

Domi stares as I fish a clean set of clothes from Darcy's bag, and I have to stagger down the hall and into the small bathroom to find some semblance of privacy.

I barely recognize the woman staring back at me from the mirror. She's old. She's haggard. Piotr's mark taints her skin, spreading like cancer. Even with the dark curtain of hair shielding part of her face, she won't be able to hide from him. Maybe she doesn't really want to.

Moya lyubov.

I rinse my mouth out with water and spit every ounce of my fear into the sink. Using my wet fingers as a makeshift comb, I ease the worst of the tangles from my hair. Out of the clothing Darcy picked, I settle on a white tank top and a pair of denim shorts. In the end, I don't know if it's modesty or something else that drives me back into the bedroom for Espisido's jacket. It's long enough to cover even the shorts, and when I zip it up to my chin, it's almost like I'm wearing nothing else.

"Let's go," I tell Domi, who's still watching me from a corner.

She leads the way out into the hallway. Down below, the bar is deathly silent. It's also a fucking wreck. Broken glass and plastic cups clutter the floor while a lone figure attempts to clean it all up.

"Grab a broom," he snarls the moment we approach. "And I don't want to hear shit about how it's 'not your job.'"

Domi and I obey without argument. An hour later, the floor is clear, at least.

After that, I help Francisco restock the shelves behind the bar with liquor from a storage closet while Domi attempts to make whatever drink he calls out within a specified amount of time.

She's good—a realization that surprises him more than it does me. Piotr probably kept her at his personal table on the nights she worked inside the club. I recognize the unnaturally steady way she manipulates the bottles and how her dead eyes disguise all emotion.

He trained her well, too.

"The girls don't go on stage until nine at night," Francisco tells me when I hand him a whiskey bottle to set onto a high shelf. "You gonna stick around until then and make yourself useful?"

Rather than answer him, I grab a broom and work on the floor. By the time he opens the pub at ten in the morning, Domi's already poised to manage the bar, and I help to minimize the mess.

Mulligan's attracts a decent crowd, even before noon. It's like Arno's chosen thugs live by the closing and opening of the battered wooden doors. By midafternoon, Francisco has broken up at least four fights, and he's in the middle of separating another brawling pair when Arno himself walks in.

Just like that, the entire atmosphere changes, feeding off the figure who dominates the doorway. He determinedly scans the crowd with his green eyes. Searching. Hunting. When they find their chosen target, they narrow.

"You," he growls, his voice easily traveling across the bar. "Come on. We need to talk."

I don't meet anyone's gaze as I set the broom aside and follow him toward that infamous "tea party" room. Once we're inside, he slams the door shut and gestures to the table with a wave of his hand.

"Have a seat."

I do, and he takes the one across from me, splaying his legs on either side of the table while his hands palm the surface between us.

"What's your name? And don't fucking try to shit me, either. I want the truth."

The truth? It's a dangerous request. "Chloe Parker," I tell him. "At least, that's the only one you'll find in any database."

"Hmph." He sits back in the chair. His eyes are bloodshot; he's been drinking. A lot. What would make for a vulnerable state for anyone else just makes his gaze sharper. Meaner. "That doesn't sound like the name of the captive-Russian-slave-girl sob story bullshit Espi spun about you."

"That's because it's not."

He's already figured that out though; his eyes dart directly to my neck. He saw the mark, most likely during my audition. He's done a little digging.

Chances are he knows all about Piotr's infamous number ten.

"You a cop?"

"I was at Moe's on police business, if that's what you mean."

He cracks his knuckles one by one—purely for my benefit. The warning translates better than any verbal threat. *Keep talking.*

"I was supposed to get intel," I say. "Ask a few questions. Wear a wire. I wasn't supposed to go inside."

"Is that so?" There is nothing comforting in the way he smiles. "And, now, we get to the good part. Somehow, you managed to kill Vladimir Olshenkov. A lot of people wanted to claim that little honor, missy. From what I hear, you killed him fucking *dead*."

"I fucked up," I correct.

He stops cracking his knuckles and resorts to resting his clenched fists on the table. I'm not sure which action alarms me more. Unlike Espi, he's easy to read yet impossible at the same time. A bit like an open flame— You know it's burning, you know it's hot, but where will it go next? That depends on which way the fucking wind blows.

"If you're worried about me, don't be. I can't go back," I say. Not yet. Not without answers. Not without Anna.

"So, why are you *here*?"

"My handler wanted information on a gang." I leave out the part where the gang in question just so happens to be his. "In return, he pulled some strings to get the other girl out of holding."

"So you thought you'd spy on me? Is that it?"

I don't bother denying it. "A girl's gotta eat."

He swipes his thumb across his chin. I know the look. I doubt they're related by blood, but Espisido has picked up a few of his mannerisms. That glowering, thoughtful stare is one of them.

"All right. Let's say I believe you. What shit were you gonna feed your boss?"

"Nothing to blow your operation. Just enough to get him off my ass." I let him sense the part of that sentence I don't say out loud—*for now.*

"Hmph." The grunt resembles a genuine chuckle. "You do this often, huh? Just admit that you're a fucking narc?"

"And let's say I did go running to the cops with damaging intel," I propose. "I killed a man in cold blood. Even if he was a criminal. Even if he was *Vladimir Olshenkov*—I still killed him. Any investigator worth their salt would be able to prove it. I wasn't exactly careful. I turn you in, and no prosecutor in the country could offer me a deal of immunity. If I'd used a gun, it could have been self-defense. But I didn't. Not only would anything I said against you be laughed out of a court as hearsay, but I'd land my own ass in prison once some justice-happy prosecutor decided to get their name in the papers."

I wind up holding my breath in anticipation of his reaction. Coming clean to him is more than just risky. I'm laying everything on the line—my life *and* Domi's. But, when everything goes to shit—and it *will*—only one person will be caught in the aftermath.

It won't be Arno or me. But therein lies the real question. Why do I care?

"I take it you don't plan on sticking around for too long?" he asks.

"I just need to make sure my handler doesn't pay for my fuck-up."

"I guess you need something good to feed him, then?" All at once, Arno pushes back from the table and draws his gun.

I don't have the time to blink before he aims it squarely over my chest.

"Here. Read this."

Pathetic bursts of air trickle into my lungs as he turns the weapon, allowing me to make out the serial numbers carved into the side.

"Memorize that. Give it to your cop friend. Say you heard me talking about a man I killed while waving this gun around. You got close enough to rip the serial. Have him run it—"

"Won't that just lead back to you?" Better yet, it would give Grey probable cause to get a warrant for either his arrest or a search of the club.

Arno just laughs. "Trust me, sweetheart. It won't lead back to *me*. I know the fucking rodeo. But, whatever they find, you bring back to me. I want a name. I want a fucking dealer. You give me that..." He cracks his knuckles in unison. "Give me that, and I don't throw you out on your ass. For now."

"Done." It's a logical headache I'll figure out later. All that matters is…

Hell, what does matter? Running should be my primary focus. *Not* making sure a certain little angel doesn't get too burned from his attempt to save a demon from the flames.

Though it's not like I have much of a fucking choice now.

"Wait. I can't be seen at the station if I'm associated with you." Considering my status as an actual informant this time, I don't think chatting with Grey in the open would be a good idea. "How should I—"

"Here." Arno pulls something else from his pocket and tosses it to me.

A burner phone. One of many, I suspect.

"Call him on that. Then toss it. Now, get the fuck out. And one last thing…" His eyes flash with a sober-like intensity. "Just so we're clear—Stay the hell away from Espi. You got that?"

I hold his gaze without flinching, ignoring the clenching sensation gripping my chest. Maybe it's relief. "Deal."

Arno accepts the answer with a nod. His blazing expression doesn't reveal any ulterior motive for the request, other than concern for his friend. The fact just feeds the cruel part of me whispering that someone else is behind the sudden need for boundaries. Espi? Perhaps I've disgusted the angel so greatly that he can't even tell me himself to back off.

My jaw tightens at the possibility. I pegged him as reckless, but never a coward.

Alone, I find the upstairs hallway deserted and use the silence as cover to call Grey. He's pissed by the protocol breach but accepts the serial, promising to call back within a few days.

"The damn analyst is backed up to shit," he tells me.

I reenter the barroom and discover that it's packed. From behind the bar, Domi tries to meet my gaze, but Francisco sighs. He's relieved. I guess he knows what happens when Arno doesn't approve of a guest.

"Get back to work!" he shouts above the din of chaos.

Already, there's more broken glass on the floor and spills to mop up. While I set about conquering the busywork, it's almost enough…

I almost forget. I almost stop eyeing the doorway every five fucking minutes in search of a familiar pair of eyes. Blue or dark brown?

It doesn't fucking matter.

CHAPTER FOURTEEN
ESPI

SOME PEOPLE CLAIM THAT BLOOD IS THICKER THAN water—but they don't know my family. To my brother, Dante, blood can be poison. He learned to cut it out and never look back.

Call me naïve, but I just never thought he'd do the same to me.

Even now, I can't seem to call it what it is—him skipping out for nearly half a year. Abandonment? No. It's just Dante being Dante.

He'll come back. He always does.

Though maybe I'm as delusional as Arno. Rather than drown my memories with booze, I exorcise them in streaks of paint over canvas. Black for hate. Red for anger. Blue for pathetic, old Espi, the one always left behind.

It's only when I'm knuckles-deep in acrylic that I let myself think about what I'm doing. It's not too late to take more jobs and save up enough to skip town. Run. Hitch a one-way ride on a plane and never look back. I could pull a Dante-esque move, only I wouldn't be self-righteous enough to pretend like I was doing it out of anything other than selfish greed.

I'm almost twenty-one years old, and I don't know what it feels like to want something. Not really. Something real. Something worth turning my back on the whole fucking world for.

Maybe if I find it, I'll finally understand what it's like to be him.

Or maybe I'll just learn what it's like to be Espisido. Someone other than the punk kid stuck doing the dirty work or holding the short end of the stick. Someone who crawls through life alone no matter how hard it knocks them down.

Like her, Miss Yellow. She's here beneath my fingertips, judging me from the surface of a canvas. Yellow paint forms the base of her features, sharp and focused. After picking up a brush, I use hints of green and red to flesh out the details, extending the line of her mouth until she's no longer judging me.

Just watching. She stares beyond my head, seeing what I can't. Like the figure I catch from the corner of my eye, lurking beyond the screen door that leads into the backyard.

The man standing there is tall, towering nearly to the doorframe. A jacket shrouds his body, the hood drawn low over his face. The line of his jaw is visible, moving as he speaks.

"You're still smoking," he says. "I can smell that shit out here."

Sure enough, there's fresh ash smoking in a bowl on my table. I step back from my easel and swipe my hands along my pants. Then I grab the makeshift ashtray and pitch the ash into the trash.

"I didn't think you'd know where to find me," I admit without facing the door. I eye my shadow instead as it flickers along the wall opposite from where I stand. "Considering you haven't come around in six months—"

"I'm always watching out for you," he says. "You know that."

"Do I?"

He doesn't answer. Nervous energy builds in my muscles the longer the silence wears on.

Finally, I sigh. "You can come in."

My back door always creaks, and I use the sharp squeal as cover to flick my lighter. At the same time, I snatch a fresh cig from a pile on the table. Two puffs don't make it any easier to face him. The cold air ghosting the back of my neck warns me that this isn't a hallucination, at least. That's a good sign. Maybe.

Dante keeps his distance, watching me from his side of the room, I bet. Tallying up the differences in the punk he left behind and whoever he sees now.

"I'm not going to make excuses," he says.

A bitter laugh comes out of me. "You might want to tell Arno that."

"There's something I've got to take care of," he says like I didn't speak at all. "Something I don't want you being a part of—"

"I'm always a part of it." His life. His mistakes. I've always been caught in the wake of Dante Vialle. To be fair, I've never complained. Until now. "And you never give me an answer."

I look over my shoulder and find him standing awkwardly near the door, ready to slip out of it at a moment's notice. Before he can, I take notice of the things I couldn't before. He's bulked up some, and his hair is longer, falling into his eyes, the main feature we share. His narrow in a way that signals that he's not here for idle chitchat.

"So, what is it?" I ask. "What reason are you going to spew for bailing on me now?"

"Espi." He shakes his head. "Look. I know you don't understand—"

"Just tell me what you want."

He sighs. Then he nods. "I need you to warn Arno that whatever he's sticking his nose in will only bring him trouble."

Like that narrows it down. Arno sticks his nose into everything.

"Why not warn him yourself?"

His mouth twitches into something that could be called a smile on someone else. "You know Arno. It takes more than talk to distract him from one of his schemes."

"But I can?"

He shifts his weight, crossing his arms over his chest. "He listens to you."

"And if I don't?"

His mouth falls flat. "Nothing good. Trust me on that."

"It's kind of hard to do that lately," I admit. God, I sound like such a whiny punk. So desperate for my big brother's attention.

But hell, if I knew it would work, maybe I'd play that role to its fullest. Beg.

Stick around.

"I've got to go," he says, reaching up to adjust his hood. It's raining out, and droplets of water splatter my kitchen floor. Near the door, he pauses, rocking on the balls of his feet. "It won't be this way forever," he adds. "I promise. But this... this is something I need to do."

He's gone before I can even get a word in edgewise.

I utter my reply anyway, letting the rain snatch the words away. "Isn't it always."

I wipe the counters down and reshuffle the stuff on the table—anything to delay the inevitable. Arno gets antsy if I don't poke my head into the club at least once, but tonight, I'm not in a hurry to make my customary appearance. After today, I can't stomach Arno's paranoid bullshit, but he's not the person I picture waiting for me at Mulligan's.

She's still beneath my fingertips. Yellow paint. Yellow eyes. Yellow—now dark—hair.

It doesn't take remembering what happened to Vlad to suspect that tangling with her isn't a good idea. Though it's not like I've had a lot of those lately, either.

I take a seat at the table. I could find another job tonight, if I wanted. With this new gang on the loose, it seems there are plenty of gangbangers willing to be patched up off the books.

I could always chase after Dante, or better yet, I could make some money. Enough to buy a plane ticket in addition to Domi's. France. London. Someplace far from here.

No matter what, I won't get distracted again.

Not by Dante.

Not by her.

CHAPTER FIFTEEN
CHLOE

By midnight, Espisido still hasn't shown when I take my place on stage. I should be relieved; he wouldn't approve anyway. The lacy, black thong and a matching bra were one of the few sets that fit me, but they reveal the most skin. A pair of knee-high boots minimizes the damage somewhat—Darcy's idea.

"They make you look hot," she insisted.

I look deranged. From my position near the stage, I can't go a second without eyeing the door. The longer his absence stretches on, the more my anxious stomach twists into knots. But the sentiment isn't the popular one tonight. A wild energy electrifies the interior of the club, chafing against my raw nerves.

Are they all this selfish? Arno doesn't look worried, considering that he's trying to balance a busty blonde on his lap with one hand while holding a shot glass in the other. I assume he wouldn't relax if his friend were in danger.

Or so I prefer to imagine.

Admittedly, my imagination's taken a hit lately. I'm too tired to hide anymore, even inside my head. When the emcee announces the performance of "Angel," I move sluggishly, weighed down by a million guilty thoughts vying for my attention.

I should be looking for Anna. Not lying. Not hiding. Certainly not trying to evade Piotr through the art form he taught me so well. I shouldn't be *feeling*.

So I don't.

My audience is unforgiving. They boo and hiss when I circle the pole with as much enthusiasm as a dead bird croaking its last song from inside its gilded cage. I'm on my final exhausted lap when the main door flies open, and a lone figure walks in. He has his head bowed at first, and droplets of rain drip from his black curls and bounce off his shoulders.

Then he looks up, and my mouth goes dry. I'm frozen solid in the path of his stare, wobbling on unsteady heels. *Go,* a part of me urges in vain. I should collect what little money was thrown at my feet and flee. Something about his expression makes me *stay*.

It could be the raised eyebrow. The slight quirk to his mouth. Pity? No…

Interest. It consumes his expression before he can hide it, making those pink lips part and his pupils dilate. In this moment, I have his full attention.

So I take it.

I grip the pole again with shaking fingers and swing myself high. This time, he stares. Haunting blue eyes remain on my skin, viewing every ripple and twist of muscle. Stripping my tiny lace bra feels more like removing a deeper part of myself and laying it bare. Not for the crowd.

For him.

I've never been much of an exhibitionist before this, but I *want* him to see. Everything. I want to give him a real reason to disapprove of my dancing or cast his pitying looks. I'm proud of my scars and my damaged soul. Or I *was*.

He peruses those broken pieces of me as the jeers and whistles of the other men fade. Soon, there's only him left behind, and god knows what he thinks—though I suppose that's the irony of it. *He* judges me with more scrutiny than any higher power ever could.

It's not fair. I want his disgust, not his curiosity. My traitorous body reacts to it in ways I don't like. My nipples harden beneath his gaze. Muscles quake. Nerves tense and fire off at random.

He makes me sloppy.

Every limb is on fire when I swing myself around to face him again. I'm already anticipating what I'll find—a frown. Instead, he merely nods as if giving me permission to climb down, so I do, trembling and slick with exhaustion.

Then he turns and walks away, denying my unconscious wish for a final verdict.

Only now do I feel naked. I barely notice when another smiling girl prances onto the stage, and the music switches over to something more upbeat. I make my way backstage in a daze and push past the other girls for the dressing room. The two cackling brunettes inside do their best to ignore me as I find a spot near the mirror on the far wall and catch my breath.

Focus. I flatten my palm against the table to reinforce the command. *Focus!* I snatch a wad of tissue from a nearby box and scrub at the lipstick Darcy insisted I wear. It's a dark red that somehow minimizes the shadows lurking beneath my eyes.

But makeup can't minimize the desperation. I reek of it, the need to hide, the itch to run. The confusion…

Little Ksei failed at many things in her short, tormented life, but dancing for men was never one of them.

Until now.

My nostrils flare, which draws my attention back to the present. Noise comes from the opposite corner of the room, someone entering.

"Espi!" one of the other women shrieks. "What the hell?"

"Sorry," he says, his voice gruffer than I've heard it before. "You two mind clearing out for a second? I'll leave after that. I promise."

The two women sigh but gather up their things, and then I'm left alone with the intruder. Escape briefly flits across my mind, but it's already too late. The steady thud of his footsteps marks his approach, and I watch him over the surface of the mirror in front of me.

"You looked...good out there," he says once he's a few steps away.

A sigh I didn't even realize I was holding escapes in a rush, leaving me weightless.

"So do the stitches," he adds, betraying the real reason behind his visit. His breath feathers over my neck, followed by the delicate brush of warm fingertips along my left arm. He's touching me without permission, but my tongue can't form a protest. "I mean—I don't really know what I mean." He laughs. "I sound like an idiot, don't I?"

"An idiot?" My nostrils flare again, catching cigarette smoke. And whiskey? Reddened eyes confirm that suspicion. He's been drinking, but the liquor didn't chase away whatever's clouding his gaze. I'm too much of a coward to ask what caused it. "Good is not the best compliment I've ever gotten," I admit. "But it's not the worst."

"Well, that's good too, I guess." Another laugh doesn't displace his unease. The worry lingers as he runs his fingers down my arm. Long after he should be satisfied by the state of my wound, he just keeps...*feeling*.

And the entire damn time he does, the mirror mocks me with a grotesque caricature of the woman I've become. I don't recognize the way her brown eyes widen, so damn empty. I don't recognize the way her bottom lip trembles, either, or how many times she has to flick her tongue along the flesh to moisten it.

Every brush of his fingertips jolts through my skin like an electric current. Soft. Softer. *Blinding.*

So much for Arno's warning.

"I should get back..." My voice falls flat, and I don't move.

Neither does he. I find an unreadable expression lurking beyond the glass. More pity? His gaze skims my shoulders before I can be sure, impossible to decipher.

Exhaustion and nerves make for a reckless combination. He takes a small step closer, and I inhale him even more deeply —mint, rainwater, fresh air. Wherever he was during the day, he spent most of it outdoors. He's shivering beneath his jacket, but his hands feel steady. Too steady. There's nothing sexual about them—no groping or wandering fingertips. Does that make this easier?

Regardless, my lungs deflate as he pulls away. With relief, or so I tell myself.

"I should probably let you get dressed now," he says, his voice thick.

It's only now that I realize that my bra is still undone. Confusing me further, he averts his gaze as I reach behind my back to refasten the clasp.

I grab his borrowed hoodie from a nearby hook and drape it around my shoulders. "I'm ready."

He leads me out into the main bar in silence, though we don't stray too far from the stage. I go on again in an hour —and then an hour after that until the bar closes at four. Already, I can tell it's a tiring schedule, but at least it has an ending time. I even get to keep some of the money, it seems, as a stern-faced bouncer dressed in black approaches me to tuck a wad of bills into my hands.

"You earned it," he grunts before pushing his way back through the crowd.

I guess it's what was thrown at the stage during my last set. I don't bother to count it when I slam it down onto the counter in front of Domi as she struggles to pour drinks for the horde of drunks crowding the bar.

"You want a shot?"

I nod. "As many as you can pour."

She smiles mischievously and palms the cash. "Can do."

A minute later, a shot glass slides in my direction. I down it without asking as to the contents and then demand another. I'm on the third glass when my silent shadow speaks.

"Do you like it?" he wonders, jerking his chin toward the stage. "Dancing. You looked different up there."

"Did I?" I'm genuinely curious. I've never seen myself dance. I don't want to. Or, at least, I didn't. Blue eyes contain the hints of a creature I don't recognize. Someone he describes as "different," but how? I ask him.

He blushes. "I mean…you look alive." His teeth falter over the word, breaking it into two syllables. Even his hesitation sounds beautiful. "You look tired, too," he adds. "Like you've been doing it for a while."

I say nothing and knock another shot back. A warm jolt of alcohol imbibes me with fresh stupidity. I look over and meet his gaze, only to instantly regret it. "I don't like it," I say, and he nods slowly, dissecting my answer to take note of all the things I don't voice. Speaking with him is as dangerous as Arno's game of Russian roulette when drinking is involved. My lips form more words without waiting for input from my brain. "You don't seem to enjoy watching me?"

I expect him to cringe away in embarrassment, but his lips part fearlessly to deliver an answer. "I—"

"Hey!" Francisco approaches from across the bar. "Arno's looking for you," he tells Espi. "He's…cranky."

Espi rises, muttering, "See ya around," to Domi. Then that's it.

By the time I return to the platform, he's already gone, and I doubt he'll return. Maybe I hope he won't. Wait. No, I don't mean that. There are worse things to stomach than his pity.

Like the real possibility of Piotr returning at any moment to do what he does best. Destroy me.

So, even as the thought makes my cheeks flame, I hope he does come back.

He has to. Because I'll be the only one to blame if he doesn't.

And I'm not sure if I can live with that.

CHAPTER SIXTEEN
ESPI

Arno is waiting for me near the back door of Mulligan's, a bottle in his hand. He leans against the doorway, blocking my way. "You've been out a lot lately."

Damn it. My fingers clench, aching for a cigarette—any excuse to walk away. Arno doesn't do small talk, and I'm not in the mood for a fight. Not now.

"I've been busy," I grit out, but he doesn't move, not even when we're toe to toe.

"Out doing *what?*" His breath hits me full in the face, practically acidic with liquor. "More of your little side projects? You think I don't know what shit you get up to when my back is turned?"

Does he? If so, he's taking the idea of my leaving better than expected.

"You're looking for *him*," he says as his knuckles whiten over the liquor bottle.

Dante?

"If you have been," he adds before I can deny it, "I've got a lead…" He takes another swig directly from the bottle and spits the swill out at his feet.

My common sense warns me to step back, but he doesn't seem liable to strike out with either the bottle or his fists. Yet.

"A good one—so don't fucking look at me like that," he snaps. "I didn't want to let you know until it panned out, but I can't have your ass running around the city every fucking day. I need you here."

"A lead," I repeat carefully. Now doesn't seem like the right time to mention my impromptu family reunion. "What kind?"

"I need more time." He shakes his head. "I'll let you know when I hear something—"

"So I'm just supposed to take your word for it?"

"Is there some reason why you can't trust me now, Espisido?"

I don't answer. My problem never was about trusting *him*. "Fine."

"Tomorrow at the latest," he says. "I can promise you that."

He steps aside, and I push my way past him without digging any further and leave the pub. With Arno, sometimes it's better to be in the dark.

———

I WAKE UP SPRAWLED OVER MY SKETCHBOOK AND WASTE most of the day avoiding my ringing cell phone. In the end, I miss out on at least two jobs. A few sips of whiskey and I forget why I need the money.

Almost.

Alone, I head to Mulligans after midnight, and the roar of music and laughter swallows me whole the moment I enter the barroom. It's a full house tonight. Most of the crowd hovers around the stage, fighting for a glimpse of the main show. If Darcy's on, I might as well toss her a wave before asking for another favor—Domi needs clothes that cover her ass.

I look up. *Shit.* The woman approaching the pole is not Darcy; the features are all wrong. Messy, brown hair. Pale skin. Body barely covered by skimpy black lace...

I turn away, but it's too fucking late. My jeans feel tighter. The itch beneath my skin bites a little deeper. My fingers shake. It takes me three tries to lift a cigarette from my pocket as I push my way to the bar counter. From behind it, Domi tosses me a smile, but the moment I reach an empty stool and sit...

I turn around, driven by the same impulse that has me dragging on the cig so hard that I choke. She's already into the start of her set, and her eyes find mine in an instant. I inhale another puff like it's an antidote to her poison—but the longer I watch her, the more she floods my veins. She moves slowly, finding the hidden pulse within the music until her entire body is in motion, like gasoline drizzled on a flame. Just when the tempo starts to build, she heads for the pole.

I don't *want* to watch her climb onto it, but I do. She's got the crowd in the palm of her hand. The same one she's gliding down to the swell of her ass before she fingers the hem of a lacy, black thong. She tugs on the strap, and my throat lurches at the sight of creamy, pale skin underneath, marred by scars. Tainted with secrets. A heartbeat later, the material is in her hands and flung carelessly into the crowd. Some bastard grabs it, waving the damn thing through the air, but she barely spares him any attention.

Her eyes are on me as she reaches for her bra. She easily peels the material loose, slowly...slowly. In one quick motion, she lets it slip from her fingers.

Like my control. It hits the floor along with everything else.

My cig hangs limply from my lips as I take in her full breasts swaying when she swings. Her hips glisten as she gradually winds herself down from the pole without seeming to notice or care that she's naked. That hungry eyes are watching her. That her indifference only makes the jeers louder.

She doesn't even stop to gather the dollar bills flying in her direction on her way off the stage. I'm already on my feet, pushing my way through the crowd. I catch flashes of her in bits and pieces. Heaving shoulders. Pale skin.

She opened the stitches. My brain clings to that excuse as I barge into the dressing room. She's alone this time, standing in the corner and tugging on a pair of black shorts, still topless. Her fingers freeze when she spots me, her ass still bare.

"I…" My throat goes drier as I fumble for any goddamn excuse. "I need to check the stitches—"

She flings her arm out without turning around, and I can see for myself that the wound is intact. But I keep moving, ignoring how she backs up with every damn step I take. She's flush with the wall beside a vanity when I finally manage to dig my heels into the floor.

"I'm sorry… I…"

"Are they torn?" She extends her arm, and my fingers find her skin, circling carefully along her wrist. Up to her elbow. Higher, to her shoulder. More.

I should pull away. Selfishness must be another Vialle family trait. The rush I feel… It's like inhaling on a cigarette—the icy, familiar burn, the fear that I might choke if I take too much too fast. The numbing clarity that comes after. One hit of her splits my fucking brain in half. I inhale raggedly and don't even realize that I've pulled away until her free hand grabs mine, clenching tight.

I expect her to break the remaining fingers in warning. She seems like the type. Instead, she forces them open, turning my instinctive fist into a grasping claw. The pad of her thumb grazes my palm, and she stares at it as if she's counting each and every individual line and crevice.

Our gazes meet over the mirror's surface of the nearest vanity, drawing me closer. One step. Two. Three. She doesn't let up until her ass meets my hip, the back of her head is against my shoulder...and my hand is on her breast.

She holds it there, lightly enough that I could pull away. I fucking should. I can't. I don't. My fingers curve instead, sensing the heat running beneath her skin, driven by the rhythm of her pulse. I feel the gasp that catches in her throat, brief and broken.

My other hand finds her hip. My fingers have a mind of their own when they flatten against it, splayed and searching, feeling the firm bones and delicate skin. I've drawn nudes before, but never anyone like her.

She's art, scribbled and marked over in a million barely visible scars. One on her lower back catches at my fingertips, just beyond the edge of a series of tattoos—black symbols I vaguely recognize as belonging to the Russian alphabet, Cyrillic. It's another detail of her I steal away. Like the fact that, going off the dark curls I glimpsed between her legs during her show, she really isn't a natural blond.

Does it matter? Something warns me that it does. Every bit of her seems to add up to one indiscernible picture—Little Miss Yellow. I could draw her using just that one shade and never lose any detail. But it isn't long before my brain turns to more than sketching.

"They're still intact," I tell her, pulling away. "The stitches, I mean." I head for the door without looking back and keep moving until I'm in the alley behind the bar. I lean against the nearest wall, pull out a pack of cigs, and light four of them up one by one. I inhale them all down to nothing, flicking the ashes at my feet.

I fish out another cig and flick the end of it with my lighter. It's been a long time since I chain-smoked a whole pack at once. But why quit now? I'm already halfway there.

CHAPTER SEVENTEEN
CHLOE

I'm about to head downstairs to help Francisco open when the burner phone in my pocket rings. Unease pools in my stomach as I fish it out. For Grey to call so early, something must be wrong. He works fast, but not this fast.

"What kind of shit are you playing here, Parker?"

I wince. The fact that he's shouting proves my suspicion correct.

"What happened?" My throat feels tight, my palms slick. For good reason. If Arno decided to play some sick game at my expense, Piotr would be the last person I would need to worry about. "Did you run the number?"

"Yeah, I ran it," he snarls.

"And?"

"*And* are you sure you got that number from Mackenzie? You saw Arno *Mackenzie* with that gun?"

"Yes…" That part was the truth, at least. "I saw him with it. Whose is it?"

Grey sighs so heavily into the phone that all I hear is static. "That gun belongs to a cop," he breathes out a second later. "A thirty-year veteran of the force. The soon-to-be fully instated chief of police, to be exact. You know the guy. Richard Van Hallen. Someone who I know for a fact isn't dead."

Shock runs through me like a lance, and it takes me a second to remember how to speak. "You're kidding me…"

"I wish I were, Parker," Grey admits. "That gun was reported missing almost six months ago. Apparently part of the whole mess with Vincent Stacatto's murder."

Vincent Stacatto, an Italian mob boss infamous for human trafficking. His murder happened right before my transfer, exposing a corruption scandal that went all the way up to the top. Things before had been tense, to say the least, but they got much worse after Stacatto went down.

"What would a gangster be doing with that gun?" I ask. Arno or otherwise.

"I think a better question is—Why leave the goddamn serial numbers on it at all? That's sloppy. Or…"

"Or it's a bad sign," I say, picking up his train of thought. "Someone's setting a trap."

"You always were quick on the uptake, Parker," Grey admits and laughs gruffly. "Whatever this is, I don't like it. In fact…I'm not even going to go to the brass with this. Yet. You lie low and see if you can find out more. I'll continue to cover your ass here."

"How?"

He grunts out another coarse laugh. "As far as they know, you're on *vacation*—the emergency, undocumented kind."

Fair enough. I don't question it, and with a terse goodbye, Grey hangs up. I'm already staggering down the hall toward that infamous room at the back of the bar. When I throw it open, I find Arno inside, slumped over the table.

He starts when I slam the door behind me. "What the fuck—"

"What game are you playing? I had them run the serial number on that gun. Turns out, it belongs to a cop—"

"What the fuck did you just say?" He lurches to his feet, knocking his chair over.

"And not just any cop," I continue, unfazed as he advances on my position. "A gun that belonged to the soon-to-be police chief, Van Hallen."

Arno blinks and stops in his tracks, paces away. "What's his name?"

Something tells me that he already knows the answer before I even say it. "Richard Van Hallen."

"Fuck." He curls a fist and slams it into the palm of his other hand. Once. Twice. Again. "Fuck. Fuck. Fuck!"

He plunges the abused fingers into the pocket of his jeans, and I half expect him to go for the gun, but he withdraws another cell phone instead. A second later, he's snarling into the receiver.

"Get the truck and get the fuck over here. Now. You have five goddamn minutes. And *you*." His eyes cut over in my direction while he hangs up. "You're coming with me."

He grabs me by my arm. The bad one. I wince as he manhandles me toward the door, but either he doesn't care, or he doesn't notice. It takes everything I have in me not to resist as he hauls me down the hallway and out of an exit that opens onto an alley. Not out of fear. Even drunk, Arno doesn't seem like the type to be easily overpowered.

I try using logic to reach him instead. "Where are we going? Can I put some shoes on first?"

He just grunts and pulls me forward, though he loosens his grip enough so that I don't go falling down the three concrete steps after him. My foot has barely hit the pavement as a black pickup truck swerves into the alley.

I don't recognize the driver, but he lunges across the passenger's seat to fling the door open, and Arno shoves me inside, forcing me to climb onto the back bench. He muscles his way in after me and slams the door.

"We've got to visit an old friend," he says, but the edge to his tone doesn't inspire any warm or friendly feelings.

The driver shrugs. "Which one?"

"Jose, that sick fuck," Arno spits out. "Take us to the fucking bike stop."

———

THE "BIKE STOP" IS ON THE OTHER SIDE OF THE CITY from Mulligan's, situated between a rundown warehouse and the river. Most of the buildings within the general vicinity are dilapidated, vacant, or overrun with druggies and homeless.

It's the perfect place for the lair of a self-professed outlaw king. I recognize the territory from some of Grey's secondhand horror stories. Everything on this side of the bridge belongs to the *El Patrón* cartel.

Something tells me that Arno's use of the word *friend* was in the loosest sense. He tenses up the moment we near the property, like a guard dog sensing the piss of another beast nearby.

Overall, the place looks like an old gas station that once might have serviced the towering warehouse behind it. I assume from the state of the pumps that it's still in service, though I doubt to the general public. A chain-link fence encloses the space, and in the attendant's station, two men sneer at their newfound company.

"Stay in the truck," Arno tells the driver. "If anything goes down, you get the fuck out of here and bring backup. They try to take the truck? You shoot them in the fucking head."

He wrenches the glove compartment open, revealing an impressive array of weapons.

Either he's not worried that I'll snitch or he's desperate enough to ignore the caution. He grabs two guns and presses one into the driver's palm while tucking the other into his back pocket. Then he nudges the passenger's door open and climbs out. His feet hit the pavement. Then he reaches back and tugs me out after him.

I'm frog-marched barefoot to the mouth of the fencing. By the time we pass through, one of the men has left the attendant station. He shouts at us, the words in Spanish— the only language I studied in college.

"What the fuck do you want?"

Arno chuckles, his smile feral. *"Hola, ese.* Taco fucking Bell. Take me in to see Jose."

Standing beside him, I feel like a doe caught in the rampage of a crazed, wild bear tearing through anything in its path. Either he gets us both killed before we get in the door or the display will strike enough fear into the lackeys that they snap to attention.

So far, it's the latter effect. The two men share a look between them, and the one closer to us breaks away toward the warehouse. I assume we're meant to follow when Arno marches in his wake, dragging me alongside him.

With every step we take, something inside my stomach clenches up. The air here smells similar to what haunts my nightmares. The stench of decay. Of hopelessness. Whatever dark corner of hell spit out Vlad and Piotr apparently had a few other monsters running loose.

The man leading us to the warehouse's entrance is sporting the same guarded expression as one of the bouncers at Moe's, even though his attire of a white T-shirt and jeans differs slightly. He comes to a stop before a battered metal door and knocks on it once. It opens, held by a man wearing a flannel shirt splattered with a dark substance. It's oil.

I think. I hope.

"Let's get this fucking over with," Arno mumbles as he shoves me through the doorway first.

I stagger inside, catching myself against a firm surface. A wall? It's made of concrete, harsh and uneven beneath my fingertips. I blink to make out more of my surroundings and catch sight of a narrow hall before Arno grips my shoulder and drags me closer.

"What's this?" a soft voice calls from what appears to be a larger area beyond the short entrance.

I blink when we reach the threshold of the cavernous space. It must have served as a cargo bay during the building's official use. Now, it appears to be a makeshift den where a shirtless man is lounging on the floor, eating cereal out of a bowl.

The relative harmlessness of the scenario is undercut by two chilling realizations—one, the man is "lounging" on the body of a prone figure lying on the ground—make that *chained* to it. There's so much blood surrounding the body that I can't tell where it ends and the poor soul begins. Or even if they're alive despite the carnage.

The man sitting on the victim's back doesn't seem to mind the mess, however. His ass rests comfortably over their spine, his legs splayed on either side. A bowl of Fruity Pebbles balances on a rent section of back, and he calmly takes a heaping spoonful. The movement draws a moan from the body—they're definitely still alive.

"Arno," the dining man says cheerfully. He's beautiful. That's the second striking revelation.

With caramel skin and a flawless complexion, he's the golden angel to Espi's ivory. Insanely long lashes flutter against his cheekbones whenever he lowers his eyes to his meal. A dark thatch of closely cut curls covers his head, framing a face set with strong, breathtaking features that appear deceptively innocent when paired with the blood on his jeans.

"Is there a reason why you're interrupting my breakfast?" he wonders beneath a thick Spanish accent.

"You could say that." Arno's callous shrug is as close to a sign of respect as anyone's likely to see from him, I assume. "We need to talk."

"Talk…" The other man frowns at his cereal bowl and then sets it aside, unperturbed by the pool of blood occupying the same space. He wipes his hands on his jeans and then stands in a single fluid motion. He's tall. Nearly as tall as

Arno, but the slight height difference doesn't tip the scales of power in either's favor.

This man, he must be Jose. Only now does it strike me that I have heard of him before, just by another name. We called him "The Shredder of the Cartel" around the precinct. It was the nicest term to describe what he did to his victims.

The horror stories clash with his smiling façade. I'm almost fooled by it—until the moment he comes to a stop inches away from Arno and meets the other man's gaze directly.

"You come into my house, unannounced..." His tone deepens, revealing a hint of the danger lurking underneath. "You interrupt the lovely breakfast I was having with Julio here. For what? To *talk*." He throws his head back and laughs.

It's a beautiful, charming sound that serves as a violent contrast to the way his hand shoots out and finds my neck. White explodes behind my eyelids. I can't breathe. His grip is the only thing holding me upright as he yanks me closer to him and out of Arno's reach.

"Pretty friend," he says while my eyes stream and my lungs constrict.

My heart surges, desperate to panic, but an old familiar instinct keeps it at bay. It's been years since I've had to anticipate the violence, but my body remembers how to react. Stay still. Hold your breath. Count...

It's the only way to keep from blacking out too soon.

One. Two. Three.

"She smells like a Russian spy," Jose says. "Is there a reason that you brought her onto my property, Arno?"

"You kill her, and she can't tell you what she knows." There's a rehearsed calmness to Arno's tone. He's been through this before.

Jose's grip tightens, his fingers digging in. Ironically, the thoughts floating through my brain seem oddly detached given the current circumstances. I'll bruise if he lets me go. I'll suffocate if he doesn't.

Four. Five.

"You hear…about…Russians?"

I catch bits and pieces of the words as Arno spits them out. Black… I blink frantically but only see shadow.

"Who took them out?" Arno asks. "Think your fucking operation isn't next?"

My lungs shrivel, collapsing in on themselves. I'm vaguely aware of the moment death slowly begins to creep…

"Fine."

Air! My own gasp is deafening. I'm choking, down on my hands and knees, as two tan feet pad out of my peripheral vision.

"Let's hear her talk," Jose commands.

But I don't know if I'll ever find my voice again. He was careless. Spiteful. Piotr always made sure never to damage my windpipe during his attempts to drag whatever words he wanted out of me. Words like—*Fuck me. I love you. I'm yours.*

Jose got carried away. While I gasp, Arno's forced to pick up the beginning of the story for me.

"Someone set up that hit and took out nearly a third of the Russian Syndicate overnight. Shit like that doesn't happen on a lucky whim. It was planned."

"Keep talking, *hombre*," Jose says.

I glance up and find him pacing the sliver of concrete before the body on the floor. From this angle, I can see the man's face—what's left of it. One of his eyes lies loose in its socket while the other stares dead ahead, unseeing.

"You know who's behind it?"

Jose chuckles. "*Hombre*, if I knew that, I would have a few more guests for *breakfast*."

A shiver racks my spine at the gleeful, murderous tone. Even Piotr wouldn't make torture seem synonymous with…simple fun.

"Do you know?"

Arno shakes his head. "But I think I have a lead. I just need your help to follow it."

"And your little friend?" Jose smirks at me. "What stories does she have to tell? I have some stories of my own. Like about our dear little Espi—"

"You don't fucking talk about him," Arno says, his voice still dangerously level. Only a subtle cracking of his knuckles betrays the calm.

"Word on the street is that he's crawling around, desperate for cash," Jose says. "Could your boy be planning to run away? I wonder why. Ah...maybe he's figured out *your* little secret—"

"*One of the raids was carried out using a gun that belonged to the interim police chief*," I manage to croak entirely in Spanish, drawing attention to myself.

"So she can speak." Jose flashes a beautiful, dangerous smile. "Is what she said true? You think this little game might stretch higher than some punk-ass gang trying to make their mark on the world?"

If he does, Arno doesn't admit as much out loud. "You share what you know, and I'll share what I know."

Jose considers the proposal while I struggle to my feet. My eyes are still streaming. It's hard to breathe without wheezing, but I manage to stay upright.

"Fair enough," Jose says finally. "I'll have one of my men come by for a little visit when I get my information. That might happen sooner rather than later if you let Julio and me return to our little breakfast..." He nudges the seemingly dead man with his foot, eliciting a pained groan.

Let's go. Arno doesn't even have to say the words out loud, but I'm by his side in an instant. His hand finds my shoulder, steering me along as he barges through the door and past the men still stationed out front.

The man in the truck fires the engine up, and Arno shoves me inside the cabin. The moment he climbs in after me, the truck takes off.

My throat is on fire by the time we finally reach the bar. I think that will be the worst of it—a sore throat for a few days and maybe a pulsing headache.

But I'm barely out of the truck before a familiar figure appears at the side entrance of Mulligan's. He's wearing another hoodie, his hair windswept, his eyes lined with the shadows of exhaustion. He's...he's angry, and it paints a dark, terrifying picture over his features. The angel's grown fangs, but unlike Jose, he's quiet in his rage. The moment he spots Arno, all he does is shrug.

"Fuck. Don't give me that look," Arno snarls, but his plea is ignored.

"You took her to Jose."

There's a cold familiarity in the way Espisido utters that name. I take it his experience with The Shredder of the Cartel is similar to mine. My mind returns to his scars, paired with Arno's defensiveness when Jose uttered his name.

"Have you gone fucking crazy, Arno?" Espi asks.

Arno stiffens, crossing his arms over his chest. "Maybe I have? You got a fucking problem with that? I've been hearing shit on the grapevine, Espi. You want to cut and run out on me too?"

Anger smolders between them, hot and wild, but surprisingly, it doesn't seem to be directed at each other. At least not outright. Something else is fraying their bond. Jose is just the catalyst to a bigger strain.

Espisido shakes his head. His eyes drift over to meet mine, and I'm frozen in place. My hand keeps straying to my throat no matter how hard I try to pin it by my side. He sees the marks my trembling fingers try to hide, and I don't know what reaction to expect. Pity? Anger?

He just stares, his gaze unreadable, and I'm ill-equipped to decipher the elusive emotions.

"I got a lead. That's all that fucking matters," Arno says behind me. "If Dante's got anything to do with this shit, we'll know soon enough." He barges his way past, leaving me and the driver beside the truck. His steps slow before Espisido, who hasn't budged from the doorway.

For a moment, it seems like he won't. I'm not sure how much time passes before he finally steps aside. Arno pushes by him without a word, but it's not over between them. It's a strange dynamic they share. Brothers one minute. Friends the next. Enemies at tense moments sprinkled throughout. But never once do I sense the loyalty between them fade. If anything, their bond only seems stronger.

It's evident in the way Espisido merely sighs when his gaze sweeps over me again. He makes no move to rush over and fawn all over my new injuries. He doesn't even glance at my arm to ensure that the stitches have held. His eyes meet mine directly instead.

"You okay?"

I just nod. He sighs again, taking the assurance at face value. Then he turns and heads back into the bar. Within minutes, I know he'll be out on the other side, gone for the day.

I just watch him go, and he never does look back.

CHAPTER EIGHTEEN

ESPI

SOME PEOPLE CAN STAY SANE WITHOUT ART. GOOD FOR them—but I need the release that comes from spilling my emotions in color and ink. My soul bleeds onto the pages of my sketchbook, and I'm disgusted by the picture I paint.

But at least I can still feel something.

I don't run from it like Arno or ignore my baggage like Dante.

I spread it out in strokes and lines, and I feel every fucking thing.

In the end, I guess it's only fitting that I'm left with a drawing of her. This time, she glares at me. Judges me. Charcoal shading has stripped her yellow away, but she's just as conflicting. Just as volatile. Smearing the details around her eyes with the pad of my thumb doesn't disrupt their intensity. If anything, they burn brighter, demanding answers I'm too chicken to give.

Such as why hearing that she'd gone off with Arno bothered me more than it should have. Or that I felt relieved to find out they'd met with Jose. Only to feel more pissed in the end.

And guilty.

If Arno was desperate enough to go to the Cartel for information, then things are worse off than he's letting on. Suddenly, Dante's warning makes a whole lot of sense.

But it's too late. I can't just run out like he did. I have to face my problems.

Or not.

I ball the drawing up in my fist and toss it into the trash. Then I pour a shot glass of whiskey only to dump it down the sink without taking a sip. For the first time in over a day, my thoughts turn back to escape. Catching the first plane out of here and never looking back.

Not out of spite, either. Maybe fear.

I'm fucking afraid of who I'll turn into if I stick around here. I barely recognize the punk staring back at me from the basin of the sink already. He's not smiling like happy Espi should. If anything, he's scowling.

I try washing him down the drain with water, but he doesn't budge. I'm too much of a coward to see if I'll still find him if I look in the mirror.

So I kill time with violence and paint something dark. I miss the canvas and wind up splattering the walls with blank acrylic. I leave it there and let even more drops drip onto the floor.

My phone is buzzing in my pocket, but I don't answer it. Instead, I pace. Clench the air between my fingers. Kick the fridge on my way past it.

The sound of my ringtone continues to build, drowning out my frantic breathing until I have no choice but to pick up.

"We need to talk about this," Arno says before I can even voice a hello. "Come to the bar."

He hangs up, and I collapse onto a seat near the table.

The bar. She'll be there tonight, probably working. Or maybe not, depending on how badly she tangled with Jose. I grit my teeth against my own memories. I know from experience that he's a hard son of a bitch to forget.

She saw the scars on my back the first night, but she hasn't asked me about them yet. Maybe she's too polite, or maybe she just doesn't care. I can't figure out why the thought bothers me so damn much. Knowing she has ample ammunition to use against me that, for whatever reason, she hasn't yet.

I could always beat her to the punch. Tell Arno that she could be a cop. Or ask her directly where she learned to dance like that.

Instead, I return to the whiskey bottle and take a sip right from the rim. Then I head out for the pub, if only to avoid being by myself.

CHAPTER NINETEEN
CHLOE

GREY CAN SUFFER ANOTHER DAY. I'M NOT A COP tonight. I'm not even human. I'm an animal with a bruise for a shackle. It's a familiar feeling. It's a maddening one.

I'm addicted to the stage. The lure of abandon. The silence that floods my own thoughts when I'm riding so high that no one can fucking touch me. I'm ruthless. I'm selfish. Each set lasts longer than the one before it. I'm cutting into the other dancers' times without a single fuck given.

The crowd loves it. The other girls don't.

Not that I care. Ksei's regained some of that old fire. I owned the stage at Piotr's little playground. I danced for his associates to keep him happy. I danced to save myself.

My old outlook on life paints everything in front of me like I'm wearing blood-colored glasses. The world is an inferno, but as long as I move, blinded by the pulsing strobe lights, I'm safe. I can *breathe* in this sliver of heaven. I can contort my body in any fucking way I want and never feel any pain.

That all changes the moment I come down, though, and am forced to traipse backstage. The pounding headache behind my temples returns. My left arm sears at full force. My throat is on fire. Agony, after agony, after agony...

If I were a good girl, Piotr would give me something to chase the discomfort away before sending me back on stage. To dance again. To make him more money. To plunge further down the rabbit hole of viciousness and vice he'd dropped me into.

But here... One step into the dressing room, one whiff of a familiar scent, and it all comes to a screeching halt without the need for a powder to sniff. A hooded figure is waiting for me at the back corner of the room, and my chest tightens at the sight of him. It was easier to breathe while being strangled by Jose. He showed mercy. My new tormentor seems well aware of the effect he has on me, yet the look in his eyes won't let me go.

It's open. It's raw. He's had a bad day—we both have. I don't speak when I approach him though. I eye the mirror, and he silently creeps in behind me, his hand finding my shoulder.

"You're bleeding." He grits the words out against the back of my neck.

I am. I glance down and find blood seeping through the gaps in the stitches. Some of it is dried. Some isn't.

"Sorry."

Sighing, Espisido runs his hand along the wound once, but he doesn't pull away to get fresh gauze or a rag to wipe the area clean. He just stands there, inhaling me, feeling me. It's a brutal game of tit-for-tat we play. With every breath he takes, I suck in two. When his hand starts to trail down my arm again, I reach for the other, blindly lacing my fingers with his.

Consequences are easier to face when he's not around. I guide his hand higher and inch backward until he's closer—until the heat from his body disrupts every nerve in mine, and I have to lean against the table for balance. His captive hand cups my breast. The one he still has control over drifts down to my waist. I flex my fingers, forcing his to curl.

It's lightning. He's a million watts bursting through my skin, frying everything he touches. I bite my lower lip in vain, but he breaks through my defenses, drawing a moan from my throat. I don't have to guide him anymore—he digs his fingers in, clutching. Groping.

One hit just isn't enough. I need more. He already knows just how and where. One brush of his fingertips makes my nipple harden into a sharp point, but he's forsaken that needy bit of flesh in favor of a new domain. My stomach. My hips. Maybe I'm the one steering him there all along, but when his palm ghosts down to the apex of my thighs, the fingers spread, eagerly searching. Studying. He's an artist, after all.

With steady determination, he breaks me open, painting the air with the gasp I can't smother. He doesn't seem to realize just where his fingers are aiming—and that's the worst part. He's merely feeling. I'm exploding. Colors ripple beneath my skin. My head is bouncing off the ceiling. I'm higher than I've ever been.

I'm needier. Hungrier. More selfish. Feeling him through the cotton of my black shorts isn't enough. I can't stop myself from steering him lower, slipping beneath the waistband and directly against the skin underneath.

I squeeze my eyes shut, rocking back on my heels. Back and forth. Side to side. I don't even let him touch me where every nerve is screaming for stimulation. Just at the ridge of my stomach and it's still too much.

I'm too much of a coward to look up at the mirror and see his reaction. I hunch over the table instead, eyeing a tube of lipstick in a bloody shade while my traitorous body yearns for more. He doesn't resist my grip, even when my fingers tighten over his, my palm slick against the softness of his skin. He never makes a move on his own, but one firm nudge and…

It's like having an entire row of cocaine all to myself. The first hit is the hardest. You placate yourself with memories of how you used to be such a good little girl. Once the burning sting goes away and the high sets in, you lose yourself, however. The good girl makes short work of the remaining lines. Then she licks the surface underneath for any traces of powder.

And he is more potent than any hit. I shove his hand between my legs and shiver at the coursing brush of every callused fingertip. My nerves are a million tripwires he's carelessly triggering. Over and over again.

It's like he doesn't even know what he's doing to me or how. I feel him breathing against the back of my neck. His free hand comes to flick a lock of hair aside, baring my throat to him. It's bruised, and he exhales sharply against the sore flesh.

"I'm sorry."

I'm *coming*. It happens so quickly that I don't have time to catch my breath before everything tightens and clenches. My head goes back. My teeth skewer my bottom lip to keep any sound inside. It's a slowly broiling, torturous climax I doubt he even senses.

When I finally come back down to earth, it's a rough landing. I have to shove his hand away and catch myself against the table, gasping for air. He steps back, taking a cue from the way my shoulders hunch away from him as I struggle to readjust my shorts.

"I...I have to get back on stage," I croak. It's a lie, not that he counters it.

I feel his gaze on the back of my neck as I stagger past him and down the hall. A blonde is gyrating on the pole now. Maybe Darcy or someone else. I can't tell. She falters when I climb on stage and approach her. The crowd roars, but my only goal is to smother every shred of confusion as I step against her, grabbing her waist with one hand while swaying my hips.

She moves awkwardly at first until the increase in bills flying our way spurs her to move faster and grind her body against mine. We give the crowd what they holler for. Her fingers tangle in my hair, drawing my mouth to hers. She tastes like mint-flavored gum, but it's a pale imitation of the scent in my head. The shouts and jeers of the men watching us don't drown out his voice. No matter how fast I move, the slickness of sweat can't erase his touch.

It's a pathetic, pitiful attempt, but I keep fucking trying until I'm breathless and panting and it's time for another girl to take the stage. The act did nothing to counter the high. I'll ride him out all night, and I suspect that it will be one hell of a withdrawal when I finally purge him from my system.

———

I WAKE UP AND FIND DOMI GONE. HER BED'S BEEN made, the other side of the room carefully tidied. I don't find her in the hall when I finally haul myself upright and pull a pair of sweats on. Another figure's taken her place though. They're standing at the mouth of the narrow kitchen, their back turned to me, their shoulders hunched as they rummage through the fridge.

"There isn't much to choose from," they tell me tiredly before glancing over their shoulder to focus a pair of brilliant, blue eyes in my direction. "We'll have to settle for just eggs."

Before I can protest, he snags a carton from the fridge and approaches the stove. He must know the contents of the cupboards, because he easily fishes out a frying pan and a few utensils. By the time he cracks the first egg over an open flame, I've finally mustered up the energy to speak.

"I'm not hungry—"

"We need to talk." He sounds so casual. The only clue that betrays even a hint of uncertainty is how the second egg shatters right in his grip as he attempts to crack it along the end of the counter. He pitches the mess into the sink and starts over with a fresh egg and another attempt. This unbroken yolk joins the first to sizzle in the pan.

I watch him against my own better judgment. He's good with his hands—even the prosthetic fingers. He works quickly to scramble the yolks before they can set and then scrapes two servings onto two mismatched plates. He offers one to me.

I shake my head, but my stomach contradicts the refusal and makes its hunger known in a loud, gurgling rumble. Jerking his head toward the couch, Espi sits first, taking up a corner and leaving me to perch myself on the opposite end. He sets one of the plates down between us and greedily attacks the food piled onto the other one.

I watch him until my fingers start to twitch, desperate for something to do. I snatch up the other plate and balance it on my lap while taking a bite of the eggs. Then another.

"I don't want you to think I'm some sick pervert," Espisido says once I've gathered up enough of a mouthful to swallow.

I promptly choke, spraying egg across the floor. "What... what are you talking about?"

He shakes his head. "I'll stop coming into the dressing room at night." He opens his mouth, seemingly on the verge of saying more, but then he closes it.

And I don't know whether to laugh or count my damn blessings. Without him there, the world is gray again, dominated by Piotr. I'll have no excuse to dwell on feelings and needs that shouldn't matter. An addict only ever knows how to survive on the verge of needing a fix.

"Okay."

We both tentatively swallow another steaming mouthful of eggs.

He exhales sharply as the food goes down his throat. "But... I still need to check out those stitches."

Of course, he does. I shift around so that he's facing my left side. With a clinical precision, he helps me peel off the sleeve of the hoodie I'm wearing—his. He breathes out sharply when he sees my arm—bruised from Arno's manhandling, inflamed from my nights at the bar, still leaking tiny droplets of blood in places.

He rises and gets a rag from the kitchen counter. When he comes back, it's damp with the water from the faucet, and he gingerly dabs away at the area around the stitches. When all is said and done, they've held at least.

But Espisido doesn't finish his examination just yet. His hand goes to my shoulder, flicking back the hair shielding my neck from his gaze. At the moment, Jose's marks take precedence over Vladimir's little wound. Whenever I swallow, the muscles throb in torment. I know from experience that most of the danger from strangulation comes after the fact, when the sore muscle swelled and damaged the windpipe. I've seen girls suffocate a day after having been choked, but I don't have any trouble breathing. For now.

Or at least any difficulty caused by the injuries. My lungs are frozen due to an entirely different reason.

"That crazy motherfucker," Espisido says softly while his fingertips feather over the bruising.

Is he referring to Arno or Jose? I don't know, and I don't bother to ask. There's a certain look in his eyes that I vaguely recognize. Something distant and pained.

"I take it he's not a 'friend' of yours?"

He flinches, his gaze cutting down to the floor. After a minute, he shakes his head. "You could say that."

I'm satisfied with his gruff admission—until he continues to speak.

"A few years ago, I was doing something for Arno. Something stupid. Something he technically wouldn't allow me to do, but I thought I could make him some decent money, so I tried it anyway."

"What was it?"

He shrugs. "Running drugs. Look, Arno's no citizen of the year, but he's not entirely insane." He cracks a worn, small smile that doesn't reach his eyes. "I did it on my own. Thought I could make a quick buck. Make him proud so that he'd let me handle bigger jobs. I was almost out of school by then. I had nowhere else to go but the Gardai. Thought I had to earn my keep. It was stupid. I know."

"So, what happened?"

"My dumb ass cut through territory run by the Cartel. I didn't know it at the time, but Arno and Jose had already tussled over 'boundaries' before. When he caught me, Jose thought Arno was breaking their little treaty." He draws back so swiftly that my entire body resonates with the loss of his heat. His eyes shut as he tears a trembling hand through his hair, holding the black curls away from his face. "He decided to make an example out of me."

The memory of the man chained to the floor, Jose's breakfast companion, makes my blood run cold, numbing my skin.

"He strung me up against the wall," Espisido says. "He went at me with whips. Different shapes. Different kinds. For hours."

The view of his back springs to my mind—the scars, lengthy and jagged. I'm already reaching out for him. My fingers grip his shoulder and tug. After a moment's hesitation, he allows me to lift the corner of his shirt.

With single-minded determination, I paw the dark cotton away and peer at the pale skin underneath. The worst of the scars are easy to see, bulging against taut muscle and the ridges of his shoulder blades. The full extent of the damage, however, can only be felt through my fingertips. Every twitch and shudder of scar tissue. Every bumpy stretch of tendon where I assume he can't feel sensation anymore.

Jose made an "example" out of him, all right. He gave him wings—a twisted, broken mockery of them.

"Did he do this too?" My hand slides down to his right wrist. Two of my fingers slip in between his, ghosting the spaces where his are missing.

Shaking his head, he pulls away. "No. No…that was someone else."

For a moment, I can only stare, taking him in. Every inch. He wears his scars so differently from mine. Open and guarded at the same time. He doesn't cut them away or hide them behind masks and different names.

He just *is*.

I find the voice to ask when he doesn't continue the thread of the story himself. "What happened?" There is a reason why he didn't wind up like Julio, wasting away while Jose ate a meal on his bloodied remains.

"Arno happened," Espi says gruffly. He readjusts his shirt, pulling the hem back down to his waist and covering the scars. "He found out what I'd done. He came in the nick of time. I know he might seem like a hardass, but the Cartel outnumbers the Gardai two to one. It was suicide for him to go in alone, but he did. He had to beg Jose to let me go. He *begged*."

I can't see his face—I merely hear the icy, tormented edge to his words—and have to imagine his expression on my own. Indigo eyes narrowed in pain. Beautiful features chiseled and hardened.

"Even after all that, I'm not sure what he had to promise Jose to make him stop. It took me four months to heal."

The gravity of the violence washes over me. I have to brace one hand against the couch cushions to find my breath. In the midst of the tumult of emotions raging in my head, one thought sticks out.

"Where was your brother? What did he do when he—"

"Dante?" Espisido chokes out a laugh. "Dante was in prison. By the time he got out, there didn't seem to be a point in mentioning that little story."

My throat feels tighter. "Where is he now?"

I don't know what to expect. A different gamut of emotions comes over him when he speaks of Dante versus Arno. With Arno, he's angry, loyal, aggravated, and understanding all at the same time. When all thrown together, I think it's love. With Dante, there's just...*pain.*

"He got out of prison about a year ago," he says, his shoulders hunched away from me. "For a while, it was good. Then, six months later, he cut out again. Just left some money on the table for me and was gone. *Again*." He shakes his head, his dark hair flying, and fights to suck in air. One ragged breath paints the air between us.

I don't realize I've touched him until I feel him shiver beneath my palm while his heart beats furiously against his skin.

"If he got bored of me or sick of me tagging along or something like that...I could handle it. But Dante only breaks loose when something's wrong. When he's trying to protect someone."

"You and Arno are looking for him?"

He scoffs. "Something like that. We won't find him, though, until he *wants* to be found. But..." He faces me, brushing off the hand I have on his back. "This time, I have a feeling that having him back won't be as easy as him ditching an orange jumpsuit."

I don't answer in favor of scrutinizing the planes of his face and memorizing every angelic detail. Why? The act does little to diminish the inexplicable ache humming through my veins whenever he's near. It's not lust—not that I've ever felt that emotion for myself. I just watch it unfurl in the men who look at me and only see a body. A hole. A quick fuck and the loss of a maybe a few bucks.

Even after I left the Syndicate, dating didn't repair any of the damage left behind. So what I feel for him isn't lust.

It's something more pathetic than that. Something needy and aching that won't let me back away from him, even though I can tell he wants me to. I'm not his type.

Maybe he doesn't like blondes or box-brunettes. Maybe he doesn't touch dancers on principle. Maybe...

So I'm the one who touches *him*, sliding my hand along the top of his shoulder. Just once. It's not enough. My fingers curl, catching the muscle underneath. I'm pulling him closer before common sense can warn me to stop. Closer. Too close.

For some reason, he lets my lips brush his—too chaste a touch to even be called a kiss. Even so, I taste him as I breathe him in—cigarette smoke, mint, and the faintest sting of alcohol. He's virtue and vice in one conflicting taste.

I surface once I've gotten my fix, but he has other plans. I don't think he means to kiss me so much as he intends to feel. How my lips feel. What I taste like. The sounds I make when his body presses into mine. Gasps. Moans. I can't control it.

He exhales himself into me, and my tongue sneaks out to steal more of him away. More mint. Acidic smoke. Sweetness. Egg. Everything.

We're fused at the mouth, his body positioned between my legs, his hands surely on my waist. His fingertips graze my stomach while his tongue flutters against the outside of my lower lips. Soft. Tempting. I can't stop myself from reaching for the waistband of his pants, and I barely brush the denim before he shoves my hand away.

"Stop!"

I'm left panting, staring up at him as he lurches to his feet. His eyes flicker, catching the emotions laid bare in mine. He shakes his head, tearing a hand through his hair, and groans. There's nothing boyish or cute about the motion. He's more devil than angel again. Shadows drape his innocent features, adding definition to the ivory.

"It's not like I don't…like I don't want you," he says thickly. "I do."

I do. Everything in my body rides the wave of those words. *I want you.*

I'm already croaking out an argument. "But—"

"*But* you won't want me," he says.

And then he's gone. The door slams. Reality descends, and my body ramps up for yet another grueling withdrawal. Good. I deserve to suffer.

Biting my lip so hard that I taste blood does nothing to assuage the self-hate surging through my veins. God, how could I be so fucking pathetic? I look down at my fingers in disgust. Then again, how could I *not* be?

Piotr taught me that the only way to process lust is to take what you want. Demand it from those weaker than you and break down anyone strong enough to resist. I'm still his creature, so desperate for affection.

So broken.

Tears escape my eyes before I can blink them back, searing fiery trails down my cheeks. The sting of rejection shouldn't affect me so harshly. So fucking deeply.

But it hurts.

As it should. Maybe I'll learn my lesson now. I'll heed Arno's advice. I'll stay away.

I won't consume another dizzying dose from a dealer who wants nothing to do with me.

CHAPTER TWENTY
ESPI

Fuck.

I never used to smoke in bed, making it the one place that didn't reek of ash. Better to be safe than sorry. I knew a druggie once who lit up half-asleep and set himself on fire.

She changed that. I wake up with a cig already in my mouth. The first thing I do is feel around for my lighter and flick the flame with my eyes still closed. One puff and the risk is worth it—I'd burn alive rather than feel what I do when I see her face. When I hear her voice.

In a way, she makes me feel like Dante. Out of fucking control. Or maybe more like *him*... Sick. Deluded. Like father, like son.

A cold shower is the only weapon I have against her. I stagger into the bathroom while I inhale the rest of the cig, and then I wrench the showerhead on, grappling for control. The shitty water pressure won't help much. I need a damn tsunami to knock her out of my system.

The reaction doesn't make any damn sense. I've had women come onto me before. I've seen them naked. Barely a night can go by at Mulligan's without someone shaking their ass in my face.

But no one looks at me the way she does. Hell, most people wouldn't dare. Little Miss Yellow. She's a cigarette, demanding my sole attention or she'll set my ass on fire.

Kind of like the one I'm smoking now. I flinch as hot ash trickles from the overgrown end and burns through my sweatpants. I flick it off and pat myself down, but the pain lingers. Like her scent. Like this hard-on.

The burn of nicotine doesn't diminish the ache in my stomach. I'm too damn wound. I have to toss the cigarette into the toilet bowl and slide a hand beneath my waistband. I roughly grab my dick, squeezing it at the root, desperate to cut off all fucking feeling. It doesn't help. I pump my hand along the shaft, squeezing my eyes shut to block my surroundings out.

The physical touch does nothing. I have to envision it... I have to see her riding high on the pole, her legs splayed, her breasts swaying. It's not even her body that gets me off though. It's those eyes. The hunger in them. That need. Like she might actually feel whatever the fuck I do.

"Shit." My hand flies out, my palm hitting the wall. The fire building in the base of my stomach spreads, but it needs more fucking fuel. Like the feel of her skin. The gasp she let out when I touched her. The feel of her nipples grazing my palm. And then her pussy…

A grunt rips from my throat. My hand keeps moving. Faster. Harder. I only have to imagine what it would be like to thrust inside her and I come so hard that my ears pop with the force of it. I'm still in a daze when I shake the hot cum from my fingers and climb into the shower.

I stay here until my teeth start to chatter. Until every inch of me is numb. Then I climb out, get dressed, and head out. When I reach Mulligan's, Arno is already there, taking up a stool near the bar. When he sees me, he just grunts and lifts a shot glass in salute. Domi's at the bar counter behind him, and Ksei…

She's in the corner, a broom in her hand. The bruise around her throat looks even worse in the daylight, but she wears it like someone who's been through worse—*healed* from worse.

I turn my back on her and seek out Francisco. I need a job. Something to take my mind off Dante. Arno's no fucking use when he's this deep into the bottle, but Frank already has a task in mind.

"I need your expertise," he tells me when I find him in the back, moving crates of liquor into the basement, where Arno stores the good stuff. "Arno won't like it, but the fucker won't talk."

"What is it?" My stomach clenches the same way it does at the mention of any new "side job." I've tried to rationalize it in so many ways. At the end of the day, it was even a hobby of sorts. Some people fix cars in their spare time. Mow lawns. Clean gutters. The busywork no one else wants to do.

We all have our quirks, I guess. Mine's no different—I tell myself that repeatedly. Whatever helps me sleep at night.

"One of our Russian friends survived Arno's fun and games," he says under his breath. "He knows something, but he won't fucking talk. I think you should try to convince him before Arno gets bored and snuffs out this lead."

"A lead," I echo. "This have anything to do with the *real* reason why he had me try to get up Vlad's ass?"

He might have lost his shit even more than usual, but Arno's not entirely insane. He wouldn't push me toward the Russians without a reason—a much better one than the gun-running excuse he fed me when I asked. It has to be something deeper than that. Something he couldn't ask the Russians outright. Something more than just Dante.

Francisco knows what, at least more than I do. He's not willing to tell me though. His loyalty to Arno goes deeper than any favors I could ever deliver. "Just trust me on this. You know how he gets when he's desperate."

I know, all right—better than anyone. "He gets sloppy. I'll do it. I just gotta get my kit."

"Thanks, kid," Francisco says. He's smart enough not to sound too grateful though. He still has a soul in there somewhere. Maybe in any other situation, it wouldn't come to this. "I know it isn't easy on you. But this fucker is a real piece of shit. Trust me—He deserves it—"

"I'll get my kit." The excuse takes me away from him, but not far enough. If I had to get the stuff I keep at the house, maybe I would change my mind along the way. But, whether out of convenience or guilt, I've learned to keep a spare kit at the bar.

When I approach the counter, all of those old concerns I've pushed to the back of my mind rise again. I'm running low on equipment. I need new thread. New narcs...

"Hey!" Domi flashes me a smile when I slip past her and snag a black case from underneath the sink.

Someone, probably Francisco, wrote *FIRST AID KIT, DON'T FUCKING TOUCH* on the plastic surface, and I have to snort at the irony as I return to the back.

Francisco's already waiting for me near the basement. When he opens the door, moaning mixed with laughter wafts out. I can tell just from the stench alone that Arno's done a fucking number on this guy already.

"You ready?" Francisco asks as his gaze flickers over his shoulder to make sure we're alone.

I just shrug and fish a cigarette from my pocket. "As ready as I'll ever be."

———

IT TAKES TEN MINUTES. THAT'S THE FUNNY THING about the human psyche. Some people break in seconds. Some take hours. The length of time reflects nothing on the strength of the person though. It just shows how much shit they've already suffered through. Endurance is like scar tissue. It builds up over time, uglier and cruder than normal skin. A knife can easily tear through most flesh, but when it's scarred, you might have to saw a little.

As expected, the sawing can get messy. There's blood everywhere, speckling the floor and the table like sloppy graffiti. I fucking taste it whenever I lay off the cig hanging from the corner of my mouth. So I drag again, flicking ash onto my knee. The shit burns, but my hands are too busy to swipe the embers away. The left one adjusts the knife in its grip while the right pins a trembling wrist against the table.

"Last time," I say. There's no point in putting any ice into my tone. I just sigh when the bastard sitting across from me doesn't answer.

He's gritting his teeth together so hard that a vein's pulsing in his forehead, but the pathetic sounds he makes slip out. He won't take his eyes off his hand. What remains of it. Shock will set in fast if he doesn't talk soon.

I tell him as much. "I'd say you got about an hour before you really start feeling the blood loss."

The bastard whimpers, turning his head away.

"Fuck this shit." Francisco's at my shoulder. He's impatient. The longer this takes, the more likely it is that Arno might stumble down here and crash our little party. "Do what it takes to speed this up," he grunts in my ear.

The magic words. One more drag on my cig gives me enough of a hit to drown out the scent of salt. As the butt glows red, I lift the knife. The tip gleams, even beneath a smear of ruby liquid. I lower the edge close to my handiwork. The guy has one-third of his pinkie finger left, clinging by a sliver of sinew and a chunk of bone. It's not the most elegant of jobs, but it gets the point across. As long as the fucker talks, he'll keep the finger. If not…

"Wait! Wait, wait!"

So the asshole speaks. Whatever he has to say, I don't want to fucking hear it. Instead, I push back from the table, letting Francisco take my seat. He takes the knife without a word; we've played this game before.

"I'll take it from here," Francisco says.

Two other men lurk in the corners, ready to jump in if shit goes off. Stitching the guy up can wait until later.

———

It takes a shot of whiskey, and a few good drags on a fresh cig before I can push the images out of my head —far enough away, at least. The icy air helps when I shove the door to the bar open and step outside.

My fingers are cramping, but clenching them into fists doesn't help. Neither does slamming them against the rusted dumpster outside Mulligans. I have to drag my bruising knuckles against the first brick wall, the skin ripping off from the friction. The faster I walk, the deeper the pain. The reddish streaks I leave behind are a new form of graffiti. They tell the story of a pathetic punk too stupid and weak to skip town. So what does he do?

He sells his fucking soul.

"Fuck!" I shout, startling a woman gazing from an apartment building across the street. Evading her curious stare, I cut through an alley. Then another. Another.

The asshole on my tail is pretty good. They keep up no matter how many detours I take. Their loss though. I've got a full syringe in my pocket. I've got no fucks left to give, and they're not even trying to hide. I hear their footsteps. Their breathing echoes off the walls, ragged and unsteady.

By the time I reach the stoop of my place, I'm already reaching for the knife in the mailbox, and I wait while the punk sneaks right up to my front door.

"You got a problem?" I turn, keeping the weapon hidden beneath my sleeve.

They're standing just beyond the bottom step, their face hidden beneath the hood of a jacket. A familiar jacket. Then the hood falls back, and a mane of dark hair catches the light.

"Are you all right?"

The sound of her voice knocks me back against the door as everything I've been blocking out until this point comes rushing back. I want to wash the blood off my hands. I need to shower, scrub away the stink of death and pain. I finished my last cigarette somewhere during the walk here, but my hand is already pawing through my pockets in search of another. I feel more like Arno than ever—I need to drown in a vice. Anything but her.

"Fine," I grit out. Then I turn to the door, get it open, and shove my way inside without bothering to invite her in. It's rude. It's the only way I know how to save myself. "Goodnight—"

She easily muscles me aside, grabbing my chin with her free hand and angling my face toward her. A curse slips between her lips as she traces a corner of my mouth with the pad of her thumb. The slight touch stings, and something warm dribbles down my chin. Oh, that's right. The fucker did manage to land a good hit before Francisco pinned him down.

I shake my head, batting her hand away. "It's nothing—"

"You're bleeding." *It's everything,* she might as well have said.

She scans my face, hunting for any more injuries. The caring-nursemaid act isn't natural for her. I see the way her hand starts for the edge of my jacket before she presses it to her side at the last minute.

"It's deep. You're going to scar—"

"It's nothing."

"Nothing," she repeats. She has that look in her eye. The same one Dante used to get back in the day, when he would tell me to go to bed, and I claimed I wasn't tired. "Sit down." She jerks her chin over to the couch and then marches toward it, leaving me to follow.

I'm a dog on the leash of her scent. She smells clean, if that even makes sense. Clean the way an old, worn, stained T-shirt does once it's been run through the wash a few times. It's broken in and ragged, but any trace of its struggle has been thoroughly scrubbed from the cotton.

I wonder what she's tried to scrub from her brain. Her hair is wet—a fact that doesn't make sense until I notice the thunder rumbling through the walls. I'm wet too, dripping water all over the damn floor.

She grabs a towel from the counter and tosses it in my direction. Then she sets out on a determined scavenger hunt through my kitchen. Without waiting for permission, she snatches up a length of paper towel and some ice from the freezer. Another dishrag. A glass of water, too.

She approaches me, juggling her tools in her arms, and I cross over to the couch.

It feels good to sit down. I've forgotten how long I've been on my feet. They ache like just about everything else on my body. I've probably worn my sneakers out within this week alone.

"Sit still." She issues the command while she comes closer.

I expect her to stand in front of me, just beyond my reach, but no... She sinks down, right between my spread legs. I can't smother the impulse that has me attempting to bring my knees together, but I just wind up trapping her between them.

She inhales sharply at the resistance, but she doesn't pull away. If anything, she stiffens her shoulders and reaches up to grasp my chin again, each finger searing hotter than a branding iron. She makes her mark on me without even trying, every bit as brutal as the damn Cartel.

"You really should be more careful with your face," she scolds while manipulating the damp paper towel in her free hand. She's not gentle when she dabs at my mouth.

I suspect that it's by design—punishment disguised as treatment.

"I'm fine." I try to pull my head back, but her fingers tighten their grip.

"You're *bleeding.*" She withdraws the paper towel and holds it up as evidence.

Splotches of dark red speckle the surface. The cut must be worse than I thought. When I don't deny it, her mouth flattens into a smug line, and she returns to her work. I guess this is karma; it's my turn to play the role of patient.

"I suppose you need a story to take your mind off it," she adds so casually that one might expect something along the lines of *Cinderella* or *Little Red Riding Hood*. But, no, happy and sweet is not her style. "So, what will it be?" she wonders without looking up. "A story about a duck or…something else?"

The question reminds me of one of Arno's games of Russian roulette. It's not clear which option holds the bullet.

"Performer's choice," I tell her in the end.

She shrugs, but the grim expression that takes over her face is anything but casual. The words come slowly, but it's obvious where they lead.

"I…I was fifteen when I was sold to Piotr Petrov. I still remember that day so clearly. It was like a nightmare, too vibrant to seem real."

Damn it. The pain in her tone slices through me like a razor. I shake my head to cut her off. "You don't have to tell me this—"

"I want to."

No. She *needs* to. For whatever reason, the truth is burning a hole in her throat now. I never thought I'd get to hear the story of her past. I'm not sure if I want to. But stopping her would be worse. Pain is like that—it can sink into your veins like poison for years before seeping out. From your pores. From your throat. You can't pick the way it gets expelled. You just suffer through the purge.

"I was fifteen." She dabs at my mouth again and then stares down at the bloodied bit of tissue. After a second, she sets it aside and picks up the ice cubes she wrapped in the dishtowel. I grit my teeth at the icy sensation and try to grab it myself, but she evades my grasp until I let her hold it there. "My father was a boss in a drug-running syndicate back in Russia. Heroin. Liquor. He was no saint, but even now…looking back, I can still feel just how much I loved him." Her eyes flutter shut for a brief second and reopen ice cold. "One day, the syndicate fractured. Two leaders got into a power struggle. The others were left to take sides, and my father…he chose wrong." She sucks in air. Lifts the ice pack. Frowns and sets it against my jaw again. "He sided against a man named Wilhem Petrov who, once he'd cemented his power, made sure that those who stood against him realized their mistake."

Her hand falls. She's staring at the floor now, her hair framing her face like a halo of shadow. Pain paints her body in shades of gray. Her eyes seem darker. Her skin paler.

"You don't have to—"

"I *want* to." This is more than a morbid game of show-and-tell for her. She shakes her head to clear it and reaches for the bloody rag again. "They came in the middle of the night," she says. "They dragged us all from bed and into my father's study. They made him watch as they slit his wife's throat in front of their daughter. Then they blinded him with the end of a lit cigar and made him listen while they took turns…" She dabs at my mouth again. Faster. Harsher.

I don't react to the pain. I bite it back and watch her face. Her eyes are wide, haunting, and yellow.

"While they..." It takes her three tries before she gives up saying exactly what. She's up on her knees now, her hand still pressed to my face, those eyes distant.

I bet she's not even seeing me anymore. What she's looking at, she doesn't like.

My hand is on her shoulder before I realize it. I can do that much—comfort her like this and not have it mean a damn thing. She doesn't shrug me off at least. Maybe it helps.

"When the last man took his turn...they finally put a bullet in my father's brain. Then they took my sister. She was so little." Her voice breaks on a harsh gasp. She has to inhale to find the words again. "A baby who'd barely started to talk. I used to call her *little fox* because of her hair. I never saw her again. I hoped they would kill me, but they had another use in mind. Piotr, Wilhem's son, had a business in America smuggling girls to rich men for sex. They might as well make money off me before they killed me."

She swallows hard. Breathes deep. Tries again. "I wasn't like Domi. Not in the end. I wasn't brave. I wasn't smart. I was a *slave*. I surrendered my identity. I became a pet. A plaything. A toy. Whatever role helped me to avoid a beating."

"But you got out." I'm not prodding her. Just stating the facts.

She nods, steering the direction of the story. "One day, Piotr went too far." She grits her teeth, but it takes her only a few seconds to swallow the pain and keep talking. "They left me in an alley just outside the club. I would have died if a friend hadn't found me."

"Ivan Ivanov?" It's a leap of logic, but she nods, proving my hunch about why she took Domi to his territory the day we got her from the station.

"Ivan. He took care of me. He helped me get an education. Find employment. Live."

But it's not really living for her. I can see it in her face. I know that slack-jawed expression. How dead you can feel inside when you know you're powerless. How addicting the power can be when you finally vanquish one of your demons.

Even with Vlad dead, she's still not living.

"I just want you to know. I need you to understand," she says. "No matter what...no matter what. I've never lied about this. Helping Domi. Piotr. Vlad. None of it was a lie."

"I know."

She doesn't want the validation. She just needed to hear it out loud—*she* did.

"Your face looks better," she says while rising to her feet. She gathers up the bloodied rags and carries them into the kitchen. Then she wipes the counter down—a task I suspect she does to keep her hands busy more than anything. She's on her third pass when she finally addresses me directly over her shoulder. "You live here alone."

It isn't a question, but I still answer her. "Yeah. It's just me."

"Just you and no one else?" She deliberately skirts around the subject of Dante. "No roommate? No girlfriend?"

"Nope."

"Oh." She shuts the faucet off and returns the rag to the sink. "I should get going."

She's halfway to the door when I call out. "Wait."

I've never thought of myself as too much of a selfish prick, but here I am. Maybe I just want to comfort her. Let her know I'm willing to listen, good old Espi. It's all bullshit, though, when I can smell her from here. I can still taste her. Spicy, fiery red. Sharp, desperate green. My stiffening dick is a warning sign, but I would rather cut the damn thing off than have her leave while looking like that. Raw. Open. Wounded.

I'd bind my fucking hands if she asked me to, anything to get rid of that pain. "You can crash here for a bit, if you want."

She feints for the door on the tips of her toes. She wants to leave. Greed holds her back. Just like that, she's in front of me again, her gaze on the wall, her face half turned away. Her fingers seize mine though. Tugging. Pulling. I see it on her face. She doesn't want this…whatever it is. She *needs* it the same way I need the nicotine to chase out the shit I can't bear to think on.

She wants a drug to clear her head.

"Does this…help?" I don't have to explain what I mean. I just trace the inside of her wrist with my thumb.

The way she shudders could mean anything. Then she jerks her head once. *Yes.* She doesn't resist when I tug lightly on her hand, drawing her a step closer. Another.

She swallows hard, a small noise dying in her throat. That fucking sound. Whatever shred of control I've maintained until now breaks. She's in my arms. On my lap, straddling me. I take hold of both of her wrists—she can't touch me. She can only show, guiding me to her body slowly, hesitantly.

My fingers find her hips, and I watch her face to see what she wants. Soft? Hard? Her jaw clenches—*hard.* It's not enough. She raises my hands higher, her grip tight over my wrists. I cup her rib cage and follow the trail up…up.

Fuck. I have to grit my teeth and grind my thighs together to cut off the reaction building beneath my skin. This is for *her.* My dick will have to deal with my hand. This is for her.

I just let my head fall back and eye the ceiling while she writhes against my palms, her hips on my waist. I don't grab until she makes me, digging her nails into my skin. Then I squeeze. I let her use me like a rag doll to distract from whatever the fuck she's feeling inside. She makes me grope her. Tug. Rub.

I know it's not enough even before her ragged breathing shudders against my ear.

"Please…"

I can feel her lips moving. She has to lick them to find enough leverage to speak again, her mouth practically over my earlobe.

"I need you to touch me. Please. Just for a minute. I…I need you to—" She breaks off when I tug my jacket from her shoulders.

My fingers are stupid, impatient *fucks*. They don't stop to savor. They just take. Every gasp. Every moan she has building in her lungs. I fucking paw at her through the gray cotton of her shirt. My thumb finds her nipple, teasing it into a sharp point, while the other hand cups her stomach, holding her steady. Physically, anyway. Her pulse is a rapid-fire staccato. I can practically hear the damn thing beating against her rib cage, spurring me on, drowning out any rational thought.

I breathe her in and get drunk. High. Wasted.

Her shirt's off. She's braless underneath, her tits bouncing with every writhing action her hips make. I'm going to come in my pants if she keeps this up. I don't fucking care if I do. Watching her is better than my fucking hand. I'll give her the humiliation on a fucking platter if it means I get to feel her. Smell her. Taste her. It's pathetic. *I'm* pathetic.

She's desperate.

I dart my gaze to the clasp of her jeans; she's already tugging them down her hips before I can process the fucking invitation. Her legs spring apart, allowing enough room for me to spread my thighs and force hers open wider.

Her hand snatches up one of mine, leading the fingers to the waistband of her black lace underwear. I make my fucking hand limp. *She's* the one who guides me there. Who rocks her hips to feel me there. She *wants* me there.

She's silk. Hot. Wet. Goddamn perfect. All of those things I hear Arno and his men boast about when they get drunk enough to compare conquests.

The touch alone is enough to make me almost regret. *Almost* touch that place at the back of my mind I never dwell on. I start to think dumb shit. Like maybe…maybe I could control this—not get addicted to it. Maybe…

But then she moans, and it's like gasoline on the fucking fire. I stop thinking about anything but this. Her. My universe is her pussy. Oxygen and sanity don't mean fucking shit. I'm shoving a finger inside her. Crudely. Roughly.

The sharp cry smothered into my ear says it all—She craves it.

I'm consumed by it. The way her heat envelops me like a glove. It's suffocating. It's fucking intoxicating.

I don't come down until I'm sliding another finger beside the first, twisting my wrist for leverage, watching her face contort. Her eyes drift shut. Her mouth opens. She's panting, riding my hand with more abandon than she could on a pole.

I'm her plaything. A tool to get her off. And, when she does, my fucking brain explodes. My dick stiffens. The only reason I don't burst in my jeans is because she slams her chest to mine, her mouth against my throat, and the pain and pleasure short-circuit every nerve in my body.

She comes down slowly while I ease my hand from between her legs. Her breathing returns to normal. Her pulse steadies.

We stay there, a tangle of limbs on the couch. I don't think I can leave, even if I wanted to.

CHAPTER TWENTY-ONE
CHLOE

I come alive against a warm hand cupping my lower back—nothing else can describe waking up like this. One whiff of cigarette smoke and I can identify the culprit. He must have held me during the night. It's a disgusting token of concern from a man who exudes kindness without trying.

Darkness too.

The stench of it lingers on him. Like smoke. Like mint. Like blood, clinging beneath the stink of sweat and lust.

As I peel my eyes open to the cold, gray daylight painting the edges of the room, I can't bring myself to move. I'm still straddling him, my face in his neck, his hands on my waist. It's pathetic to admit, but I could come again, just like this. Listening to the sound of his breathing. Feeling his breath against my throat.

Reluctantly, I unfurl my stiff, sore limbs and roll my weight from him. He grunts when I do. I guess he's been awake all along.

"We should get back to the bar," he says.

But we don't move. We just lie here like two statues in a world of his own making.

The creations I assume he put on the canvases seem to fill every available space from this angle. Splotches of red. Black. Green. Yellow—mainly the last one. It's the color under his fingernails now, I see when I glance over. There's no substance to any of the newer pieces. Just streaks of that one hue, over and over and over.

I could lie here for hours, trying to decipher them all. Maybe I do. I'm not sure how much time has passed when he finally moves, breaking the spell. With a shift of his body, he puts space between us and tugs on the hem of his shirt, tucking any bit of stray skin away. Then he enters the kitchen and turns the faucet on. He splashes water on his face until it drips onto the floor. With his face still wet, he grabs a plastic cup from a cupboard, fills it, and drains the entire thing.

"I...I need a shower," he grits out before heading down the hallway.

I can tell from the way he walks that it will be a cold one. The realization alone diminishes whatever heat he left behind. Angels are strange creatures. He's selfless enough to touch me with his hands, but nothing more. He won't even let me touch *him*.

But why do I want to? It's a terrifying question. It's a relieving puzzle at the same time. Piotr didn't break me after all, ruining me for any other man. It just so happens that the only one to make me feel...anything isn't interested in the leftovers of the Russian Syndicate.

I hear the water running from my position. I picture the scene beneath it before I can help myself. His scars basted in the glow of the dim artificial light. The letters of his tattoo blazing on his damp chest. His hair slicked back.

A hard swallow doesn't dislodge the tightness at the back of my throat. It's funny. Now, I might have a faint idea of what drives men to frequent places like Moe's. Cheap, easy sex with no strings. With him... Maybe I'd consider it. Debase myself just to get him out of my skin. Out of my goddamn head.

The only way to block the idea out is to stand and pace. *Remember.* I shake my head to reinforce the command. Remember. Think. Why am I here? Because of Grey. I upheld my end of the bargain. My next step is to outsmart Petrov. Keep moving. Find Anna. Devise a new plan. Be ready.

The bathroom door opens down the hall, but the water's still running. I turn and find him there, sandwiched between the doorway and the door.

"I need to grab a towel," he says, his gaze on the hallway across from him. It's like he's asking for my permission to traipse around his own house naked.

The polite thing to do would be to turn my back and let him. Better yet, I should leave and return to the bar on my own. Francisco would be expecting me around now. Maybe that's what I plan to do when I start in his direction.

But, somewhere between him and the front door, I change my course of direction.

Inside the hall closet, I find a stack of towels and washcloths. I grab two of each and turn for the bathroom. He extends his hand, angling the door to hide as much of himself from me as he can. The only clue to his shock when I slip past him is a widening of his eyes. He steps back. Maybe in confusion. Maybe in invitation. Either way, I keep going and set the towels down on the floor beside the tub. Then I strip my shirt and my pants off and climb inside.

I hear the door close through the spray. For a moment, it's so silent that he could have left. A layer of steam has flooded the room by the time the shower curtain is finally drawn back from the outside. Damp curls shield most of his face from view. I can only make out the stern ridge of his jaw as he braces one hand against the tiled wall of the shower and enters the stall. He's cautious but doesn't shy away from standing too close. Tempting me.

I back away, freeing enough space for him to stand opposite me. But not much. I take his hand, feeling the shudder that runs through his skin. I don't need anything else. Just this. His nearness. This closeness. Everything else in my head is a distant murmur when he's near. I *need* that silence.

It's like he knows that. He doesn't resist my touch. He humors me and my silent request for more of him. More nearness.

Maybe it's enough.

Maybe not.

———

It's afternoon by the time we get dressed and return to the bar. Francisco shouts at me to, "Give me a fucking hand!" the moment I step over the threshold, and Espisido just keeps going, probably searching for Arno.

Wading knee-deep into a sea of broken glass and spilled beer should help take my mind off him.

But it doesn't. Withdrawal is a cruel fucking thing. Coming down from whatever shit Piotr had injected into my veins during those long, dark years was easier than this. I still remember the unofficial detox. Ivan had to strap me down while I writhed and screamed obscenities at the wall for days.

I would eagerly return to those vices rather than become an addict to a drug I've only gotten hits of. A full dose might kill me. Maybe it's a good thing I'll never experience it.

My time is running out. I know it. I feel the inevitable sense of urgency—like there's an invisible clock ticking the minutes down. Piotr's still coming for me.

But, once the lunch rush hits and I'm swamped with work, I can almost forget. Almost. I'm sweating by the time I join Domi behind the bar. I slink past her for the faucet, but her hand on my shoulder keeps me in place.

"Your phone rang all night," she says around a yawn. "I didn't answer it, but here." She reaches into her pocket and tucks something into my hand. "I had to turn off the noise, but I think they're still calling."

When I rouse the phone from sleep mode, the notice of twenty missed calls flashes across the screen. They're all from the same number—Grey's.

I leave my broom in a corner and slip away to the back while Francisco isn't looking. Only when I'm safely in the alley with no one else in sight, do I hit the redial button. Grey picks up on the first ring.

"It's bad," he says without wasting time on pleasantries. "Either you return from 'vacation,' and try to find some way to cover your ass, or you stay gone."

I swallow hard. It's quite the dilemma to be faced with this early in the day. "What happened?"

Grey inhales raggedly and releases the air on a sigh. "I got an email last night," he says. "It contained a certain little video…of you."

He doesn't have to describe it. I can picture it easily enough. Piotr's grown impatient, it seems. Apparently, he thinks I need incentive to run.

"It's bad, Parker," Grey says. "I think I'm the only one who got it so far. But if the brass sees that—"

"Who sent it?" It's a pointless question. I'm just stalling for time. I need to think. I need to plan. With one hand braced against the wall of the alley, I start walking.

"Blocked address," Grey says tightly. "I'd have to enlist IT to track it, and I don't think you'd want me to do that."

"What do they want?" There's always a catch. Always a hook to the bait.

"They want me to give you a letter. I found it in my mailbox this morning. Your name's on it—"

"Which name?"

If he heard the hollow note in my voice, he doesn't question it. "*Your* name," he says. "Chloe Anne Parker. The note says I have twenty-four hours to give you the letter before that video goes department-wide. I got it at four p.m. last night. You have two hours to get your ass down here."

"Where?"

"Not the fucking precinct. Maybe… Meet me down by the harbor, near the docks. Look for the station wagon. Don't bring anyone and I won't fucking call for backup, got it?"

"Got it."

He hangs up and I…breathe. I try to. My steadying hand against the wall grapples for leverage. It feels like I've run a mile, but I've only gone a few feet away from Mulligan's. The feeling building in my chest should be grim acknowledgment—I've known that this was coming—but it's not. It's a different pinching sensation I recognize all too well—fear.

This isn't like Piotr. He doesn't set traps for his victims and invite them to spring them. He is a hunter. A predator. He sent me his little gift and should have waited patiently for me to run, allowing him to track me down. *That* is how a wolf operates.

It used to be our favorite game to play.

Not this. He's impatient, but not in the way I'm used to. Though, hell, maybe the bastard learned a new trick over the years.

I consider running anyway. I could hop on the next plane and leave Grey and my reputation to ruin but buy more time. Chloe Parker would become an outlaw, wanted for the murder of a criminal, yet Ksenia could be free for just a little while longer.

Then the truth hits me.

There is only one way this will end. One outcome…

A pair of blue eyes chase the dark thought away before it can really take hold. It's been hours since I left him and I'm still high on his scent. How funny. How pathetic.

I do my best to hasten the withdrawal as I return to the bar and mount the staircase to the upper level. I enter the borrowed apartment and rummage beneath my bed just long enough to find the gun. It fits perfectly in the pocket of Espisido's borrowed jacket.

Maybe he'll miss it. But he won't miss me.

CHAPTER TWENTY-TWO
ESPI

"You gonna ignore me all fucking week?" Arno spits out while pouring himself a shot. He overfills the glass, and the liquid sloshes over the rim, tainting the air like gasoline. "How many times do I have to fucking say it?" He downs the shot and grimaces at the taste. "I'm fucking sorry."

"I hope this means that I won't have to fight Jose for the title of your best friend forever." I step farther into his office and nearly trip over a trail of empty bottles.

It's like he spends more time in this damn room than he does at his own place, not that I can blame him. After all this time, he can't bring himself to sell that house. He can't even empty out her room.

"Don't even fucking joke," he snarls, already pouring himself another shot. "You know me. I wouldn't go to that piece of shit without a good fucking reason—"

"I would like to think so."

Arno isn't one to hold grudges. Jose, on the other hand, doesn't just cling to a vendetta. He cuts it into pieces and hangs it on his wall.

"Let's just say I took a gamble and got more than I goddamn bargained for," Arno says, his jaw clenched. "I found a gun at the warehouse of the cartels that got hit. I figured some idiot from the other side dropped it, and a good trace would lead back to a dealer at least. Maybe I could neutralize this new threat myself."

Suddenly, Dante's warning reads loud and clear. "And?"

The dark look he shoots my way prefaces the gravity of the answer. "The gun belonged to a cop." He doesn't bother explaining just how he found that out. "It wasn't a lead. It was a plant."

"You're serious?"

"Damn right," Arno agrees. "They'd find that fucking gun, and it wouldn't just end there. They'd have 'just fucking cause' to open up an entire FBI investigation. They could arrest and interrogate at random. Whoever is behind this isn't just happy with burning shit down. They're leaving a sniff trail for the goddamn Feds."

I almost swallow the question that springs to my tongue. "You...you think it's Dante?"

Arno shrugs, tearing a hand through his hair. "He wouldn't be that stupid to bring that shit down on me—not so close to the fucking Gardai." But he doesn't sound very convinced of that.

Am I? My head spins with the new information, but at least one mystery might be solved by this shitstorm. "Is that why you've been acting so weird lately?"

"Part of it," Arno admits. He knocks the next shot back and chases it with a swig directly from the bottle. "About the Russians... You deserve to know why I really sent you there. Not whatever bullshit I told you before."

"You mean you *aren't* looking to muscle in on the human sex slave trade?"

Arno's had his fingers in some shady shit, but never that dark.

Yet.

"Fuck no," he says, "but have a seat. You're not gonna like the real reason, and I don't need your fucking pity."

"All right." I take the seat across from him and try to keep an open mind. More drugs? Guns? Something worse? With Arno, you never know just how deep the rabbit hole will go. "Lay it on me."

He swipes at his mouth with the back of his hand and eyes the wall behind my head. "You remember what happened to Mack?"

"Mack?" It's a weird change of subject—his ex-partner who ran an underground fighting ring. "Mack got stupid. Tried to fuck with the Syndicate. Either he got ghosted, or he skipped town." According to the rumors, anyway—which Arno never corrected.

Until now. He scoffs and takes another swig of liquor. "Mack. You really think that fuck would just walk away and let *me* have all of this?" He gestures around to the peeling wallpaper. The chaos from the main barroom reaches us even here, a distant pulse through the trembling walls. "Fuck no. That bastard wouldn't run. But whatever happened to him, you can bet your ass he had it coming."

"So, what happened?"

Arno breathes out and tears a hand through his hair. "You know that shit with Vinny Stacatto?"

"It's not like I can exactly forget." My fingers flex at my sides before I manage to clench them into fists.

"Ah, fuck." Arno notices my hand and grimaces. "I'm sorry. I didn't mean it like that. Look, Dante didn't want you to know, but Mack's the one who turned you in. He offered you up to that sick fuck on a platter. Everything."

Given Mack's history with Arno and Dante, the news isn't exactly a surprise. I uncurl the fingers of my left hand and eye the ones remaining on the right. A ruthless criminal, Mack was never my favorite person. I still wouldn't have pegged him as a goddamn traitor, no matter the payoff.

"So you two killed him?"

"No," Arno says. "We didn't kill him. That would have been too good for that piece of shit. We did him worse." He sighs and pours another shot. Then he slides the glass over to me. "We sold him out to the Russians. They don't take too kindly to traitors."

"I can imagine."

"I thought he did it for money, you know? For power. Some dumb shit. You never fucking know with Mack—"

"Why does it matter what he wanted?"

Arno looks up, and I almost pour myself a shot. I've never seen the gleam in his eye before. Not like this. He inhales the liquor, finishing off the rest of the bottle, and winds up coughing most of it back up. He has to pound on his chest, his eyes streaming, just to speak again.

"We watched," he croaks. "While they pummeled the shit out of that sick fuck. He should have been begging for mercy, but he...he was laughing. At me. He said, 'That Italian fucker bragged at how fucking easy it was. You didn't even look for her. You didn't even try...'" He breaks off, his hands clenching into fists. One of them strikes the surface of the table, knocking it off-balance. Again. "You should have seen him. Laughing even with a busted fucking jaw and a fucked-up eye. Just laughing. 'You never gave a shit about her,' he said. 'She's better...she's better off without you.'"

"He was lying." I try to make my voice soft, the way Dante did when he told me that Santa wasn't real. Soft but firm like a good slap to the face. "Parish is gone, Arno."

"You didn't see him," Arno says, shaking his head. "You didn't see the fucking look on his face. I know Mack. I know that look."

"*This* is why you've been so out of it." Underneath everything, it was always her. "She's dead, Arno."

"You think I don't fucking know that?" He lifts the bottle and starts to take a sip. Halfway to his mouth, he turns and hurtles it against the wall, sending broken glass flying in every direction. "You think I don't fucking *know* that?"

"You saw her—"

"I didn't." Admitting that makes him brace both hands flat against the table, his knuckles white. "I... Fuck, I couldn't. I couldn't. I sent in someone else. They said her face was t-too —fuck!"

"Mack got inside your head," I say as gently as I can. "He wanted to fuck around—"

"I tried to let it go. But too many fucking things made sense. That's how Stacatto operated, you know? Those fucking Italians. They loved keeping things around for 'insurance.' If she's alive, the Russians would know where. Hell, she could be in any fucking one of their bars—"

"Arno, don't do this."

"Don't fucking lecture me, Espisido. If it were Dante, you'd be doing the same fucking thing."

I don't have a comeback for that. The sick, ironic thing is that Arno has a better shot of finding his dead sister alive than I do of finding Dante when he doesn't want to be found. The joke's on me.

"I just wanted you to know," he says, hauling himself upright. He has to take a few steps before he can balance on both feet.

"Okay." I stand and turn for the door.

"Wait," Arno says before I am halfway there. "There's something else. I got a little message from Jose today. It's not much, but it's something that's for sure."

I can tell from his tone that I won't like to hear whatever it is. "What?"

"Apparently, there's word about a new gang in town. They're recruiting, but get this—not the usual criminals and punks. They're targeting ex-police. Informants. People who've been fucked over by the Cartel, or the Mob, or the Syndicate."

"And the Gardai?" I say, taking a shot in the dark.

Arno just chuckles. "It seems like someone wants a war, little brother. You better keep your fucking head down. Got it?"

I leave him there to hunt for another bottle, but I can't shake what he said. Maybe I don't want to shake it. It gives my brain something real to focus on. Something important.

After all, a war just means more business for me. I even manage to laugh at the bitter irony. Business. If only I could afford to keep my fucking kit stocked in the meantime.

I hunt for the current cause of my low supplies, but I don't find her sweeping at the corners of the bar. It's only later that night when the girls take the stage that I realize she's gone. I know without even having to go up and check that she took the gun.

I tilt my head back to eye the ceiling while I fish my final cig from my pocket and light it up. One hit and I don't feel anything, just a burning taste in my mouth. Two drags don't help, either.

I've gotten hooked on something harsher than nicotine. The funny thing is that I can't go five minutes without a cigarette, but without her?

My feet twitch against the pavement. I could go after her. But the key question is, does she want to be found? A woman like that, with so many damn secrets. She could have a lover out there. Someone who doesn't hesitate to touch her—or more.

Someone she wouldn't leave in the middle of the night.

I try not to let the fact sting. I'm a big boy. She's a big girl. I'll get over it.

But finishing the pack doesn't make me feel any better. Despite the acrid taste of ash in my throat, her flavor remains, stubborn as hell.

CHAPTER TWENTY-THREE
CHLOE

PIOTR LEFT ME A SINGLE WHITE ENVELOPE WITH MY name written on the front. It looks so clean, so harmless. No one would ever guess that it has my soul inside it.

I put off opening it until after I've left Grey, when no one is else around to witness my reaction. When no one is around to see me break. He kept the message simple this time, Piotr, scribbling only the name of a hotel, the room number, and a time.

It's an amusing game to convince myself that he couldn't possibly have been there, watching through the windows of the bar. With each attempt, I lose. How soon could I forget his favorite pastime when he wasn't lording over his club—haunting me. He's not here now. I take the gun from my pocket and scan the alley I'm in just to be sure, searching for him behind an old dumpster or a car parked on the side of the road.

But no. Stealth was never his style—and, apparently, he has a more upscale setting in mind for our reunion—a hotel on the north side of the city. But it's not just any destination. My heart tightens at the sight of the gleaming, silver façade towering against the skyline like a castle formed entirely of steel. Once again, nostalgia forms a noose around my soul. He chose well. Outside of the club, it was our special place, a venue that caters almost exclusively to Piotr's branch of the Russian Mob.

I clear my mind of everything before I step through the glass doors lined in gold. I'm a blank slate when I cut across the lobby and ride the elevator to the top floor, guided by memory alone.

It's suicide; I know that. I'm oddly resigned to my fate as I travel down a hallway lined in ebony carpet and ruby-red walls. The memories... They're harder to bite back here. I can feel him, that harsh, bitter sting of him inside me. In my soul. My head. My body.

That old impulse to escape rears its head once I approach the last door at the end of the hallway. I can practically feel the word hammering against my skull. *Escape.* I can taste it, poised at the back of my throat like a scream. *Run, Ksei. You don't have to face him now. You need to be stronger. Faster. Quicker. Braver.*

At the moment, I'm just tired, and exhaustion makes me bolder than any bravery.

I don't bother knocking. I try the handle and find it unlocked. It opens easily, and I step inside while drawing the gun. My eyes instantly hone in on a shadow flung against the wall—someone approaching the entryway from down a dimly lit hall.

My finger finds the trigger. I don't even bother closing the door behind me. There's no point in wondering why he's without some protective thug or bodyguard. Maybe the bastard is ready to die.

The shadow grows larger, gradually taking on the shape of a human figure. But they're smaller than they should be. Thinner. When they finally appear at the mouth of the hall, it still takes nearly a minute for me to process that the stern-faced blonde in a modest, gray dress isn't Piotr.

"Welcome," she says, her accent thick. "He is expecting you. You dress first." She starts back down the hallway, leaving me to follow. The rest of her words reach me from over her shoulder. "He said you can keep the gun."

I don't move, still aiming the gun at the wall. The woman never calls me or beckons me in farther. It's like she knows without a doubt that I'll follow.

And I *do*, closing the door behind me.

He picked his favorite suite, and I know it well. This scent. These dark, innocuous colors. It's barely changed in all these years. The walls are still gray. The furniture sleek and modern with a slightly old-fashioned twist, just how he likes it.

The woman is waiting for me in a modest guest room, where a black dress lies in wait on the bed. It's satin, tailored in his favorite style—a tight shape and a low neckline.

I gesture toward it with a flick of the pistol. "I'm not wearing that—"

"You change first," the woman insists. She steps back expectantly, refusing to bat so much as an eyelash when the gun is aimed over her chest. The stern set to her jaw reveals all—She's used to it. "He's waiting."

"You can take me to him like this." I thumb the trigger once, twice. The unsteady sound undercuts the threat. With every second that passes, I might wind up shooting her by accident.

Despite the danger, she just stares back. God, I know the cold, empty look on her face. I recognize the role she's been forced to play. The slight twitch of her eyes to the doorway gives her away—I stall, she dies.

Maybe I've grown since my old days, but Piotr is the only one whose blood I want on my hands.

As if sensing the moment I break, the woman lifts the gown from the bed and approaches me. I stand there woodenly as she strips Espisido's jacket from my shoulders and tosses it aside like it's trash. She slips the dress over my head without being hindered at all by the gun I'm still pointing at her. Sighing, she steps back and observes me with a sweep of her gaze.

"Your hair." She says it almost mournfully, as if merely pointing its state out. Then she retreats back the way we came without another word and turns down another hallway that opens onto an expansive dining room. There, a lone man is sitting at a table set for two.

Unlike the ageless revenant of him haunting my nightmares, he's grown older in real life. Gray streaks his hair, catching the light while he scans my body from head to toe. Every nerve prickles with recognition. It's that slow, perusing look I used to live for. The one I almost died for.

The one that threatens to kill me again.

My hand shakes, fighting to keep the gun trained on him as I will myself to pull the trigger. Kill him. *Run!* I hold my breath, but my nostrils flare to breathe him in anyway. Wolf Blood. My blood. God, he smells the same.

"It's been a long time," he says, his accent catching over the syllables in every word. It's the gentle tone he rarely used, only when at his most content to lull me into a dangerous sense of security. "You still look so beautiful."

He should look dead. My finger twitches, but for some reason, it won't bear down. Yet. My heart beats with more conviction, straining against my rib cage. Pounding. It hurts. It's greedy. Only with him so close can it ignore the shackles my brain has strapped around it for all these damn years. *Moya lyubov.*

"I knew it would be like this," Piotr says, his tongue lingering over each twisted syllable. "When I saw you again.

I thought maybe…" He shakes his head sadly. "I was wrong. This moment. *This* makes it all worth it."

He folds his hands and pushes back from the table. I flinch when he stands. He's just as tall, wearing the same brand of black suit he always did. Everything is tailored, down to the black loafers on his feet. He takes a step toward me.

I finally squeeze the trigger. The deafening roar of the gunshot slams into my eardrums, but Piotr doesn't collapse in pain like he should, and something made of glass shatters over his shoulder. He doesn't even blink. He merely sighs. My protector, my lover, my tormentor.

"Put the gun down, Ksei."

"No." I grip it tighter. My hand trembles. I can't keep it steady. I can't pull on the trigger again, either.

I can't obey him.

I can't resist.

"I don't want to hurt you," he says. "I just want to talk."

I want to laugh. I try to, but the only sound that trickles out is weak. A moan. A gasp. "Talk. You want to talk."

"And you want to hear." He pauses as if waiting for me to argue. When I don't, he smiles. That cold, icy smile that used to serve as a focal point of my nightmares. And the highlight of my day. "You came to me for a reason."

"A good one," I echo. "I…I came to kill you."

"Did you?"

My grip on the pistol slips in my sweaty palms. I have to grip it tighter. "I *will* kill you."

"Have a seat, Ksenia, and I will tell you the real reason why you came to me."

I laugh again. The sound echoes off the walls, violent and unsteady. I sound like Arno right before he put the gun in his mouth and pulled the trigger. *Pow.* Maybe he had the right idea all along.

"You didn't give me much of a choice."

"You've always had a choice." Something in his voice warns me to back away from him. He steps forward.

I scramble back another step. My shoulders strike the wall —there's nowhere farther to go.

"Put the gun down, Ksei."

"No."

He reaches out and I will my finger to pull the trigger. I scream the command inside my head. *Kill him!*

His palm settles over my hand, the touch electrifying my skin. He gently lowers the weapon until I'm aiming it at the floor. There's no ounce of fear in him. Just a look I know well—possession. He exudes it in everything he does, from the way he appraises me to how he breathes me in, leaning close so that I can hear each ragged intake of air.

"You fixed your hair for me." He fingers a tangled lock of it.

I see it happen from the corner of my eye. He still wears the thick, silver ring on the thumb of that hand. I have scars from how deeply the insignia bit into my skin whenever he struck me with it.

"I didn't even have to ask—"

"Get away from me."

He doesn't let go of my hair. If anything, his grip tightens, forcing my head to tilt in his direction. Burning pain creeps across my scalp like an old, forgotten friend.

He inhales me again, and I know what he'll find—cigarette smoke, spray paint, and Espisido. "You remember how much I loved this color on you."

This color. "It came out of a box," I tell him, but the words fall flat. My hair has been blonde for years.

With every salon appointment, maybe I forgot the original shade of it a little more. I see my reflection in the glass window—a girl I last saw ten years ago, her dirty, brown hair limply framing her face while she cowered beneath Piotr Petrov's scrutiny.

I raise the gun again, aiming the barrel somewhere over his chest. "I didn't do it for you."

Yes, you did. I don't know if he murmurs those words to me or if I just imagine them. Like roaming fingers, they trickle over unseen parts of me. Only he can do this—violate my body without even trying. I hate it. I crave it…

"You don't know how beautiful you are like this." He lets my hair fall and steps back. Just an inch, but it's like the difference between touching the sun and being near it. I'm still broiling beneath the heat. It's still lethal.

"Get away from me—"

"You came to *me*." He almost sounds surprised. As if I magically arrived on his doorstep unannounced. Surprised, but not alarmed. "Just like I knew—*hoped*—you would."

"So that I can kill you?"

It's a laughable concept. Piotr's been waiting patiently for me to put a bullet in his head. So why the hell can't I pull the trigger?

He chuckles darkly. The tone of his voice alone used to control me like a puppet on a string. I studied every cadence. How soft he could sound when I pleased him. How utterly brutal when he was angry.

Now? I can't tell. His voice wavers when it should be steady. He's soft when he should be terse. My heart picks up speed, sending my pulse surging through my skin. The flavor of fear is a lot more familiar. My body knows how to react to it.

I raise the gun.

Piotr smiles. "You love me," he says, his voice a gruff rasp against my skin. "*That* is what this means. Of your own volition. You came back to me, Ksei. And, when you are ready, I will reward you."

"Bullshit." I have to choke out another laugh. This time, the sound gets stuck in my throat. Now, it strikes me—Piotr isn't worried because the bastard's gone insane.

"Oh?" He releases his own chuckle and strokes his chin with his thumb. "You could have run. You know it. I know it."

"And you would have had me arrested for murder—"

"And you could have had Ivan erase that video, had you told him about it. But you didn't. Oh. You thought I didn't know about your little friend."

This is the point when I really should kill him. Concern for Ivan is like a living thing wrapped around my throat. One wrong move and I'll suffocate.

"H-how?"

"He never was good at hiding his loyalty for your father. Even when he signed off on the order to have him killed. Good old Ivan could never shake that guilt. I always knew that he would do anything for Milo's daughter—just as long as he could still slither within the shadows like the snake he is."

"You knew," I say thickly. "So why   "

"Who did you think alerted Ivan's men that night, Ksei?" He poses the question in that commanding tone that warns me he wants a direct answer.

I'm punished by him advancing another step. When I don't respond, his voice deepens.

"Who do you think lessened the guard patrol to allow them into my territory?"

It's a dangerous picture he paints. It's a maddening one. I still remember the pounding rush of clinging to life as Ivan's men hustled me through the streets. Was he really watching them, laughing as my blood painted the earth behind me?

"You're lying."

"It was a gamble," he admits coldly. "Had the bastard been even a second later, you would have died. I was too…thorough."

I cringe when he reaches out for me. I dodge his first touch, but he comes again, trailing his thumb along the top of my forehead.

"My little beauty. Still unmatched, even while flawed."

"You're *lying*."

"I will admit that it wasn't easy," he tells me while his thumb drifts down my jawline. "Watching you all those years. How you destroyed your hair. Became a new woman. *Chloe*." He scoffs at the name. "My men were always within reach of you. Always. I could have had you back any second, but I withheld. I endured. It was a necessary pain, but it was pain nonetheless…"

I shake him off. He's close enough now for the barrel of the gun to brush his chest directly. The nearness of the weapon only makes his grin widen. God, that expression… The pathetic girl I used to be would have cherished it—done anything to make it last. She would have sold her soul for a hint of his smile.

"You tried to kill me."

"I needed to *restrain* myself. For you. For us. My beautiful little Ksei." He cradles my chin in his entire palm this time.

For the love of God, I can't move.

"I knew you were loyal. But was it love?" he asks. "Would you die for me? Live for me? Forgive me for anything—even the worst of betrayals?"

Would I?

Did I?

A burning sensation consumes my eyes. There are two of him now, laughing as I try to distinguish between them. The barrel of the gun drifts left...right. I fire and splinters fly from a sideboard across the room. I missed again.

Or did you? He might have whispered the words to me. Or maybe I was just taunting myself.

"I had already loved you then, Ksei. But when you finally came back. When I saw what you did to Vladimir..."

Now. I want him to pull the gun I know he has hidden in his breast pocket. I wait for him to strike me with it and try to avenge his friend by putting a bullet into my brain. I wait.

And Piotr watches me. "I knew then who you really are. *Moya lyubov*, willing to do anything to see us reunited. Anything."

"You're sick." Spittle flies with how harshly I grit the words out. "I killed him because I hate you. I bashed his brains the same way you tried to kill me. I used the same damn weapon—"

"*Our* weapon." He lets his tongue linger on the word, and it serves as the password to unlock the memories I've struggled for seven years to suppress.

The feel of the ashtray in my hand. His voice in my ear. "*Strike them hard… Draw it out.*" The stench of blood in the air. I never could seem to scrub it from my fingers no matter how hard I tried. Maybe I never really tried at all.

"You remember it. How good it was between us."

I remember…

I remember the beatings. The rapes. The awful things he made me do. I didn't want to do them.

Lies.

I remember the feel of his weight on top of me. The hungry way he used to kiss me. Touch me. Possessively. Demandingly. How his scent would fill my lungs more than oxygen would. Wolf Blood.

"You remember the fun we used to have."

Nostalgia taints his voice in a way I've never heard it. It almost sounds like he's humming.

The fun. Him goading me on while I...

"Stop!" I'm shouting. I'm begging. Him. Myself. The gun flails—it finds a new target. My wrist aches as I twist it so that the barrel is against my stomach. "Stop."

"Ksei." His voice regains that commanding edge. For once, he seems afraid. "You think killing yourself will keep you from me?" He throws his head back for a sharp bark of laughter that pierces me deeper than any bullet ever could. "You are mine, Ksei. You came to me. But our reunion might be too much for you to bear at once. I can understand that." He gives me another smile. Another lethal blow. "I will give you a few days to remember our love. How about seven?"

I'm panting. I'm breathless. He seems so unconcerned. The only time he so much as flinches is when I raise the gun to my heart rather than my stomach.

"Seven days," he tells me. "In the meantime, you may have the run of the city. Go back to that hovel you've found yourself in, though I would prefer the apartment. I will not contact you."

"You've been watching me." My voice breaks as the truth spells itself out before I even see him nod.

Every move I've made. Every pathetic attempt to convince myself that I had the nerve to really do it—kill him. He's been watching. He's been waiting.

He's been amused.

"I could keep my distance," he admits. "But I couldn't go another moment without seeing you dance again."

His words are the equivalent of someone revealing that my entire life has been played out on stage. All of those private, secretive moments that I thought were my own merely served as someone else's entertainment.

"You were there…"

"I have my ways, Ksei."

I swallow hard. For some reason, it's easier to thumb the trigger with it pointed at my soul. Maybe the blow of a bullet could scrub him from it. Drive him out.

"Why?"

"It's already too late, Ksei." His eyes drift over my throat and then up to observe my face like it's one of the many pieces of property he owns. "You already came back to me."

"Get away!"

He takes a step, and I train the gun on him again, holding it unsteadily while I inch toward the doorway.

He lets me go, his eyes darker than midnight, his jaw clenched. "When you need me, I'll be here. You *will* come back. In the meantime, remember me. All of it. We have much to discuss when I see you again."

I turn on my heel and run. The suite becomes a maze. I wander it for what feels like an eternity before I finally stagger out into the main lobby of the hotel. Once I hit the street, I pick a direction and keep going. My bare feet slam against the pavement, driving me forward. I never stop to put the gun away. It's my only protection from the memories. It's my only shield from the eyes watching me with every step I take.

Moya lyubov. Moya lyubov.

I hear him. I smell him. I taste him.

I'm dying again. I'm drowning. He's bashed my brains in, and there is no one here to scoop them back up and tuck them neatly into my skull. Just silence. Just my own pulsing heartbeat.

Just him.

CHAPTER TWENTY-FOUR

ESPI

"Bang." Two ice-cold fingers graze the back of my neck. "You're dead."

Giggling, Domi steps around me. Her eyes glow neon blue in the dim light of the bar. Her teeth are bared, a partial smile, partial snarl. She's feral tonight. The way she used to look when Vlad made her turn so many tricks that she could barely walk before he threw her out onto the street.

Something has her worried, but I'm too tired to ask. No. Fuck that. I'm too drunk. I snatch a shot from the counter and down it without so much as a sniff test to tell what it is. The shit burns going down, but it doesn't come back up. Yet. Two more shots don't chase my sanity away though. It's still here, lurking like poison, as Domi returns to her post behind the counter and starts wiping it down with a wet rag.

In all the chaos of the week, I've barely checked on her. Really checked. Francisco's taken good care of her, protecting her from the shitheads at the bar; I can tell that much. Whatever's gotten her antsy lives inside her head. She never stops fiddling with her hair. Tugging at it. Pulling. It's like she's trying to yank something out, but damn. Don't I know better than anyone? Dark thoughts can only be buried beneath liquor and nicotine.

Or confessed to someone so tormented by their own shit that they just might hear you.

Another shot chases the thought. Not far enough away though.

With a sigh, I settle my focus on Domi. "What's up?"

She stands beneath a puddle of bluish light, and I've never realized just how young she is before. I know her age, but she's *young*. A tiny little girl with no clue of what to do.

"It's nothing," she says, shaking her head. "Someone just asked me something. That's all."

In an instant, I'm sitting straighter as anger washes through my stomach, neutralizing the alcohol. "Arno?"

Domi shrugs but doesn't deny it. Tonight, she's wearing another outfit of Darcy's. Something so fucking skimpy that I can't even dissect it in pieces. I just stare at her eyes. The bruise around the one is healing up, but they look even more haunted than before. Blue and Yellow. Piotr's hell sure did churn out an unusual pair.

"They just asked me about a girl is all," she says, her accent thickening the way it does whenever she talks about the past.

I wasn't stupid enough to pry about her family or her life before America. In a way, I never really had to. Domi always was an open book—a fucked-up graphic novel with the scenes depicted in violent, glaring colors.

"She was blond, they said. Green eyes. American. Five foot two…"

I grit a sigh back and shove away the bottle of whatever I was drinking. That definitely sounds like Arno. "You don't have to—"

"I said no," Domi says, staring down at the counter. Her fingers twitch against the rag as if she's fighting to cling to the present. Her eyes reveal the truth though. She's already back there, living and breathing in the stench of the club. "But that's not the truth…"

I wait without saying a damn thing. Hope. It's a bitter fucking taste that burns worse than nicotine. I can still see Parish slumped over the end of the bar, too doped up to carry on a conversation. I would never say it to Arno, but it's better if she's dead. Honestly, she already was.

"You saw her?" I ask while Domi just stands there, her palms braced against the countertop.

"I don't know." She's barely loud enough above the shouts of the last stragglers to stagger out of the bar. "I don't remember. I never saw their faces, the other girls. I can't tell you what the girls who shared my room looked like. You go through that life blind. You focus on you. Only you. I don't know if I… I don't know."

With a sigh, I stand and circle around the counter to where she's standing. She doesn't resist when my arms go around her. She just coughs, her nose wrinkling at the stench of cigarette smoke. I'm no good at the nitty-gritty of comforting people. I just wait until she stops shaking.

Until she stops muttering nonsense into the front of my shirt—*I don't know. I don't know.*

She sways on her feet when I finally let her go and send her upstairs to get some rest. But then the real fun begins. Because, after calming her, I don't even know how to comfort myself. Arno's way isn't working tonight. I'm all out of cigarettes. I'm out of fucks left to give. In the end, I just leave the bar, pick a direction, and start walking.

It feels like hours before I find myself somewhere familiar. Even this goddamn early, there's a man still on the corner, his hands tucked into his pockets. I shove a fifty beneath his nose, and he hands me a vial, full and unbroken.

I'm doing a mental count of just how many extra syringes I have by the time I start home. The moment I reach the front stoop, I lose count.

Someone broke into my house again, but I don't go for the knife this time. I shoulder the front door open instead and find the culprit in plain sight, slumped against the wall. I blink as my eyes adjust, making out a slender frame. Pale. A woman.

I'm on my knees beside her before I even realize I'm crouching. She flinches when I touch her, cringing against the wall. She's shivering—so cold that the chill bites through my fingertips. I try to withdraw my hand, but she grabs my wrist before I can, her nails digging in. Scraping. I let her hold me as I wrestle the door shut with one hand. I don't say a fucking thing.

I'm just here. She pulls me closer when she's ready. Her head finds my shoulder, her breath hot on my skin. There's something in her hand, I realize, held to her chest. It's metal. It's oddly shaped. Her finger is on the trigger.

Stitches won't cure this newer pain. No. I have to reach into another box of tricks this time.

"Which one shall it be, huh?" I wonder out loud as I lean back against the wall and stretch my legs out in front of me. "*Little Red? Sleeping Beauty?*"

She tilts her head just enough for me to make her eyes out through the shadows—wide, empty, yellow. They drift down my chest, and I sigh, reaching up to follow the line of her gaze with my fingers.

"All right. Listener's choice it is." I eye the ceiling as the sound of her breathing counts the seconds. I grit my teeth at the realization that she's crying, gasping at the air.

I have a feeling that the tears aren't because of sadness. In my experience, the real waterworks start flowing once you lose every fucking shred of control. When your emotions turn against you and all you can do is just feel your body fall apart.

It looks like I'll have to dig deep for story time. Maybe play a game of *Show You Mine* because she already showed me a bloodied bit of hers.

"Do you know the difference between a murderer and a killer?" I ask to no response. "Animals kill. Hunters kill. Diseases kill. It just happens. Sometimes there's a reason behind it. Sometimes not. Murder is different…"

She doesn't react when I reach for the gun and pry it from her grip. It's the one I gave her. I sniff and catch the telltale scent of residue drifting from her fingers. She used it.

"You have to want to murder," I say, continuing my story as I tuck the weapon against my side. "You do it on purpose. There's no reason behind it. Just rage. You want the fucker to suffer. You need them to die. I…I've never *killed* anyone in my life."

She swallows noisily. I know the question she wants to ask. Maybe she's too tired to. Maybe she already knows the answer. Either way, she says nothing, and I let her lie here beside me. I let her heat sink into my skin. But a promise is a promise, after all. I owe her a story.

"My brother is a *killer*," I say to kick off my little fairy tale. "He does what he has to, when he has to—no questions asked. He doesn't think about it. I think about everything."

It's a sloppy way for the story to start. I take a deep breath and try again.

"My dad…if you want to call him that. He was a doctor. Had a nice house. Nice car. I barely even knew the guy, even though I got sent to live with him when I was eight. My mother died in a car accident not long after I was born. I had an older brother, though, who stayed with my dad while my grandparents raised me. I never really saw him growing up. He was always in a 'special home' or out on the streets. By the time he was eighteen, he'd moved out of that place, and our dad always said he was on drugs. A runaway. But he came back. I never knew why until I got older though."

I've never been a good storyteller. The fact must run in the family. All the words run together. It's hard to keep it all straight. My captive audience doesn't seem to mind though. Her eyes never leave me once.

"As it turns out, my dad wasn't as squeaky clean as he seemed. He did stuff to Dante…" I have to suck in air as the words stick in my throat. I grit my teeth and force them out—that bastard doesn't deserve any sugarcoating. "He used to sneak into his room when he was a kid. Touch him. Hurt him. He was a fucking pedophile." I flick the word out the same way I flick the dead ash from a smoke. This flame continues to burn me up though. I smolder.

She doesn't react to the minutes-long pause that comes after. She listens, and it takes me a while to hunt down the thread of the story again. I'm fishing in my pockets before I even register craving a cigarette. I'm all out though. I have to inhale the air and use the rage in my blood as fuel rather than nicotine.

"I didn't know. All those years in that house and I didn't know. Dante came back to keep me away from him. Every waking moment. It killed him, being near that sick fuck. It killed him. He did it for me. When I finally found out, I was sixteen. He…my dad, was drinking in the kitchen. He looked at me, the bottle in his hands. He *really* looked at me."

I still see him. Eyes bloodshot. Lips slick with drool. Tears drying on his fucking face. Real goddamn tears—not a single one for Dante, only for himself.

"He begged me for forgiveness. Said he was sick. Said he was sorry." I laugh.

The sound makes her stiffen, and something in my chest tightens up. Apparently, she's disgusted by my show-and-tell. I wait for her to flinch away. Her fingers seek mine out instead, clenching me tighter, and my entire body thrums with the latest dose of her.

"Sorry. Can you believe that? *Sorry.* I wasn't sorry. All I really remember is that I grabbed a hammer from the table. He'd been fixing something, but I don't know what. I remember the first hit, right across his mouth to shut him the fuck up. It knocked him off his chair. It didn't dislocate his jaw though. He was still blubbering."

I couldn't help it.

God, I tried…

I gotta tell him I didn't mean to.

"I hit him again." The story's gone rogue. It pours out of me, broken and tactless. I can't sprinkle in pretty words to decorate the gore. I tell her everything. "He got scared then. He begged me to stop. I hit him again. And again, but...I never blacked out. I never stopped to think about what I was doing. I didn't have to do it."

The admission paints the air black as coal. The only source of light is her eyes, like embers in the ashes. My ragged breathing makes them glow. Spark. Catch fire. It's like she goads me to go on. Spit the truth out. Admit it all.

"I *wanted* to do it."

So what the hell does that make me? I had the answer inked onto my chest. I wouldn't hide behind a lie. I would never forget what I am.

My lone audience member silently digests the end of story time. She doesn't offer up a glowing review. She doesn't pat my head and try to comfort me with meaningless phrases like *you didn't really mean it.* She listens.

And that silence is more numbing than anything I could inhale. Go fucking figure.

———

I INSTINCTIVELY KNOW SHE'S NOT BESIDE ME WHEN I wake up. I'm already lurching toward the door when I spot her watching me from a seat near the kitchen table, wearing only black underwear.

She got a cigarette from somewhere and managed to light it up. My throat goes dry as she drags deep and releases a plume of smoke.

I still have the gun, I see when I glance down. I test the weight of it. It's loaded. She had quite the night, it seems. A puddle of silk is on the floor beside me. A dress. Fancy. Expensive. Black.

"I'm sorry." She tosses the words at me between puffs. "I didn't mean to—"

"You don't have to apologize to me." I haul myself upright, clutching the wall with my free hand for balance. I tuck the gun into the waistband of my jeans. Then I join her at the table.

It's not set up for entertaining. My sketchbook is open in the center. Apparently, she's been flipping through it. The sketch she's on now stares up at me. One of Dante.

"You're good." She flicks the ash into the ashtray in front of her and turns the page.

"It's nothing." I reach over and flip the book shut.

There's no judgment in her gaze. No pity. None of the shit I'm used to.

"Seems like you had a rough night," I say to change the subject.

She drags on the cigarette, making the end glow red. Whether by accident or intentional, she exhales the cloud of smoke directly into my face, and I breathe her in like a fucking addict. Smoke. Fire. Yellow.

"I just… Tell me something," she says.

It's a plea, not a question.

"What?"

She thinks for a minute. Whatever drove her here kept her up at night. Shadows line her eyes. Her hands are shaking. In the end, she grits her teeth and sighs, settling on a single question. "Tell me… How would you define love?"

My mouth quirks, ready to deliver a laugh, but she doesn't even attempt to return it. She wants a serious answer, it seems. It just so happens that I have one.

"It's pain." I eye my sketchbook, picturing the drawings I've scribbled inside it. Dante. Arno. Danny. "It's getting addicted to someone's own personal brand of the shit. It's letting it fuck you up. It's wanting to be fucked up. Love is poison."

"And hate?" She sounds even more desperate now, like a student seeking the right answers for a test. She's trying to make sure our papers match. For some reason, she thinks I've paid more attention in this damn class than she has.

"Hate isn't much different, but it is way more addictive," I tell her. "It's all the shit you told yourself you don't ever want to feel. Anger. Rage. Jealousy. Every fucking temptation rolled into one. You may convince yourself you despise that sting, but that's a lie. You crave it. It's power.

You can't be hurt by someone you hate, so it lets you forget. And when you finally lose control… Well, you have something to blame, don't you? All that hate sets you free. Free to fucking feel…everything."

She's silent for a minute, letting each definition sink in. "And what do you hate?"

I shrug. "Is that a trick question?" I try to play the response off with a laugh, but it trickles from my throat as a sigh. The real answer lurks within my skull. That voice only nicotine or whiskey can smother these days. *Yourself.*

"Do you hate…you hate when I touch you?" Her free hand flattens against the table.

I let my gaze trace every single pale finger. I've never been much of a liar. "Yes. I hate it."

She's envy and rage wrapped up in one tormented package. Her touch brings about everything I don't want to feel. Everything I crave. Everything I fucking hate.

She inhales sharply, relishing the sting of the confession. Her gaze drifts up to meet mine above the burning embers of the cig between her two fingers. She finishes it with one hard drag and puts it out amid the pile of ashes in the tray.

"Show me?"

I don't know who moves first. Maybe she stands up. Or maybe I beat her to it. Either way, I have her backed into a corner, her ass striking the edge of the counter. She grasps the ledge with both hands and hauls herself on top of it.

Her gaze never breaks away from mine while her knees clamp onto my waist, pulling me in. Her breath trickles against my lower lip, harsh and unsteady.

I want to steal every hit of nicotine from her. That's why I claim her mouth with mine. That's it. She's a living, breathing cigarette. She'll burn me just as badly if I'm not careful.

It's not a kiss. She bites me. I inhale her. Blood. Ash. Smoke. We're addicts desperate to salvage whatever the fuck we can from each other. I already know her poison of choice. She just wants to forget.

Her fingers fan out along my back. Feeling. Flexing. I copy her, only my hands aim too low, and she groans into my ear. Angry. Pissed.

She hates me. I hate *this*.

I show her how much. I lose control, if only for a second. My hands are beneath the lace of her thong, grasping at her skin, tearing through the curls between her legs. I find her pussy and sink in, and she nearly comes off the damn counter. I have to use my body to pin her flat against the bottom of a cupboard. I hold her like that. I trap her like that. She's captive, held by my fingertips. I own her. I'll break her.

I release her.

She's panting when I do, her yellow eyes damp and unfocused. I can almost hear the plea she's too proud to say. *Not yet. Not yet.*

I have to inject her into my veins again. Just a little. One more hit.

I slide a hand between her legs again and tease her with the pad of my thumb. The sounds she makes work on my control like a hammer, and I come apart bit by bit by fucking bit.

I kiss her again. I bite her. Hard. Harder. She moans at the pain, raking her fingers through my hair, her nails digging in to pull me closer as she writhes against my dick. I can feel her through the denim. Fuck, I need... I want...

No.

I push away from her, my fingers pawing at the counter for leverage. She doesn't attempt to pull me back. She stares up at me, her head braced against the edge of a cupboard. Everything she's thinking spills from her eyes. She thinks it's her. She's not pretty enough. Sexy enough. Whatever.

That never used to bother me before. Control was all that mattered. All that does matter.

With one fucking needy, desperate look, she shatters it.

I'm on her again, my mouth open. I let her show me where to touch her, her hands clawing at my shoulders, pulling me down. My teeth graze her bare breast. Her stomach. Lower. I don't hesitate to sink my fingers beneath the lacy fabric and drag it down. Her legs spread for me, her hands fisting in my hair.

I take her hard, like a fucking shot. All at once. No drop of whiskey has ever burned me worse. I've never tripped this badly on liquor. She's in my head. She's in my fucking skin. Her heat. Her moans. I'm too fucking weak to block her out.

I drag on her. Greedy. Hungry. I take everything she has to give. I take, and I take—every last drop. Every last gasp. My pants feel like a fucking vise, but I still have enough shred of control to pull back before it's too late.

Withdrawing from her is like surfacing from underwater. I'm gasping. She's panting, still riding the high of whatever she feels in the aftermath of…this. Her eyes find mine, watching as I stagger back against the table and throw my hands out to brace my weight against it.

It's hard to come down when I can taste her. It's hard to come, period. My jeans are too tight. My fingers clench, aching to rub one off. The bathroom's too fucking far away though. Her scent is too damn much. I almost crave the humiliation of coming in my pants. Right here. Right now.

Whether intentionally or not, she won't let me. Her legs tremble as she brings them together. Her hands claw at the countertop as if she's worried one ragged breath might be enough to pitch her off it. Her eyes slide down my face, right to the front of my jeans. She can see how fucking pathetic I am.

One of her hands flies to her mouth, and she chews on the broken nails. "You said your father never hurt you." The words spill from her throat, broken and hoarse. She's afraid I lied to her.

"He didn't." I clench my jaw against the inevitable question that flashes across her face.

But?

"But…I don't want to be like him."

She blinks, her eyes widening. "You're afraid that you'd hurt someone."

"No." I shake my head. "I'm afraid that I'd *enjoy* hurting someone."

She climbs down from the counter on trembling legs and has to clutch the end of it with one hand to keep her balance.

I expect her to run. She staggers forward—toward the kitchen table. To me. Her pale knees strike the tiled floor as she lowers herself down, just out of my reach. Her head is barely visible above the rim of the table.

"Can…can I touch you?" Her fingers flutter against the floor while she eyes the waistband of my jeans.

It's like she's teasing me on purpose.

"I just told you why—"

"I'm asking for permission." She reaches out for me with one hand. Her tongue flits across her bottom lip. Pink. Wet. Glistening.

The sight makes my dick throb. I'm harder than I've ever fucking been, and it's nearly impossible to think straight.

"If…if you want me to stop, I will."

I don't say a damn thing. My hips jerk and my thighs spread apart, just enough for her to slip in between while I snatch the gun from my pocket and shove it away. She rises slowly, using her fingers to grab my zipper. It's like she's peeling my fucking soul open. I try to bite back the sounds that threaten to tear from my throat. I hold them back. I hold my goddamn breath, too, as she takes her sweet time, undoing the fastenings bit by bit.

I suck in air when she finally gets them undone, and I spring forward against my boxers. She takes me in with a single sweep of those yellow eyes. I can't tell what she's thinking. I know from her own sordid little story time that she's been hurt. A lot. By many different men. Am I bigger than they were? Smaller? Less threatening? I don't know how long she drinks me in.

There are tears in her eyes when she finally looks up. Tears of pain? Relief? Exhaustion? Her lips tremble as she fights to suck in air and release it all on a single question. "Can…can I touch you?"

My answer rips from my throat. "Yes." *Fuck yes.*

Any control I had is gone. I'm already lifting my hips from the table when she moves her hands to the waistband of my jeans. She slowly tugs them down, carefully, unwrapping me like a fucking present.

It's torture. It's drawn out. It's for her.

Telling myself that while my teeth skewer my lower lip makes it bearable. Barely, but I'm still in control. By a thread. By a fucking hair trigger. But I don't reach for her.

I let her ease my jeans all the way down to my ankles. I bite my lip harder when she starts on my boxers. The head of my dick is already leaking precum by the time she gets me bare. It's pathetic. I wait for her to laugh or maybe make some joke about innocence.

She stares instead. She inhales raggedly, shifting her weight so that she's balanced on the tops of her knees. "Can I..."

"Yes."

I breathe out as she takes me in the palm of her hand. There's no gentleness. No hesitation. She grips me firmly. It's like she knows my dick inside and out—better than I do. When she starts to pump her fist...

I see light. Colors. Reds. Greens. Yellow. Fucking yellow. She knows how hard. How fast. It's like she's in my goddamn head, getting off on how well she matches the gut instinct I don't even have the nerve to say out loud. I just groan, my head rocking back against my shoulders. My gaze flutters up to the ceiling at first, but then it drifts right back down. She's staring up at me, gauging my reaction. She pumps faster. Harder. *Shit.*

I grit out a noise that might be a moan, and she slows just for a second. Long enough for her to readjust her grip and lower her head.

I feel her breath on my shaft. It's like the first brush of a lit lighter against the end of a cig. You've got to hold it there for a second before it catches fire. Before the flames bite deep.

One touch of her tongue is all it takes for this new flame to bite *deep*. I'm on my heels before I know it, curses revving in my throat. Her hair parts between my fingers as I seek out the shape of her scalp. I know it's wrong, even before I hold her steady and arch my hips to sink in even deeper. I feel the entrance of her throat. Tight. Hot. A part of me needs to sink in deeper, but the sound she makes... It's a choked gasp, and I pull back. I'm nearly free of her mouth when her hand clutches my hip, her nails digging in. I look down and right into her eyes again.

Don't. I'm okay.

Gritting my teeth, I go back, letting her set the pace. I don't last long. Not even a minute later, I'm already trying to shove her off again. I'm coming. I feel the impending release in every fucking inch of my body, but she doesn't take the hint. She stares me dead on. She sucks me in deeper. Her cheeks hollow...

And I'm on another goddamn planet. I lose my sense of gravity; that's how violently the world shifts. I'm on fire. I'm full. I'm empty.

She takes everything I have and then some, swallowing it all down like it's vital. Like she thrives on this. She needs me more than fucking oxygen. More than sanity.

We're *insane*. I could get off again just from watching her. Knowing that, I wrench my jeans back up and turn around. I set my sights on the fridge, and I stare at it until my breathing slows and I feel in control.

CHAPTER TWENTY-FIVE
CHLOE

Fate is a blank slate. So how fitting is it that my angel is an artist, painting beauty out of darkness and destruction? Taking an act I've always reviled and making it seem...vital. Even worse, forcing me to crave it.

Only he can make hate so appealing. For five minutes, I forgot about Piotr—that's the longest I've ever gone. For five minutes, my used, broken body felt something other than pain or disgust.

It's like the formless paintings streaking the canvas around us spell out the truth—Fucking him is *art*—even if it will never happen in the traditional sense. I'm resigned to that. I'll take him in any way I can, like a dog content with the scraps from a banquet table.

It's selfish.

I'm putting him in danger.

I can't help myself.

I succumb to the high, and it feels like hours pass before I manage to stand up and hobble over to the sink. I turn the faucet on and drink directly from the spray. The water doesn't erase his taste, however. It doesn't even make a dent in the flavor.

I'll choke on him all night.

Touching him is like dancing, only without the restriction of the cage. With him, my cage is everywhere. The world seems open. I'm unreachable. Just as long as he holds me. Just as long as his fingers tangle within my hair to keep me steady. Just as long as his eyes peer into mine.

Though, hell, maybe I'm not the only woman addicted to him. There was one in his sketchbook, her features carefully detailed in pencil and ink over crumbled paper. Dark hair. Flashing eyes. I'm not skilled enough to decipher whatever emotions he might have felt while drawing her.

I don't want to. Is this jealousy? Guilt?

When I finally turn the sink off and face the rest of the narrow room, he's barricaded himself inside the bathroom again. The water's running, betraying what he's doing without my needing to see it for myself—his hand on his shaft, grinding me out.

He'd rather use nicotine as his crutch than me. Apparently, angels don't see the power in dominating another. This one is so afraid of becoming a monster that he denies himself pleasure altogether. He surrounds himself with pain instead—curing it, inflicting it—going so far as to tattoo a reminder on his chest as to just what he's capable of.

I don't need another brand to remind me. Piotr's stench is in my skin. I will never erase his touch. I can forget for a minute, maybe longer. But he always comes back to me.

Moya lyubov.

I shiver as my mind scuttles away from the thought. I need to move. Think. Thankfully, the house remains silent as I haul myself upright and pad into the bedroom. I take a T-shirt and sweatpants from his closet and pull them on without allowing myself to feel any guilt. When I realize I left my shoes behind at the hotel, I have no choice but to take a pair of his as well, along with another sweatshirt. That particular item I don't need, however. I want it. My nose lowers into the sleeve, inhaling the stench embedded within the cotton.

One hit is enough to soothe whatever nerves the thought of leaving stirs up as I head for the front door. Fear, my old friend, has returned in full force. *Escape. Run.* My plan is sloppy, compiled on the fly—I'll catch a train and ride it as far as I can. Piotr can have his seven days—and many more after that. I won't go back to him.

I won't.

I can't...

"You think it's really going to be this easy?"

I glance over my shoulder and find him leaning against the doorway to the bathroom. Water drips from his hair into the cotton of the gray T-shirt he paired with jeans. His arms are crossed over his chest, those blue eyes honing in on mine without mercy.

"You think you can just come to me and walk away once you've gotten your fix?" He shakes his head and heads into the kitchen. "Uh-uh. I gave you a story. Now, it's your turn."

I'm forced to speak to his retreating back. "And if I don't want to talk?"

He shrugs and lifts something from the kitchen table. I know what it is even before I see it clearly—his gun.

"Just tell me what you were doing with *this*." He points the barrel at the ceiling, his back still turned to me. There isn't an ounce of tension in his posture.

I could make a break for the door and run before he could stop me.

A part of him might *want* me to.

But I don't, prolonging our mutual high like the selfish girl I am.

"I was going to kill someone with it." I wring my fingers together as I pad closer to the circle of light he's dominating.

The damp fabric of his shirt clings to his shoulder blades. If I squint, the ripples look a lot like wings.

"Kill?" His tone reminds me of his own "story." The phrasing he used. The rationale for why he has *murderer* tattooed across his chest and nothing else.

"No," I hear myself admit while I advance on him three more steps. "I wanted to *murder* someone with it."

"Here." He faces me and holds the gun out.

I take it, pointing the barrel at the floor.

"I assume you're not planning on sticking around." He doesn't sound disappointed, merely resigned to the fact that I might leave. I need to leave…

But, like a good addict, I seek his eyes, holding his gaze. One more prick of the needle. One last snort of my drug of choice.

"What you said about love… You made it sound worse than hate." It's an odd topic for conversation, but it almost seems fitting given our current trajectory for the morning—jumping from fucking to violence to murder to love and hate.

"Did I?" His lips slant in a thoughtful frown. "Well, I guess they're close enough. But, with hate, at least you're in control. You can fight it. You can resist it. You can forgive, or you can walk away. You can choose *not* to hate whenever you fucking want."

Love has the opposite limitations. I know them well, in fact. You can only resist its allure for so long before it sucks you back in. *Moya lyubov.* Love is poison. There is no choice in how it destroys you.

"Have you ever been in love?" I know even before I see the slight shake of his head that he hasn't, and I'm sure it's by choice.

He may care for his brother and his friend Arno, but he's never been a slave to obsession. He's never been addicted to the burning sting.

"Don't want to be," he says. "Like I said, it's easier to hate. You can turn your back on it. It doesn't own you."

"And what if...what if you hate yourself?" I ask him, my tongue flicking out to dampen my dry lips. His potential answer intrigues me more than I care to admit. Do I want him to agree? *You should hate yourself.* "For the things you've seen, the things you've done?"

He observes me for a long time. When he takes a step forward, I'm not sure how to react. I just stand here, allowing him to tower over me, his breath on my face, his heat on my skin. I'm unprepared when his hand flies out, and two of his fingers start an electrifying path down the length of my arm, skirting the stitches holding me together.

"Then I guess you just have to ask yourself—Do you really hate that you've done those things, or do you just hate the fact that you can't let yourself enjoy *doing* them?"

I draw back, stepping out of his reach. My first instinct is to write him off. *Silly little boy.* The worst he can probably come up with is stealing or committing petty crimes. He has no fucking clue as to the horrors that paint the edges of my memory.

On the other hand, he saw me kill Vlad, and the neckline of his shirt rides low, revealing a hint of the word emblazoned on his chest. When I look into his eyes again, the darkness lurks in plain view.

"What do you mean?"

"The way I see it, loving yourself is overrated." Another step and he's closer, forced to tilt his head down to maintain eye contact. "Nature. Do you love everything about it? The sun and stars, yeah. Maybe. But what about when the sun burns? What about the storms? The lightning? What about when that storm comes for you? You just have to admit that sometimes you *need* the push and pull. The good and bad. Life doesn't need your approval all the damn time. Why should you?"

Indignation rises, thick in my throat. I want to argue. *You're a boy. You know nothing.* But…after everything he's been through, it may be easy for him to accept his own hell. Live it. Breathe it. But I can't afford that luxury.

"Sometimes you can do unforgivable things," I tell him, turning to stare at the wall rather than face him directly. Shadows flicker over it—mine, his, Piotr's. "Things that don't deserve acceptance."

Warm breath fans the back of my neck. "Says who?"

He's even closer now. Those searching fingers return, drifting up and down my shoulder blade. A tempting scenario of what could happen next plays out in my mind. All he'd have to do is curl his fingers and tug to have the jacket off. The shirt would easily follow. The table alone could support our combined weight.

But we can't. I can't.

I take a step back, and I can breathe again. I can fear again. When I turn for the door, I know he won't stop me this time. Words don't have any power in this moment. Still, I find myself spitting something out—"Thank you."

He grunts in acknowledgment. "Don't mention it. And..."

My footsteps slow, tethered to the sound of his voice. "Yes?"

"If you ever need me, you know where to find me."

My entire chest constricts at that word. Need. I've endured people before. My father's death. Piotr. The men he made me screw. I've never *needed*.

When I finally reach the door, I don't look back. I just tuck the gun inside the pocket of his borrowed sweatshirt. Hate is control, he said?

It's the only emotion I can bother to spare now—hatred.

Piotr wants my love. This man has already taken something else. I'm not sure which one is harder to give up.

———

I REACH THE BAR ON FOOT AND SLIP IN THROUGH the back, taking stock of everything I touch.

Everything I see. Within a few short hours, I've left behind a real dwelling and entered the stage of a play. Piotr's aura lurks in the shadows, rearranging scenery and adjusting the spotlight. All eyes on me. His star. His angel.

Moya lyubov.

Does Arno know? The question scuttles through my skull as I wander the back hallway and don't find him slumped over a bottle. Maybe he does. Maybe he even let Piotr in with open arms. Birds of a feather. After all, it's what a part of me has suspected all along.

"Hey!" A heavy hand lands on my shoulder, snapping me from the reverie.

I'm on the bottom step of the staircase without even realizing it. A quick glance over my shoulder reveals a familiar face, albeit rougher around the edges than I'm used to. Bloodshot eyes. Uncombed hair. This morning, he looks almost as haggard as Arno.

"I need your help today," Francisco says through a yawn as he swipes at the stubble on his chin. "Those fucking idiots trashed the place last night and Arno's got something *special* planned for this one."

A welcome-back party perhaps? I scan Francisco's eyes for any hint of the truth. Any sign of Piotr's hand lurking behind the dark irises. Instead, I find nothing but the dilated evidence of booze and exhaustion.

"Hey! You hear me?" He lifts his hand and lowers it, nearly jarring me off the step altogether. "Go finish what you were doing and meet me back here. Bring the mop."

He retreats down the hallway while my brain sluggishly processes his words. *"Finish doing what you were doing."* And what was that? Oh. Dying...

Poor Chloe Parker feels further away. Did she ever really exist? I can't tell. My outstretched hand holds no answers, just pale skin riddled with scars. Burn marks. Bite marks. He loved to suck my thumb between his lips and bite down hard the moment I mistook the action for one of affection. He's painted me in his ownership, leaving a million claims I've been forced to explain away in my new life. Oh, that mark on my hip? I fell. I touched a hot stove. I knocked over an ashtray.

I nearly beat myself to death with one—haha, silly me.

I'm laughing out loud as I haul myself up the remaining few steps. Did anyone ever buy those excuses? Did I ever really believe them? The lies get harder to tell from the truth. Harder to remember. I dyed my hair blonde because I hated being a brunette. I never let men see me naked because I was shy. I rarely have sex these days because I simply don't enjoy it.

It isn't because I am already owned. My mind isn't already taken, my body sold. My soul still belongs to me.

I shiver as my forehead meets the cool surface of a closed door. I draw back and jerk forward just enough to feel the pain. *Thwack!* Then I stay here, leaning against it for what feels like hours, trying to reprocess my entire life. Trying to breathe. Trying to forget.

It's the breathing that saves me in the end. I'm choking on cigarette smoke. It permeates everything he owns, every bit of him I've stolen. I can still taste him, heady and almost sweet. I can still see him—the fear, the pain, the wonder when I took him deep. My body throbs in ways I've never ever felt, every part of me aching to take him *deep.* Maybe it's the only way I'll ever be able to push Piotr out—let someone else shove himself in.

Focus, Ksei! My fingers shake as I finally pry my hand loose from my side and open the door to the apartment. I'm so damn sore; an old woman waddles her way across the threshold, clinging to the wall for balance, not me. I manage to wrench the gun from the pocket of Espisido's sweatshirt and toss it onto the couch before hobbling into the bathroom without bothering to strip.

I turn the water to scalding hot and climb into the shower fully clothed. Only here, hunched on my knees against the side of the stall, can I hear myself again. Just whispers. *Focus, Ksei. Run, Ksei. Breathe, Ksei.*

I play those pathetic phrases over and over, clinging to the fragile shards of my soul. The three women inside me clamor for supremacy. I'm not sure just which one I'm supposed to be anymore. *Chloe? Ksenia?* I think I almost find my true identity when I finally shut the water off and drag myself upright. But then I make the mistake of looking at myself in the mirror—empty brown eyes, no soul to speak of.

What a waste.

I leave the bathroom dripping wet and aimless. My stomach growls, and the thought of finding something to eat is oddly appealing. Maybe that's what I need. To stuff myself so full that there's no room left. I stagger over to the fridge and pull it open, scowling at the offerings inside. There's a dubious carton of milk with a faded expiration date and a carton of eggs. I reach for them anyway, my fingers brushing the rough surface just as a telltale noise catches my ear. *Click!* I know it well.

"Never panic when there's a gun pointed at your skull, Parker," Grey used to tell me. "That's how you get your fucking head blown off." There is no need to turn anyway. I smell her—fear, hate, and rage. She reeks of them all, just like I do.

"You were supposed to kill him," she says, her voice ragged and unsteady. "You said you would. You said you would do it—"

"Domi?" I almost want fate to prove me wrong this time. It's not her. Piotr's web isn't really this cruel.

I risk glancing over my shoulder and find her anyway. She's barely upright on trembling legs, fighting to hold the gun she's pointing at me steady. Tears spill down her mascara-stained cheeks, stripping the tough outer exterior away and revealing the little girl she really is underneath. With her brilliant hair gleaming, even in the dim lighting, and those eyes…

I wonder if Piotr planted her specifically, using her appearance like a blunt reminder of everything I've lost. Everything his family took from me.

It stings to blink the memories back. *Focus.* "Domi. You don't want to do this—"

"I believed you!" The gun sways, the barrel drifting from left to right. Her finger shakes over the trigger. Unchecked, she'll pull it, whether on purpose or by accident.

Maybe I should let her. My fingers shake, and I'm unsure of whether to grab for her or beckon her to just do it. Kill me. Save me.

"You've known," I force myself to say instead. "You know he's back." I'm not surprised, even as the guilty flush creeps across her cheeks.

"No one leaves Piotr. *No one.*" Her eyes swell with the terror sparked by those words. She's trapped in the same hell I've always been in—but she's braver than I ever was. She fights it, shaking her head to clear the memories. "He made me watch you. Stay close. I was going to kill myself before he could… For Espi—"

"Does he know?" The pain I feel at the thought nearly knocks me over.

Would Piotr really be that sadistic to use another man to feed me snippets of hope? A newer drug? The answer rings through my skull, and a part of me almost wishes it were true. It would save me the agony of succumbing to a more potent poison than him. *Yes.*

"No." Domi shakes her head again. "He doesn't know. He doesn't deserve..." She bites her bottom lip, and more tears coat her face, falling unchecked beneath the low neckline of her sheer black top. "I wouldn't bring him into this. I wouldn't. But you said... I thought..."

She sways, and I know that look on her face. That grim acceptance of the inevitable.

She turns the gun on herself, pressing the barrel against her temple while her eyes seek mine out, cold and resigned. "I thought you were brave enough."

"No!" I lunge, throwing my weight against her.

She buckles, dropping the gun. Her nails sink into my arm, ripping through flesh, as I knock the weapon from her reach and pin her to the floor by her shoulders.

"Let me go!" She kicks out, trying to dislodge me. "There's no point. There's no use—"

My palm burns as it connects with her cheek, stopping her mid-shout. "Enough." I'm panting. Judging from how badly my arm's throbbing, she drew blood. I can feel it seeping through rent flesh as I ignore the way she tenses and wrap my arms around her.

Her arms go rigid. Limp. I hold her even as her shoulders begin to heave with suppressed tears she can barely smother with her hands.

"You're not alone." The words aren't mine, but stolen from a memory. Maybe they're what Ivan told me that very first night he set me free. "You're not alone—"

"He'll find me." Her body trembles with the knowledge. "He'll kill me."

"No." I slowly draw back from her, already forming a plan in my head. "You're already dead. I know someone who can make you disappear."

"Why?" she demands, tears in her eyes. "After what I did…"

I stand, flicking loose hair away from my face with trembling fingers. "Because it's not too late for you." I grit my teeth to reinforce that statement. It *has* to be true. "Otherwise, there's no hope for any of us."

———

THE HOTEL APPEARS DIFFERENT IN THE LIGHT OF DAY. Piotr wears darkness like a cloak, but the glow of broad daylight always seemed more painful to witness him in. Blinding.

The moment I enter the lobby, I spot at least three figures lurking within the shadows. Their posture alone betrays them as one of Piotr's trained *soldaty*, his personal bodyguards. Either I missed them last night in my moment of nostalgia, or he purposefully hid them from me.

He's grown paranoid in his old age, Piotr. He must have pissed off someone big this time. Someone powerful enough to drive him into the arms of a low-level Irish gangster with a lone bar to his name.

I'd forgotten about the connection to Arno, but as I head for the elevator and ride it to the top floor, it shoves its way into my mind again. Could the Petrovs have crossed the Cartel? Jose certainly seems like the type of enemy to warrant an increase in security, but Piotr always worked hard to soothe his allies in the drug trade. No, I suspect that another enemy has him spooked. Any other day, I'd consider finding out who.

Now, it's all I can do just to focus on breathing. Living. Fighting.

My fingers are slick with sweat. *Breathe.* I do, keeping the gun tucked inside the pocket of my jacket. His jacket. I smell him even here, clashing with the growing stench of Wolf Blood and real blood in the air. I still taste him, faint at the back of my throat like a memory, one I cling to as my past looms ahead of me.

The door to the suite is locked this time, and a scowling man in a black suit answers it when I knock. He takes one look at me and mutters something into the headset affixed to his bald head. A reply comes a second later, laced with static.

"Let her in."

The man steps aside and leaves me to wander the maze of corridors alone. I find Piotr in a study. The same one that used to serve as his base of operations back in the old days. Once again, nostalgia has me rooted to the spot. The floors are still dark wood, the walls a familiar shade of black. He even kept it furnished the same. I used to sit on his lap while he sat on that chair and snarled orders into the old-fashioned rotary phone on his desk. *Make me more money. Kill that bastard. Bring me their heads.*

Today, he seems to be in the middle of bookkeeping. A ledger is open in front of him. When he sees me, he lets a silver pen fall from his hand and rises swiftly to his feet.

"Ksei—"

"I discovered your little spy. You won't bother her again," I throw at him, but the words don't land with the impact I want. My voice is a pathetic rasp and he just...stares.

"Did you kill her?"

I would sell my soul to never see that look on his face again. Hope. Hunger. He inhales sharply, seeming to grow larger with every breath of air he takes, feeding off mine.

"No." I clench my fingers together. "I'm not a monster, like you."

"Ah, but you *wanted* to." His tongue seems to caress each and every word, gently driving them into my skull. *Did I?* He advances a step before I can convince myself of the opposite. He's wearing black again. Another tailored ebony suit with a blood-red tie to draw the eye. "Another obstacle between us gone."

I back away until I'm on the other side of the room, leaving a leather chair between us. "Was she the only one?"

Of course not. His eyes take on that cunning, predatory gleam.

"A diligent man uses more than one eye to see with, Ksei."

My own gaze fights to stay clear. My eyes sting. My vision is a sloppy smear. Who else? Darcy? Francisco? Who else does he have in his pocket to *watch* me and whisper back in his ear?

I can't smuggle them all to Ivan.

"Is this why you came to me now, Ksei?" he asks in a dangerously soft tone. "Or is that just what you told yourself?"

It's like he's inside my head, pulling the strings to my emotions—broken puppets manipulated across a stage doused in gasoline. The savoring looks he casts at my body serve as the lit match tossed on it all.

When his tongue shoots out along his lower lip, I'm ablaze.

"I thought you were brave enough," Domi said. My heart pounds, striving with every beat to prove her wrong.

"I wanted to ask you one thing before I kill you," I tell him, fighting to make my voice stronger. It breaks. My hand shakes. I don't pull the gun just yet, but I can. I will.

"Of course." He folds his hands over his front, continuing to smile that wolfish grin. "You may ask me anything. Anything you wish."

Anything. It's a dangerous prospect. I need to shoot him in the head and be done with it. Hope is an awful fucking thing. It seeps into your conscience before you can smother it, tipping the scales between fear and hate.

"Tell me…" I swallow hard and fight to suck in air. I won't go back there. I won't be sucked into the memory.

As if to taunt me, the images appear anyway—my father dead, my stepmother lying bleeding and broken, my sister.

"Anna…Anastasia." Just by saying her name, I'm clawing decades-old wounds open in one fell swoop. "My sister. Where is she?"

I wait for Piotr to shrug me off, but a curious thing happens. His smile falls, but his eyes still gleam as an ominous sensation clenches in my stomach. I learned to grit my teeth and pray to God whenever he got that look.

"Your sister." He shakes his head sadly, though he's not really concerned. In fact, I've never seen him look so happy. "She's alive, Ksei. She's safe."

"W-what?" Pain. Agony. Relief. I feel it all like a kick in the stomach. I've told myself that reality for over ten years, but finally hearing it…

"How? Where is she?" I picture her as a child, little Anna. Her impish little smile and sweet kisses. I don't find her in the office, and Piotr stops me when I head for the doorway.

"She's not here," he says. "I brought her into the country a few months ago. That's why you came back, isn't it?"

My roller coaster of grief comes to a screeching halt and then implodes. So it wasn't a coincidence that I stumbled across the redheaded girl in the database all those months ago. She was bait, used to lure me here.

"Where?"

"Somewhere safe." Noting my confusion, he explains, "She wasn't put into the trade, Ksei."

My lungs flood with so much air at once that I nearly choke. Is this relief? Or terror? "Then...then where?"

"My father and his wife at the time had a young child who died. They took her." He could be referring to a doll for all the emotion his voice holds. "They raised her, but my father has his own enemies who attacked their compound and killed his wife, so he put the girl into hiding. I offered to bring her to America for safekeeping, so to speak. It upsets you to learn this," Piotr says almost as if in awe of the gauntlet of emotions a normal human can feel in the face of grief. He takes a step toward me, and I nearly blow a hole through Espi's jacket in my haste to draw the gun.

My eyes throb, my vision nonexistent. But I aim the gun in his direction anyway. I won't miss. I can't. "You're lying." Maybe Ivan was right after all. I'd rather face the fact that my sister is dead than have her memory used as a pawn to trap me again. "Tell me where she is or I'm gone."

"I will," he promises, and the thud of footsteps trails off. "But you must earn your present from me."

His voice drips like liquid honey, the same way it used to whenever I did something or someone well enough to please him. *My perfect little Ksei.*

In his world, a "present" equated to a test. A tough client to win over or an impressive amount of drugs to imbibe, snort, or inject. Anything to make him happy. Anything to make him smile.

Fearless Chloe Parker should demand that he elaborate, but I...I can't. I just wait, and he mulls the silence left in my wake like a wolf savoring the bloody trail of its prey.

"I promise you will enjoy it...but I do not have it ready, and frankly, I was not expecting you to arrive so soon." He frowns, and my heart lurches. Piotr is predictable when caught off guard.

I wait for my punishment. Hands or fists? However, he doesn't move. For now.

"Come back tomorrow night," he tells me. "Apparently, seven days is too long a wait—"

"Like hell, I will." I trail the gun over his forehead. *Do it,* I tell myself. "Tell me where my sister is, or I'll kill you." My wrist throbs with tension, but my finger won't pull the trigger.

"When you return," he tells me. "And you *will.* Like hell, it is inevitable. But I promise that you will regain your lovely smile again."

My mouth flattens in spite. He's lying. "I won't come back."

"Until then, Ksei." He turns back to whatever business I distracted him from.

I don't know how long I stand here with the gun trained on the back of his head. Minutes. Hours. I feel numb when I finally turn away without firing a single bullet.

It's a silent walk back the way I came. The bouncer grunts in acknowledgment when I leave. By the time I make it to the lobby without a knife in my back, I realize he's really letting me leave unscathed for the second time within twenty-four hours.

I came *back* to him for the second time...

It's a thought I can't bear to face alone. Not sober. Not painfully, achingly clean. A million lines of cocaine couldn't give me the hit I need though.

I dig my nails into my palms. Hard...harder. I'm desperate enough to do anything and everything to escape the pressure building within my skull when I finally remember.

"If you need me, you know where to find me."

But he isn't in Mulligan's when I finally slip through the front door. Francisco is manning the bar alone.

"Thanks for fucking bailing, kid!" he shouts above the din of music and drunken laughter. He must not be able to see the blood. "Where's your little friend?"

"I…I think she's gone." I watch my fingers fidget with the frayed edge of my sleeve. "Ran off with a boyfriend or something."

"Hmph." Francisco eyes the counter with what could be deemed a disappointed frown. "I needed the fucking help. Anyway, if you're looking for Espi, he's gone. Arno's closing the bar down for business, so Darcy took him out."

Is it that late already? I glance over my shoulder and spot the dark sky visible beyond the windows. I didn't even notice night falling during my trek across town. I'm that desperate. That needy.

"Where?"

If he's surprised that I'm curious, he doesn't mention it. "Davey's. It's on Fourth. Not far from here. I guess someone else can take your spot tonight."

I nod and then exit onto the street. It takes me an hour to track the club down, which is tucked between a warehouse and an alleyway. The pulse of the music is audible a block down, and when I finally approach the battered door serving as an entrance, the bouncer doesn't even bother asking me for ID.

Apparently, this isn't the kind of establishment that gives a damn about the legality of their clientele. Inside is a mismatched cross between what appears to be a makeshift bar at one end and a full-blown club at the other. It's packed, filled wall to wall with sweating bodies gyrating to the deafening bass.

It doesn't take me long to find Darcy. She sways wildly to the beat, catching eyes from even the drunkest spectator. Surprisingly, she isn't approached. It's as if even the sleaziest pervert can sense the watchful blue eyes on her from a corner. I catch glimpses of him at first through breaks in the crowd and the sparse illumination of pulsing strobe lights. He's red one instant. In shadow the next. It's a haunting transformation that has him shifting from demon to angel with every step I take. He's a demon when I push past a man in a wife-beater, grinding against a half-naked blonde. He's an angel again when I'm just beyond his reach. The next moment, he's the devil.

I feel him before I register reaching for him. His hand, scorching hot. His fingers greedily lacing with mine. His startled breath on my throat as I step in closer. Closer than he's comfortable with. More distance than I need.

"Hey..." His voice sounds rougher against my ear, loud to combat the noise around us.

I can sense the questions he doesn't bother to ask. He can feel the gun still tucked inside my pocket—but he doesn't move. Not until I take his hand and lead him deeper into the center of the dance floor.

I've never danced away from a stage. I've never willingly danced with someone. Not like this. He takes the place of the pole, his hands on my waist when I move them there, his body like an anchor. I stop thinking. I stop feeling. I just move, breathing in time with the pulsing beat. I let him set the pace. I let him inhale me. With every dose of me he takes, I steal double the amount from him.

I know that this won't last. That it can't. The fear only drives me faster. I grind on him. I know that it's more than he can stand. More than he can take. Maybe I want him to push me off.

He doesn't. He lets me touch him as I slide my hands down his chest. I glance up and find him already staring down at me, his eyes unfocused but still so damn piercing. I don't know who initiates it, but the kiss is deeper than the others. Harsher. More desperate.

My fingers are in his hair. His claw at me through the fabric of my clothing, touching, owning. I *need* to be owned. He doesn't resist when I pull back and drag him through the crowd. I need to be somewhere—anywhere—away from the people, and the noise, and the watchful eyes. I just need him.

We barge into a bathroom. Men's or women's? I'm not sure which. It's cramped and filthy with toilet paper wadded on the floor in dubious puddles. He tenses when he follows me inside, and something I can't even decipher tears from my throat. Maybe I beg him. Plead. Moan. Either way, he reacts by backing me into a corner by the sinks. I flail for leverage and haul myself up onto the rim of one.

My heart thunders when he steps between my legs, his eyes on mine. We share a revelation without words—This can go however far he wants it to.

I have to grit my teeth against any sound when his hands go for my sweatpants. He peels them down almost reverently before sliding his hand between my legs. With every brush of his fingers, he sends me on a slow, gradual high.

But it's not enough.

The moment I see him reach for his jeans, I lunge forward and help him tear them open. His boxers next. My knees clamp over his hips to drive him closer—drive him in—and when he does, I don't give a damn who might hear me.

It doesn't last long. I'm too wet. He's too raw. Too perfect. Too wound up. The first few thrusts slam me back against the streaked mirror, drawing sounds from me I've never heard myself make. He goes slower after that, savoring the connection rather than striving for friction. It's so damn considerate that I can't take it. I come with only the grinding of his pelvis against my clit for stimulation, dragging him down with me.

I'm distantly aware of a door opening and a stumbling figure spotting us there. They shout something, but I can't tear my gaze away from Espi to give a shit.

His eyes seem so damn blue in this moment. I've never seen anything more beautiful. I've never seen anything more dangerous

I don't know how long we stay like that. Maybe it's only a minute later that he finally pulls away. I wince as I slide from the sink. The faucet bit into my back, and I move woodenly to adjust my clothes. I've only managed to straighten the hem of my borrowed shirt before his hands are there to assist. He dresses me slowly, reverently. His touch alone can make rough cotton seem like silk, transporting me far beyond our filthy, reeking surroundings.

My fingers shake as I help him adjust his pants in return. He won't let me pull the zipper, but my rebellious fingers linger over his waistband as he leads the way back out into the club. We hunt aimlessly through the crowd for Darcy and spend the rest of the night watching her from the sidelines. He doesn't touch me, and I don't touch him. He doesn't have to for his presence to resonate within my body anyway, more potent than any drug.

———

WE DON'T MAKE IT BACK TO THE BAR. INSTEAD, I follow him to his house, where he doesn't even bother to switch the lights on once we're inside. With the prompting of one wordless plea, he strips me down right here in the middle of the kitchen, and we fuck on the floor. It's sloppy. Messy. Our bodies don't know how to meld, so we make them fit.

I hook my knees around his waist, driving him into me, clawing at his back, moaning in his ear. There's no fear as to what might happen if I orgasm too soon—or if I don't. There's just feeling, sensation, breathing. And then he's spilling himself inside me, grunting with the force of it, and I come undone.

We lie here afterward, a pile of sweating limbs, when we should redress and regroup. Reality lurks beyond the stained walls of his house, threatening to swallow us whole.

But I'm weak. He's tired. We sleep in bits and pieces, and then we fuck again, slower, harder. It's only when his mouth latches onto my throat that I realize it's not *really* fucking, at least not as I know it. He's not shoving his cock into me, using my body as a hole to get himself off. With every touch, he's making me... Making me feel. Making me moan. Cry out. Scream.

In his own way, maybe he's making something close to love. Making hate.

My battered, bruised soul swells and shatters beneath his ministrations. I'm the bloated, grotesque remains of someone once living, and he showers that broken corpse with worshiping fingers, groaning at the feel of my skin. He does his best to come only when he knows I'll follow.

It's too much.

We lie side by side, catching our breath.

We fuck again.

Dawn is painting the sky with streaks of pink and red when I wake up, my head on his chest, his hands in my hair. I know he's awake, but I'm not ready yet. Not ready to face the world. Not ready to remember the clock counting the hours down.

He told me that he'd be there when I needed him. That promise woke something inside me that I only have one word to name. I *need* him. I slide my leg over his hip and straddle him in earnest. He's hard already, nudging my inner thigh. A sigh escapes his mouth, ruffling strands of my hair loose. One of exhaustion? One of relief? The lazy smile that tugs on his lips gives me a clue.

Holding his gaze, I reach between us and guide the head of him inside me. Three…four times and the sensation never changes. The pleasure never loses its potency. He fills me like nothing else. *Perfectly.* My body doesn't strain to accept him. It swallows him, hungry for him in every goddamn way—and only like this can I fucking forget.

I move on him slowly, letting him adjust to the feeling. Once he starts to thrust up into me, I arch my back, brace both hands on his chest, and swivel my hips, riding him deeper. His hands go to my waist, guiding my pace, letting me keep control. His surrender alone makes me come so hard that I see colors. Reds. Blues. Yellows. Greens.

I keep moving until he groans out his own release and fills me up all over again. I flush with the realization that we haven't used a condom one single time. And I don't care. There's no guilt on my part. Chloe Parker's yearly exams reinforce the fact that I'm clean. And even if he's not…

There are worse ways to infect a person. Fates more damning than any disease. I'd take anything and everything he could possibly ever give me, just as long as it means I never have to go back.

"Arno's been calling me."

This is when I register the telltale buzz of a vibrating cell phone.

"He's the only one who would this fucking early."

With a sigh, I roll off him and onto the cold tile, but he doesn't move. He just stares up at the ceiling, his expression thoughtful, his arms at his sides. He's an angel contemplating the depth of his fall, the loss of his wings. The buzzing has trailed off by the time he finally hauls himself upright.

He staggers down the hallway, still beautifully naked. The muscles in his thighs ripple as he stoops for his phone and brings it to his ear. When he finally hangs up and returns to the kitchen, his halo has disappeared. Shadows line his eyes again, feeding off every ounce of light in the room.

"Jose found something out," he says while he hunts for something on the floor. When his gaze lands over his sweatshirt, he lunges for it and pulls it over his head. "I've got to go—"

"I'll come with you." I'm already on my feet before he can argue, if he even would.

He watches me fish my panties from the floor, his expression unreadable. Once we're both fully dressed, however, he holds his hand out to me. I take it, gripping it tighter than necessary. Tighter than I should.

He lets me cling to him as he heads for the door. Beside him, the daylight isn't harsh and revealing. It's cold. It's calm. It paints our skin in shades of yellow and gray, and I have never felt more human.

CHAPTER TWENTY-SIX
ESPI

"Where the hell have you been?" Arno snarls the moment we enter Mulligan's.

Shit. The set of his shoulders alone backs up the nerves I sensed in him over the phone. He's awake before dawn, without a bottle to show for it, too. Either the bar's entire stash of liquor disappeared overnight, or something's got him riled so badly that even beer can't fix it.

I don't spot Francisco behind the bar, either—another bad sign. Arno only leaves him out of shit when he doesn't want to be put on a leash.

"What's going on?"

"Well, you would know if you answered your damn phone. I've been calling you for five fucking—" He breaks off once he notices the woman in my shadow and his expression falls flat. "Never mind. I can guess what the fuck you were doing."

He's gone before I can muster up a comeback, marching toward the center of the bar. Then I realize why he's so edgy —We have company. I spot the guest of honor seated on one of the stools near the end of the counter. The next second, Arno shoves me back before I even register taking a step.

"Relax," he grunts while I catch myself against the end of a pool table. "He's just here to talk. I told you that he found something out."

"Yeah, well, I didn't think you'd invite him over for goddamn tea."

Jose put his big-boy clothes on today—a leather jacket and jeans.

"*Hola, mi amigo,*" he says. He brought a knife along to play with—Arno wouldn't dare let him bring a gun. Knowing damn well that I'm watching, the bastard twirls it between his fingers, his eyes reflecting hints of silver. "It's been a long time since our last chat—"

"Don't," Arno growls to me. "Don't give this fucker any bait to help him get off at night." He cocks his head the same way most men would a gun. His eyes narrow, and my nerves spark, painfully alert. I haven't seen this version of Arno in a very, *very* long time. His eyes aren't even bloodshot, and there isn't an open beer can lying around. It's as close to stone-cold sober as he can get. "You came here to talk," he says to Jose. "So open your fucking mouth."

"Watch yourself, Arno… " Jose drags his thumb along the edge of his blade, leaving a reddish streak along the metal—a warning. "There are a lot more important things that I could be doing with my fucking mouth, *ese*." When he looks up, the mocking humor from his expression is gone. Good old Jose is just as pissed as Arno. "It seems our new friends are using tactics similar to the Italians—"

"You mean the shot-back-to-hell Italians?" Arno interjects. "The same fucking Italians that scattered like roaches when their queen, Stacatto, met his goddamn maker?"

"*One* Italian in particular," Jose goes on as if never interrupted. "That man had close dealings with the Russians, but you see… I don't particularly favor the Russians—"

"You don't trust them," Arno says, cutting him off. "Cut to the fucking chase."

"Hmph. Cut." Chuckling, Jose tilts his knife so that it catches the light. While holding Arno's gaze, he leans forward and flicks his tongue along the edge to capture any wet droplets of blood.

To his credit, Arno doesn't even flinch.

"There is one particular son of a bitch who knew the inner workings of the Mob better than most, however," Jose continues. His eyes get that dark gleam again. He's thinking. It's the same look he was wearing while he palmed his whips, trying to gauge which one best suited his needs while I bled out, chained to the wall. He made a game out of it. How to go deep into the muscle. How to draw the most blood. "I brought him home for dinner, but he doesn't seem willing to really enjoy himself."

"So what the fuck do you want?" Arno demands, his arms crossed. "You losing your touch when it comes to wining and dining, Jose? Want some fucking pointers?"

"Him." With a seemingly lazy shrug, Jose gestures in my direction. He never stops twirling that knife, tossing the blade up and catching it by the handle every single time. "I want *him*."

A laugh trickles out of Arno, darker and more twisted than I've ever heard. "You better be fucking joking—"

"You think I don't know what little Espi gets up to while his daddy is away? Do *you* know...*Daddy?*"

Arno just stands there, his gaze flicking from Jose to me and back again. *Does* he know? Jose's guess is as good as any.

"What the fuck are you talking about?" Arno asks.

Jose just chuckles, the sound mingling with the warm breath ghosting my shoulder. She's gripping me tighter than ever, her nails grazing my skin. I suffer every unusual bite of pain, letting it sink deep to counter everything else.

"Rumor has it that another one of my warehouses might be 'shot back to hell' tonight," Jose says, apparently taking Arno's advice by cutting to the fucking chase. "I suffer, and I'll make sure the whole goddamn city suffers. So I suggest you take my advice, *amigo*, and convince your little friend to lend a helping hand. Let's do brunch."

"Hell no." Arno shakes his head, his red hair flying, his eyes gleaming. He's armed; I can tell that much from the way he's standing alone—which is ironic considering that Jose would never walk into an open trap.

"Stop." I step forward between them. My gaze lands on Jose. The bastard looks smug for a damn reason. "What are you planning?"

"A surprise," he says, not even trying to deny it. "While we've been chatting, I had one of my men do some interior decorating in your cellar, *ese*," he says to Arno over my shoulder. "You have six hours before the bomb goes off and blows your little bar...well, back to hell. I die, and the fireworks happen sooner," he adds before Arno can draw his gun. "As I said, let's do brunch." He slides from the stool, tucking the knife into his pocket. "When little Espi helps me persuade our guest to tell what he knows, I'll deactivate my present, and we'll call it a day. But if you feel like trying to fuck me over...just keep in mind that you can tear this fucking piece-of-shit place apart, nail by nail, and never find my little surprise. At least not before you do some 'interior decorating' yourself. *Comprende?*"

"Fine," I say, beating Arno to the punch. "Where is he?"

"Wonderful." Jose beams. "Allow me and my men to escort you back to my home. Our meal should be ready any minute."

———

From the outside, the bike stop looks the same. The same rundown buildings. The same piece-of-shit chain-link fence surrounding the entire property. Jose's switched up his interior decoration though. He's into open spaces now, unlike the clusterfuck of boxes and equipment that littered the place back when he strung me up. The middle of the floor is cleared, the perfect focal point for his latest piece of artwork—a man dangling from chains hanging from the ceiling.

Recognition shoots through me like a lance. Despite the blood caking the bastard's face, I know that bulky shape. The flashing, dark eyes. That telltale chuckle. Like Arno said, Mack always had a certain look about him. Though the cocky bastard's taken quite a few hits these past few months. Scars riddle the skin not covered by overgrown stubble on his jaw. Arno and Dante got their revenge, all right.

"Well, lookie here," he rasps the moment he sees us approaching from the end of the warehouse. One of his eyes is swollen shut, but he does his best to sneer with the good one. "The Mex brought along some little friends..." He trails off once he recognizes one "little friend" in particular

Arno returns the glare directed his way with one of his own.

"The traitor and the puppy," Mack says, turning his attention to me. "Shouldn't you be licking Dante's boots, little boy?"

I don't react to the taunt. My eyes are on Jose; he's grinning. Without a single glance spared in Mack's direction, he heads to a table against the wall. Even from the short distance, I can clearly make out what's on it. Knives—sharp ones.

Fuck. My fingers clench. I can't shake the murmurs of a conscience I long thought had been snuffed out by blood and nicotine. *Walk away. Don't do this.*

"So, what shall it be?" Jose wonders out loud, slicing through the drone. Only the look he directs my way reveals just who he's speaking to. "Word on the street is that you prefer another method over the typical slice and dice."

"I prefer to think of it as freelance art," I counter, taking a step forward.

Mack's still laughing, spouting some more dumb shit, but Arno… He's watching me. I feel his gaze on the back of my neck. I know that look. It's the same one he used to shoot Dante whenever he went nuts and started a fight in the bar. That one of fear. That one of goddamn pity.

"Espi, what the fuck is he talking about?"

"Business, *Daddy*," Jose says. "Don't worry. Your little baby is in safe hands." He looks at Mack, and the playful grin falls flat. "Let's see how you work. Get him to talk."

I look up at Mack again, and I don't have to strain my neck too far. Hanging by two giant hooks caught right at the indents of each shoulder blade, he's only about a foot from the ground. Blood drips down and forms a puddle underneath him. The bastard has to be in an insane amount of pain, but he just grins.

"Don't fucking tell me. Little Espi. *You're* going to try to make me talk?" His body jerks on the hooks as he throws his head back and laughs, long and loud. "You must be losing your fucking touch, Jose—" He breaks off in a grunt of pain.

I glance down as his body twists in grotesque slow motion and see why—Someone jammed a knife into the meat of his upper thigh.

"I gave you a head start," Jose says, shrugging when my gaze finds him by the wall. "But we don't have all day to play around, boy. Show me what you've learned."

The words work like a trigger on my memories. Oh, I learned from the master. How to break someone. How to push them just far enough for them to beg for the end. Only to slowly reel them back...and then push them again. Harder. Further.

They're past praying for death at that point. They'd endure anything to make the merry-go-round of agony stop. Say anything. Do anything

I learned from the master—and he wasn't Jose.

"Espi." Arno comes up behind me, his footsteps heavy. "Fuck this shit. You're not doing this." He jabs a finger in Jose's direction. "*He's* not doing this—"

"Arno—" I cut myself off, unsure of what the fuck I'm even trying to say. *Shut the hell up? Let me think.*

The bastard knows something. I can smell it. I can see it in his eyes, which glow with a mixture of pain and just plain smug fucking arrogance. Mack, the Mad Dog, was more cunning than the average dumbass punk. He covered his bases and did nothing without insurance.

"I thought this piece of shit was already dead," Arno adds, spitting at Mack's feet. "Where the fuck did you find him?"

Jose shrugs, his expression revealing nothing. "I have my ways. The Russians dealt with him…uniquely, but as you know, I'm not particularly fond of the Russians." He leaves it at that, and Arno doesn't ask him anything else.

Frankly, I don't think he wants to know. And Mack… The bastard just laughs. And laughs. And laughs.

The sound ricochets off the inside of my skull. Loud. Insistent. I doubt even another knife in his flesh would shut him up.

"Darcy…" Her name trickles out of me before I register the guilt. It draws a reaction from Mack though; he shuts the fuck up. "You seen her lately?" When he doesn't take the bait, I aim low. "I guess not. She's been fucking half of the Gardai since you 'left.' I guess it is true what they say about you. You like getting screwed in the—"

"You watch your fucking mouth," Mack bites back. "You tell him the truth, eh, Arno boy? About how you and that fucking cunt-eating brother of his turned on one of your own? Or maybe how you couldn't even bother to make sure your own fucking sister was still alive—"

"Enough of this shit." Squaring his shoulders, Arno turns on his heel and starts for the door. "Espi, come on—"

"Yeah, run, run, little Arnold," Mack taunts. "You always were a pussy little shit."

One second, Arno's still walking. The next, he's halfway to Mack, and only Jose is fast enough to get in between them.

"Not so fast, *ese*," he says, shoving Arno back. "Don't damage the merchandise. Let's see what our little friend can get out of him."

"No...no." Arno shakes his head as his hand flies out and lands on my shoulder, dragging me closer. "Hell no. He's not doing shit."

"Why don't we ask *him*?" Jose turns to me, still smiling even though his eyes have lost the playful gleam. He's all serious again, bathed in the shadows of the warehouse. "What will it be, little Espisido? Run away and let your friend's little establishment get blown sky high? Or...show us what you've learned."

Anger and disgust flutter down my spine. My toes flex in my boots. *Run. Stay.* I don't fucking know which course of action seems more appealing. A part of me wants to tell Jose to fuck off. Listen to Arno. I've *always* just listened to Arno. But another part...

My gaze drifts over to the knives, and my fingers flex, remembering the feel of the ones in my kit—specifically designed for…special work. Flaying. Slicing. They were the tools of my trade, after all, helping to create a new form of artwork Dante wouldn't approve of.

It's funny. I don't even remember the first time clearly. Maybe it was when some asshole on the streets pushed me too far. Or maybe it was that night when I picked up a hammer and didn't give a fuck as to what I had to do with it. Just that I wanted to.

I don't know how long I stand here, staring at the wall. How long before I feel her fingertips ghost the back of my neck. *Her*—I know it without even having to turn around and see her there for myself. I can smell her. Feel her. This woman is in my blood, feeding off the parts of me I don't have the stomach to acknowledge. She can fucking take them. All of them.

"Tell me." Her voice nudges my eardrum, soft and hoarse. "What…what do *you* want to do?"

My shoulders slump. That's a question I don't get asked too often these days. *What do you want, Espisido?* Not *What do you need? What do you feel?*

What do you want?

My fingers flex, my knuckles still raw from the other night. The sound of my voice doesn't even seem familiar. "A knife."

She's already moving across the room, her hair flying out behind her. Whether intentionally or not, she lets her fingers flutter from blade to blade to blade, taking her time before finally settling on one. When she returns to my side, she presents it blade-edge first.

I only see her. I don't hear Arno. I don't hear Mack. Jose's a fucking speck.

Only her. Yellow. She hands me the knife when I reach for it. That's it. No words of encouragement. No look laced with pity or doubt. Just the ice-cold scrape of metal against the flesh of my palm and the knowledge that this is all me. My choice.

My goddamn burden.

Mack's still running his fucking mouth when I face him again. He spits out a taunt I don't bother to decipher, his bruised jaw standing out in stark contrast against the rest of his skin. Jose did quite the number on him, but even he went easy. This was a part of his game all along. Why? I don't fucking care.

I just *feel* in this moment.

I don't hold back when I swipe the knife against Mack's bare side, catching the design of a tattoo. I go deep, letting the blade hiss the words I don't have the energy to say. Blood tells all. In rivulets. In drips and drops. I'm painting the floor with my own pain, and it feels…so goddamn *good* not to have to fucking think.

So I don't. I tune the world out—everything but the cold fingers resting on my forearm. It's a new kind of torture session—How far can I go before she flinches back? Withdraws? Pulls away from me?

How much blood does it take to dilute yellow?

I make another cut. Another. Another. I see the picture I'm making in my head rather than on the flesh itself. Letters. Seven of them.

T R A...

Two fingertips flutter against the crook of my elbow, and I slow the motion of my hand. But they only press deeper. The nails graze my flesh, silent and commanding. *I'm here. Keep going.*

Do it.

One more strike.

I

Two more cuts.

T

Another.

O

I have to shake my head to snap out of this hell. Hell— because nothing in heaven could ever feel this good. This fucking right. There's nothing holy in the complete lack of guilt I feel as I take in the bleeding, gaping marks I've made right across another man's rib cage. I went deeper than I had to. He's going to fucking scar.

Good.

Her hand is still there when I raise my arm again, controlling the blade with the perfect fluidity needed to finish off my creation.

R

Mack's howling when I finally shake that black-hole concentration off. Threatening. Cursing. Blah, blah, fucking blah.

I don't bother to trade his barbs this time. I just hold the knife up, staining the air with a new form of paint. Good old Mack will never forget what the fuck he is. Neither will I.

I wait until he falls silent to feel. Arno's disgusted. Jose's amused. Yellow… She's just waiting and watching. Nothing I do seems to surprise her. Nothing shocks her.

She's in my fucking soul, crawling through the filth and garbage. She doesn't wrinkle her nose at the smell. She breathes me in deeper and runs her fingers along the mess. She calls it art.

"Tell us what you know," I say to Mack. I sound so tired. So goddamn old. So much like Dante that my ears sting.

"You think you're some kind of badass now, you little—"

"Tell us what you know, or I'll kill you."

Arno scoffs. Jose laughs. But I'm not joking.

Maybe Mack can see it, because he's not so quick to counter me this time. Could I do it? I look at the knife, my bloody fingers gripping the handle. The answer is obvious, but it doesn't make me feel proud or even ashamed to admit it. Yes. I could. I will. The sick part is that I wouldn't even like doing it. Not like Jose. Not even like Arno.

I just *would*, and that's all there fucking is to know. She makes me admit that to myself, right here and now. She makes me hammer that truth into my skull. I am what I am —*murderer.*

"You're really fucking serious, huh?" Mack chokes out a long, dark chuckle. "You want to know what the funny part is? I don't owe that bitch a damn thing. Yeah." He chuckles again when Arno steps forward, his eyes glowing with renewed interest. "Who else would play the game just like fucking Stacatto? She's using all of his damn tricks. Fuck, I know you dropped out of high school and all, but you really are fucking stupid, Arno."

Gritting his teeth, Arno lets the insult fly by. "Start talking."

He does. I don't understand a word of what he says. I don't try to. Adrenaline creates a fuel-soaked prison more sustaining than nicotine. Much more addictive, but with way harsher side effects. I'm shaking. The remnants of rage war with what little bit of control I have left.

I'm angry. It feels strange to admit that. To feel it all without trying to write it off in some way. I'm tired. I'm pissed. Arno. Dante. Jose. All they do is spill their own shit out onto the world and expect someone else to clean it up.

"Espi!"

I don't register turning until Arno's hand is on my shoulder, dragging me back.

"Wait. We need to—"

"Let me go." I shrug him off, but not before Mack can get in the last word.

I'm not sure exactly what he says. Something about Dante. Something about how proud he'd be of his little candy-ass brother.

It's funny. The only time I ever hear her gasp is when I lunge for him and draw the knife. I hit him high. I hit him hard. Too hard. Blood goes flying. His eye... It's a mess in the socket. His neck chords—he screams so loudly.

And I don't even hear him. I don't fucking register the way my fingers loosen, dropping the knife. I turn, and I leave without a fuck given for the chaos I've sowed behind me. I'm selfish. I'm needy.

Just like Dante.

CHAPTER TWENTY-SEVEN
CHLOE

He makes me chase him for blocks without slowing down. My calves are throbbing by the time he finally mounts a concrete stoop and disappears through a doorway. His own.

I find him pacing in the center of the kitchen, shoving the table out of his way, knocking loose pages and his sketchpad from the cluttered surface. The way he moves stops me from reaching for it, however. Shadows flicker over his shoulders like living appendages. Broken, corrupted wings.

In one swift motion, he forms a fist and pummels it into the fridge. "Fuck!" His knuckles leave a telltale smear across the white surface. He goes pale when he sees it, and the offending hand falls to his side. "Shit…"

"Come here." I don't think. I don't have to. Instinct guides me over to him, and I let my body take control. I shove him toward a chair and make him sit. Then I wet a rag from the sink and wipe the blood from his hands.

Drip by drip. Smear by smear. He never stops looking at me while I do so. It's an expression I can't decipher—part darkness as shadow falls over his face, part light from his eyes, which never seem to lose their brilliant glow.

It's his eyes that save him.

"You think I'm sick," he tells me, his voice a gruff composition of timbre and baritone. "You...you think I'm crazy." He grabs my wrist, and I stare at his injured hand, the fingers tan against my skin.

Crazy. I almost wish I felt those things. Almost...

With a sigh, I force myself to swallow before disentangling my arm from his grip. Without a shred of hesitation, I run my fingers along his forehead, pushing the thick curls back from his face, further revealing that beautiful gaze. "I think you're tired," I tell him around another sigh. "I think...I think you're exhausted."

My heart pounds to punctuate the words I can't say out loud. *So am I. So am I.*

"Exhausted." He frowns.

It's not the scathing assessment he wants. It's not loathing. It's not disgust. I've been willing to give him so many things these past few days, but this is the one thing I'm surprised to find I *can't.* I can't fear him. I can't blame him.

My murderer.

My angel.

My monster.

His eyes tell the story he's fought. The control he's battled for so long.

"That's how you learned to do the stitches," I say carefully. But that's only the half of it. It's how he learned to stomach the horror he's seen—by wearing masks. By finding his own release.

By dancing between heaven and hell on threadbare wings.

"Learned," he scoffs, choking out a laugh that doesn't reach his eyes. "Sick, huh? I'm fucking *sick*—"

"You're not." I dig my nails into his skin before he can argue. *You're not.* My throat works woodenly. Another story time is in order, but I can't seem to get the words out. "I...I did... I've done..."

His fingers clench, cutting me off. Minutes pass before he finally takes advantage of the resulting silence.

"It was almost a game, at first," he says. "I wanted to know. After...after him. I wanted to know if I could do it again. If it was a fluke. If I really am..." He inhales sharply, shaking his head. "I *remember* now. The first time was some meth head who owed Arno money. Arno had already beaten the shit out of him, but I...I went into the room, and...he started laughing. Calling me names. The usual shit. It didn't faze me. At least not until Darcy walked in by accident to get an extra case of beer and the bastard started listing out all the ways she could 'make his day.'" He pauses again, his hand clutching mine so tightly that my fingers go numb.

I let them. The odd buzz eats its way up my arm, the same way his words eat through my soul.

"I carved a P into his forearm," Espi says thickly. "For 'pervert,' the sick fuck. I stitched him up real nice after. Gave him a hit of dope. And in the end...I didn't feel a goddamn thing."

He's lying. Or maybe he can't admit the truth, not even to himself. He felt something, all right. The same thing I feel when Piotr's near—that voice I can't shake. That unholy itch I don't ever want to scratch.

Power and fear combined is an awful fucking thing. My touch alone won't make him forget his latest taste of it. I can't help him with the physical scars, either, or even the mental pain. But I can at least help him find some way of release.

I take his hands in both of mine and guide them down to my hips. Our gazes reconnect as I step in closer, right between his legs. This is a new mask I'm putting on, a different woman from the three I'm used to playing. She's a willing sacrifice, something I never offered even Piotr. Maybe it's the only thing I have left—possession.

"Hate me," I tell him. *Not yourself. Use me. Punish me.*

Recognition dawns upon him slowly though. He stands, using the motion to step in closer, drag me closer. He's lost his halo once again, his eyes gleaming like indigo fire. Perfect. Beautiful. Consuming.

I'm still in awe when he spins me around and presses me up against the table, making me lean over it. My heart slams against my rib cage, harsh and violent. It remembers this position. The heavy hands against my lower back. The panting breaths grated out on the air as my panties are yanked down my legs, and some stranger's cock is shoved inside me.

But never with permission. Never with this hungry, raw need.

I *need* him.

My palms flatten against the table's surface as he peels my pants and my underwear down my legs. He takes his time, even though tension resonates through his skin. The anticipation—it's different from anything I've ever felt. Even the terror doesn't feel the same. When he finally trails a finger between my legs, I just moan, already wet. Already ready.

I hear him swallow, unsteady, unsure, and I barely recognize the sound of my own voice when I grit out a plea. "It's okay. I can—"

He slams into me, grunting with the effort. The pleasure... The pain. It takes him three thrusts before he finds his stride, setting a pace that has me writhing beneath him, my hair caught between his fingers, his mouth on my shoulder, teeth scraping, nails digging in.

He shows me more violence than he ever showed the man he tortured for Jose, ripping back every layer of his soul to reveal the mixture of light and dark underneath. I take it all in. Every inch. Every thrust. I let him use me as a receptacle for the twisted emotions he can't bring himself to face. For everything he doesn't want to feel.

Piotr used me in this way often. But it never felt like this.

I never grew hotter, wetter around him. My thoughts never splintered like shards of jagged glass, sinking in with every broken moan to leave his throat. Piotr never caressed me, even as he fucked. He never buried his mouth into the crook of my neck, murmuring a million words in a raspy cadence. *I'm sorry. I'm sorry. Fuck. I... I'm sorry. Sorry.*

Back in those days, I never willingly came—so hard that I see stars. And, even in the breathless aftermath of his release, Piotr never spun me around, hauling me upright, forcing our lips to meld, kissing me. Long. Hard. Soft. Gentle pecks. Around my lips. Over them. Plunging his tongue inside.

I kiss him back, running my hands down his arms and over his shoulders. I arch my hips against his, riding out the remainder of his erection. I pant. I moan. I make *hate* to him, even if I don't know how.

I cry out when he finally spills his release into me. Some part of me seems to be keeping a mental tally, and it woefully remarks, *No condom.*

On a bone-shattering sigh, he pulls back. "I...I didn't mean to do that—"

"You don't have to apologize," I say automatically.

But it's funny. I used to risk beatings to ensure that my johns wore condoms. Piotr was the only man I couldn't sway, but he made sure to secure birth control for me, at least. In his own words, he wouldn't put off fucking me for nine months out of the year.

"Do you…" He licks his lips and swallows hard, his Adam's apple bobbing. "Do you have it covered?"

Is that guilt that sweeps through me on a dizzying wave? I shake my head. Chloe Parker didn't care for the pills, those tiny multicolored reminders of hell. It was never an issue before, and only now does the danger, other than an STD, sink in. He could get me pregnant—if he hasn't already.

Does that scare me? I think on the answer as he braces both hands on either side of me, leaning forward so that our foreheads connect, our bodies still entwined. The answer is probably more terrifying than the prospect. A baby —*his* baby, wouldn't be Piotr's, but something he could never taint. Someone he could never own. *Mine.*

"I know from Darcy that…that there are ways you could." He breaks off without revealing exactly what. He sounds so damn tired.

I just tilt my head so that our lips touch, our breaths mingling, our air shared.

Five minutes. Ten minutes. We linger like this. But some emotions can't be fucked out, requiring to be expelled another way.

"I never wanted to be a part of this shit." He pulls back, gritting the words out toward the wall. The muscles in his forearms chord, and I can't stop myself from running my fingers along them, sensing the tension coiled underneath. "Arno. Mack. Dante. I never wanted a part of any of it." He laughs coldly, shaking his head. "Funny how that turned out, huh?"

"What did you want?"

He looks down at me. Really looks as his eyes narrow and he processes the question. "I wanted to go to school. Do art. Be normal, whatever the fuck that means. But then Dante —" He breaks off, clenching his jaw as his halo flickers again. On. Off. On. "I couldn't leave Arno to deal with his mess alone."

There's pain in the way he says it. He put his own dreams on hold for his friend. But that's only half of it. The rest of the truth takes longer to spill out, lingering over his tongue.

"I got sucked in," he admits. "This life... There are no consequences. No real rules. No law. It's the only kind of environment where someone like Arno could ever judge someone like me."

"You think he's disappointed in you."

He sighs and rakes his fingers through his hair. "I wanted to go to France one day, you know?" he says. It seems like he's speaking to me, but the eye contact is merely for my benefit. The words come from his soul. "I thought I could make a living drawing tourists around Paris. Learn from some pretentious fucking art school. I even took classes." He laughs. "I'd grown up drawing on the back of notebooks and napkins, whatever I could get my hands on. But these people… They had 'art tutors.' They took trips to Europe to learn how to copy shit from fancy art museums. Their stuff was a mockery of what they thought looked pretty. It didn't contain an ounce of their soul. Their pain. So I dropped out, and…"

His gaze drifts down to my face, and his thumb grazes the corner of my mouth, feeling the wet hint of himself lingering there. He opens his mouth. To talk, I think. To reveal more of his past. In the end, he just kisses me again, more deeply than before.

We wind up flat against the tabletop, with me on top of him, writhing to feel him harden up against my thigh. This time, it's quick. We both use each other, grinding ourselves into one another's skin. When we finally break apart, panting, I don't know what makes me say it, my cheek partially pressed against the cold tile floor.

"You had dreams. I had…goals. A checklist of things I had to do in order to make it through each day." I can see them flit across my mind, even now. *Obey. Resist. Submit. Survive.* Over and over like clockwork.

He stiffens up beside me, running his hand down my back. "With Vlad?"

I inhale the question and exhale the truth. I tell him everything. Every dark, twisted, sordid detail save Piotr's return. I don't hold a single damn thing back. I spill it all.

He breathes it in. Like smoke. Like nicotine. He's high on me, hating the buzz even as it burns through him.

My face feels wet when I finally trail off, and he's holding me, his body braced overtop mine, his breath warm on my shoulder. It's enough. Against Piotr and his madness, his touch is enough. I can overcome it, just for now. I can relish the sore ache of him and the brutal spice of his scent. I don't have to worry about the consequences.

I don't even have to feel. I let him own me, this angel. For a brief moment, he flies me out of hell.

———

ARNO ISN'T CONTENT TO JUST CALL THIS TIME. HE attempts to break the front door down, and Espisido has barely managed to draw his pants up by the time he barrels inside.

"Espi…" His gaze flickers over in my direction. "Can we talk in fucking private?"

"No." Espi reenters the kitchen to grab his shirt from the floor and pulls it on over his head. "Anything you want to say to me, you can say here." There's no anger lacing his tone. That's because I'm carrying it all. His confessions linger on the air like wild electricity, sparking and alive.

"Fine, then." Arno slams the door behind him and stalks forward. He has his head lowered, but it's only when he comes closer that I recognize the motion as more contrite than aggressive. "About what happened back there… I'm sorry if things got a little—"

"It's okay," Espi says. He even looks like he means it. Twenty sordid minutes could purge him of his darkness and let him pretend again.

Am I jealous? Impressed? I'm too tired to tell, haunted by my own demons. Piotr's waiting. With Anna? Or chains…

"Did Jose get what he wanted?"

Arno's eyes flash a dangerous green. "Oh, hell yeah," he says. "More than enough. He, um, *persuaded* Mack a little bit more to make sure he wasn't fucking around. We think we know which warehouse will be hit next. The plan is we get there tonight. Ambush."

Espi sighs, his jaw clenched. "Do you think Dante—"

"Don't know," Arno says tightly, cutting him off. "If you need anything, see Francisco. He'll stay back at the—"

"I'm not letting you go there alone." It's final. Decided.

Arno doesn't bother to argue as Espisido slips his jacket on and pulls the zipper up to his chin. He looks back at me, his eyes questioning.

It takes everything I have in me to shake my head.

Arno observes the exchange with barely any reaction. "You ready?" he asks.

Espisido follows him.

Once they're what Arno must assume is out of my earshot, I hear him say, "We have got to work on your taste in women."

This is when I realize I'm not wearing my sweatpants. Or underwear. With I sigh, I sink to the floor and fish them from the tile. Then I creep into the bathroom and shower, doing my best to scrub myself clean, wiping away every last drop of him. I have to make myself presentable, after all. There isn't time to savor—but I do anyway.

It could be the last time I have the luxury. So I relish the feel of him inside me. The aching soreness that flares whenever I move. I let it wash the taint of my past away for a little while before I'm finally forced to shut the water off, face the world again, and redress in the same clothes. I blindly return to the kitchen and pull drawers open at random, searching. Hunting. It isn't until I'm standing on tiptoe and lowering a black case from the top of the fridge that I find two knives, thin and made of steel. They fit easily inside the pocket of a borrowed sweatshirt. I take a syringe too, filling it to the brim with liquid from a vial.

I blink a burning sting back. There isn't time for guilt.

I replace the case and then leave the house, locking the door behind me. It's a long, quiet walk to the hotel where Piotr is waiting. This time, I don't placate myself with fantasies of killing him. I just remember…everything. The pain, the beatings, the fear. Mainly the fear. The way he used to hold me, the words he would murmur into my skin. The way my heart used to crave his approval. Was that love?

If so, then I prefer hate. Caressing fingers and searing looks. Letting my body go wild. Not having a checklist of requirements to tick off with every encounter. *Smile. Simper. Wider. More. Let him touch you. Moan—but not too loudly.*

I let the darkness of those days sober me from the very last dose of my latest addiction. He leaves me for good the moment I enter the lobby of the hotel. Or does he? A man is lingering near the entrance, his head covered by a low hood. He's wearing jeans and a sweatshirt in a building that caters to men who lap at the Petrovs' wealth. Did Piotr change the uniform of his *soldat*?

I try to catch a glimpse of his face and flinch. Flashing blue —but the features are all wrong, what little I see of them. The body is too big. But those eyes…

I step closer, aiming for another look, but he turns and crosses over to the other part of the lobby. I dig my nails into my palms to keep myself from following. I'm stalling. The delay only buys me a precious few seconds of sanity before I take the elevator up. The door to the suite is unlocked once again, but this time, I find five guards lounging in the entryway.

One of them spots me and reaches for his gun. "Name?"

I don't bother to give him one. Rather by recognition or sheer confusion, he doesn't pull the trigger as I brush past. Piotr is waiting for me in his study, but tonight…he isn't alone.

My nostrils flare, catching a feminine scent that belongs only in my memories. Not here. Sweet like roses. Soft like the sunshine we used to play in as children. *Anna.* Her presence floods my body seconds before I register her standing there beside his desk.

Her slight frame is balancing upon an impossibly high pair of white heels. He dressed her head to toe in the color—a gown that swallows her slender body, formed of swaths of white chiffon and lace. The maid must have arranged her flaming hair into a single braid that drapes her shoulder.

But no amount of expensive silk or hairdressing could disguise what lurks behind those unique navy eyes. Nothing. Blank. Emptiness.

"Do you like your present, Ksei?" Piotr gestures from my sister to me. There's something in his other hand. Round. Metallic. He raises it when I don't answer and strikes a button on the front with his thumb.

A buzzing sound hums in my eardrums. Then Anna jerks back, her fingers twitching at her sides. There's something around her neck that I notice only now. It's tucked against the neckline of her dress. A thin strip of black leather, secured by a metal buckle. A collar.

"Say your name," Piotr commands.

"Anna," the girl says woodenly on cue.

God. It's exactly how I always imagined her sounding had she lived to be old enough. Soft. Delicate. Little Anna. Everything is the same but the pain.

"What the hell is this?"

"Tsk tsk," Piotr remarks, shaking his head. Seven years later and I still recognize the dangerous signs of his disappointment. So does Anna. She inhales sharply as he speaks again. "Your *full* name."

"Annastasia Olenova." She sounds so young. So terrified.

"What are you doing?" I don't know how I speak. Piotr's last assault was child's play. *This* is death. My heart stops beating. My lungs seize. Somehow, I'm still standing. Still able to listen.

I can't help but listen.

"Well." Piotr flicks the button on his tiny remote, ensuring I see each deliberate motion. "I will ask you again. Do you like your present, Ksei?"

"Y-yes." I spit the word out, unable to move. Unwilling to scream.

Anna stares beyond me. From her posture alone, I sense that the trigger to her pain is virtually in my hands.

With sickening dread, I realize just what game he's chosen to play.

"Say it again," he says sharply. "Like you mean it, Ksei."

"I like my—" A high-pitched wail pierces my words. "Stop!"

The girl's whimpers are abruptly cut off and the only noise to flood the room is that of my own erratic breathing. And my sobs. They rip from me, unable to be contained—breaking the one rule I always maintained in Piotr's presence. Never show weakness. Never let him see your pain.

I won't. I am.

My legs can't hold me. The stench of cigarette smoke fades, and my fingers flail, searching for something. Anything.

Cool fingers grab mine, yanking me upright before I can hit the floor. "Ksei…"

I look up.

His smile is beautifully restrained, even as his eyes glow with a predatory gleam. "My precious angel." His hand lands on my shoulder, the tips of his fingers lingering over my skin. It's like the world's purest cocaine laced with arsenic—the difference between his touch and Espisido's is night and death.

My skin crawls, goosebumps forming. My heartbeat quickens. I want to move. My body refuses; she'll suffer.

"Tell me—Are you pleased?" he asks. "Now, we can be together, always. A perfect family."

Family? Bile coats the back of my throat at the prospect. "I…"

Anna flinches, reacting to something beyond her collar. A noise? Then I hear it. Loud. Sporadic. Gunshots. There are too many of them to be just from Piotr's small group of *soldaty*. The floor vibrates with a million differing sensations. Footsteps. Thuds.

There's no time to think. I lunge, wrestling a smaller body to the floor as nearly a dozen figures burst into the office.

"Clear it out," one of the strangers commands. A man. His voice is deep, resonating down my spine. I can't see his face, but there is something familiar in his tall, imposing build.

Four of the men take off through the rest of the suite. I hear more gunshots. Shouts. Screams. My mind races as I try to picture a fitting scenario. It's an attack.

From whom?

Jose? They aren't wearing the beaten leather duds of the Cartel or the stained, brutal clothing of Arno's Gardai. Just black. Like shadows.

"Clear!" The shout comes from somewhere deeper in the suite, and the man I assume to be the leader heads for the main door.

The moment he pulls it open, another figure steps inside. Someone smaller than he is. Slender. Unlike the rest, she's not wearing bulky, nondescript clothing.

A dark sweater and jeans cling to her slender frame. Paired with black hair cut to her shoulders and wide, hazel eyes, she could be a student who's wandered into the wrong suite. But, even from the yards of space that separate us, I can sense the darkness in her gaze. It shines like a beacon. A demon knows another demon, after all.

"Did you find him?" she asks the taller man beside her.

As if on cue, two of the intruders approach her with none other than a smirking Piotr Petrov marshaled between them. He's bleeding from his lip but otherwise looks none the worse for wear, even as his captors shove him to his knees. Behind him, at least a dozen trembling women in maid uniforms are ushered through the foyer and out into the hall.

"Hello, Piotr." The woman in black smiles, but with her face half bathed in shadow, it resembles a snarl more. "You don't remember me," she says. An accent laces her words, though I can't place it exactly. "Maybe this will refresh your memory?" She takes a step closer and lifts the front of her sweater, heedless of the men, dead and living, who crowd the room.

She doesn't reveal anything more than her torso, but I suck in a breath when I see what mars the golden flesh.

"After all," she adds before lowering her shirt, "Vinny did get the idea from *you*."

My lower back throbs in sympathy, recognizing the ache of an owner's possession. That name she said... It rings a bell. Vinny. Vinny. Vincent.

"Stacatto's bitch," Piotr says in English. "I remember you. He used to pick out your toys himself."

The woman flinches. One of her hands flexes, and as if following some telepathic command, the man beside her places something in her grasp. Her fingers close over it securely, and seconds later, another feral smile shapes her mouth.

"I thought I would return the favor," she says, her soft voice adding an ominous edge to her words. "Vinny said that you always preferred to mark your women on the face to create the best possible effect. I have to admit. I've seen your work. It suits you well."

My throat feels raw with the memory. *Fight it back, Ksei.* Swallow it... I can't as my trembling fingers graze my forehead. A mark on the face was the equivalent of a death sentence in Piotr's world. It was the stamp of a discarded product. You were nothing.

"What do you want?" Piotr demands. Even with his men lying dead around him, he doesn't bat so much as an eyelash. He's thinking.

I know that look. It's as if the entire universe knows it too, taunting me with a low buzzing sound that hums through my skull.

"Wait," Anna hisses into my ear the moment I tense. Her tiny hands grasp my arms, drawing me tight to her side. "Wait..."

"I don't want anything from you," the woman declares. She approaches him slowly. Only when she's just beyond his reach does her hand lash out, catching his cheek with the end of her blade. Digging deep. Blood flies, painting those handsome, chiseled features in shades of red. "I just wanted you to know," she explains as his head jerks to the side with the force of the blow. She left him with a present he will always remember—a jagged edge to his infamous smile. "I just wanted you to see who pulled the trigger."

"Is that so?" Piotr laughs, spitting blood as he fights to stay upright. His voice is a snarl, but it's his unstable chuckle that rouses every flight instinct in my body.

The buzzing grows louder. Swallowing me. Smothering me.

"Wait!" Only Anna's weight is enough to pin me down.

"Don't worry," the woman says. "Your helicopter is still on its way, filled with your skilled guards." She pauses for a delicate laugh when he doesn't interject. "Your plan was to have them come in through the roof, yes? I've only changed their course of entry by a hair."

She smiles. Piotr doesn't.

She extends her free hand and the man beside her places something new onto it—a two-way radio like the kind used by a patrol officer on the beat.

She brings it to her mouth. Inhales. "Now."

Two things happen simultaneously. One, the distant buzzing grows into a deafening roar and streaks of colored light flood the room. Greens. Reds...

The massive bay window provides an impressive view of a helicopter headed straight for the building. Piotr's private escape route, the one he only used in the direst of circumstances. I can make out every nuance of the ebony shape before it suddenly rears up and...

CRASH! The entire building shakes. The lights flicker. A lion roars. A monster. The sound claws through my entire being as glass flies in every direction, and in the midst of the chaos, the strange men start to leave. They move quickly, unconcerned by the cacophony of sirens going off. Door alarms. Fire alarms. *Fire?*

The dark-haired woman stands tall amid the chaos, her eyes seeming to glow as the lights flicker and dim. "When you see Vinny in hell, tell him..." She draws her own weapon this time from the back pocket of her jeans. A gun. She aims it surely over Piotr's forehead. "Tell him that I understand now. I understand just what kept him going. What fueled him. What terrified him. It was never me."

She raises the gun...and, suddenly, Anna weighs nothing. I'm scrambling out from under her, crawling over bloodied bodies in my haste.

"No! W-wait."

She and Piotr both turn to look at me. Her face is emotionless, but my tormentor is smiling. Beaming. Even through the blood. Through the humiliation of being outsmarted. He's still won the only prize he seems to want. I can't bear to watch him be killed.

Not when I'm the one who should do it.

"P-please."

The woman just eyes me, her gaze a twisted reflection of everything I see in myself when I look in the mirror. That rage. That hate. The *pain.* God, the pain. It swirls through her irises. It consumes her. This Vinny may be dead, but he lives inside her, haunting her every waking moment.

She's still not free.

Without a word, she hands the gun to me, and I take it, my fingers shaking over the metallic surface.

"We need to go." The tall man returns to place his hand on the woman's shoulder.

She glances back at him and her face changes. It's that bitter salve I've learned to crave—hate. Light. Some of that darkness clears for a second. Maybe it's long enough.

"Okay." She turns back to me. "You have ten minutes."

Ten minutes. It's longer than any ounce of freedom Piotr has ever allowed me.

My thumb caresses the trigger of the gun. Bound as he is, Piotr doesn't have a chance in hell of overpowering me. Not with his kingdom turning to ashes around us. I can already feel the heat. Smell the smoke. Fire. Brimstone.

There are only a handful of unoccupied floors that separate this suite from the roof. At least, now, this dwelling will resemble what it has always been for me—hell.

"Put the gun down, Ksei," he tells me. "You don't want to hurt me...and even if you did...I will *own* you, my love, even from hell." He sounds tired as he says it. So sure. I can't hurt him. I can't even kill him.

I don't have to.

"Ksei…" His dangerous tone is back, my old lullaby.

"You won't own me ever again." I drop the pistol at my feet and meet his gaze fully for the first time in so long. I stare deep and see myself reflected back as the lights flicker on and off, off and on.

By the third flash, I almost see her again. Ksenia, before the brutality of his reign over my body. The girl I used to be. Maybe I will one day find the rest of her again. To give myself a head start, I draw the syringe from my pocket, freeing the needle.

"You won't own me or Anna," I tell Piotr Petrov as I plunge the tip into his neck before he can stand, flooding his veins with the narcotic. It won't slow him down for long. I know that, even as I turn on my heel and leave him there while the building pitches and sways around us. "Never again."

Howls echo around me, those of an angry wolf denied his prey.

He'll never stop.

I'll always have to run.

But he won't haunt me anymore. I won't carry him within my skin. I won't be like her…

A monstrous roar shatters my eardrums, and I flinch in recognition. Gunshot. Whirling around, I find Anna, clothed in white, holding a gun between both hands. Piotr's in front of her, still kneeling despite the hole blown clear through his head.

"Holy shit—"

"He didn't deserve it," she says, her voice high-pitched and broken. "He didn't deserve it."

My footsteps falter as I reach for the gun. Inches from touching her, I change my mind and grab her arm instead, pulling her into me. She drops the weapon on her own, and it falls without going off. I know at the back of my mind that there isn't time for this now. Still, I can't resist breathing her in, sensing her familiarity despite the stench of death and smoke.

"We need to go."

Together, we move, following an unseen path through smoke and flames. The intruders must have set new fires as they left, because there are too many. Everywhere. Screams fill the corridors. Shouts. There are more people in this building than just the scum the Petrovs command. Innocents. Bystanders.

All dying nonetheless.

"Move!"

I can't see. I can't breathe...

"This way! Move!"

My feet flex on command, one in front of the other as my hand flails for any surface it can use for leverage. Glass. The wall. Cold concrete.

It feels like an eternity before I blink and find myself exiting through a doorway. Sirens pierce the air amid a deafening array of shouts and screams. One single emotion overrides my shock, however.

Piotr is dead. I wait for the pain. The memories. Yet I feel nothing. Just the ache as my lungs fight to clear themselves of smoke and a painfully tight grip marshals me away from the building.

Anna must have made a habit out of escaping from danger in her time living with the Petrovs, because she moves assuredly through the chaos. Like a fallen angel almost, at home in this inferno of death and fear, faltering however as more first responders arrive on the scene.

"I know where we can go. Somewhere safe," I add as her eyes widen fearfully. I can't resist the impulse that makes me finger a red curl escaped from her braid. It's real. She's real. "I'm going to keep you safe."

CHAPTER TWENTY-EIGHT
ESPI

JOSE'S WAREHOUSE IS ON THE SOUTH SIDE, NEAR THE river. Arno doesn't take any chances, placing at least a dozen men around the perimeter while we wait in the shadows.

Three hours pass before he realizes it's a setup, when none of the Cartel show.

"Fucking Jose," he snarls before forming a fist and slamming it against the wall of the alley. The thud resonates like a gunshot, but if any men are lying in wait for an ambush, they seem to be deaf as well as invisible. "Where is that motherfucker?"

He doesn't have to wonder long. Sirens wail in the distance. Fire trucks. I cock my head, pinpointing the sound as coming from the west end of the city. Apparently, the party got started without us.

"Shit." Arno reaches into his pocket for a cell phone and snarls into the receiver the moment someone answers the other end. "You fucking son of a bitch—"

"Relax, *amigo,*" Jose says, his voice drifting from the speaker. "Our deal is still good. Your piece-of-shit bar will stand another day. I just needed you out of the way…"

Arno glances at me, his jaw clenched. "For what?"

"The fireworks," Jose replies. "Thanks for babysitting, but I'll let you in on the secret."

Arno hisses between clenched teeth. "Son of a bitch. You gave me the wrong spot."

"For insurance," Jose says. "I know you run with the Russians, but something tells me that you won't be too sad to learn that one of *their* strongholds was hit instead of mine."

"By who?" Arno demands. "You fucking owe me that much."

"Do I?" Jose chuckles. "Relax, *Papi.* I think you're well aware of who's behind this little bonfire. I'll give you a hint. He looks a bit like little Espisido. *Adiós.*"

"The fuck?" Arno tosses the phone against the pavement when Jose hangs up. "That goddamn son of a bitch—"

"The Russians," I echo. Namely the Petrovs. "I need to go."

"Espi? What the hell?"

I'm already halfway down an alley before Arno catches up.

"Slow the fuck down!" He tugs on my shoulder, stopping me in my tracks. "The first fucking thing we need to do is make sure that Dante…"

It's like flipping a switch. *Dante.* If Jose gave Arno the wrong location, then his "ambush" might be lying in wait somewhere else. If Dante really is behind all of this shit, then he'll be caught in the crossfire.

"I know where the Russians had their main headquarters," Arno says, jerking his chin toward that very direction, I assume. "A hotel downtown. We need to go."

I follow him without asking questions. We take one of his trucks while the others head back to the club in case Jose decides not to keep his promise.

I don't know what to feel as Arno cuts through alleys, running through several stoplights, in order to reach the part of town where the Petrovs reign with an iron fist.

In the span of just a few hours, someone set their kingdom on fire.

"Holy shit." Arno has to park at least ten blocks back from the building that I assume is the hotel. What used to be one, anyway. A plume of flames paints the sky orange, streaked with hints of red and splotches of yellow.

It's more than the typical blaze. It's a fucking calling card.

First, Moe's. Now, this. Someone's starting a goddamn war.

"You take the left," Arno tells me. "I'll take the right. Find out what you can. We meet up in the center."

There isn't much to find. The cops barricaded the area closest to the hotel, fishing out stragglers who manage to escape the flames. There aren't many.

Someone wanted revenge—that much is fucking clear. There are no signs of sabotage, and something tells me that any money, drugs, or other shit Piotr had tucked away inside the place has been lost to the blaze. This wasn't about dominating.

This was obliteration.

Who's next? The question crosses my mind just as I see him. A man lurks far back from the crowd, in an alley, his face partially covered by a hood and shadow. I can't make out any definitive features from this distance, but I know that it's him. The same way I know, deep down, he won't wait for me to catch up.

I'm already shoving my way through the crowd anyway. Past police. Past civilians choking on the smoke-laced air.

He sees me. I know he does. A flashing siren illuminates his face in red for a split second. I see his eyes.

"Dante!"

He turns, disappearing into the alley before I can bolt across the street. By the time I pass an overflowing dumpster, he's already gone.

I can't even muster up the energy to feel pissed or angry. I don't feel like hunting him down tonight, the way I have for months now, either.

I'm too damn tired.

I watch him go. I find Arno, and when he asks me what I found…

I tell him nothing.

———

Within minutes, Arno has the pub resembling Fort Knox. Men are patrolling every inch of the block, guns in hand. There isn't a fucking beer in sight.

"You know what this means," he tells me the moment I walk through the door. His jaw is clenched, his eyes searing; he's still sober. "You *know* what this means."

I don't say a damn thing. It's a packed house tonight, but one person is missing. One face. One Russian.

"I've got to go."

It feels like déjà vu when I race out onto the street and head for my place. Turns out, there's no point in running. The house is empty. She's not here.

I tear it the fuck apart anyway, ripping through the cheap, mismatched furniture. Throwing everything out of my damn closet. Flipping the mattress over. With every hole I make in the wall with my fist, I don't find her.

Or Dante.

Like always. Chasing after people is what I do best, after all.

I don't even have a goddamn cigarette to chase the self-pity away. I wind up staring at a pool of my own blood as it drips from my fingers instead, desperate for relief. My kit might hold the answer. Half a vial. A full hit. One push of the syringe and I wouldn't have to feel a damn thing anymore.

Maybe I'll do it. Maybe I could.

I already have the needle in my hand when I smell her. Smoke, blood, death, and fire. A perfect mixture of fucking yellow. She strides through the chaos of the kitchen, her gaze hunting, searching. It finds me, and the next minute, she's in my arms, holding me. Crushing me.

"Are you okay?"

I'm too fucking tired to play nice; I kiss her. Hard. Brutal. She can slap me if she wants to. Maybe I'll feel guilty tomorrow.

She kisses me back instead. Harder. More. I already have my hands down the front of her shirt when she pulls back.

"Wait—"

When I let her go, she's halfway across the room before I can grit out a half-assed apology.

A part of me has to laugh. Go fucking figure, I have to go and repel her too. "I'm sorry…"

Tears run down her face. I try to catch one with my finger, and it winds up dripping wet. Her pain fuels me like nothing else. Nicotine in the purest goddamn form.

"What's wrong?"

"I need to leave the city," she says in a rush. "My sister…
She's alive." Her eyes gleam gold at the thought, shining
with hope and pain and fear. "But I have to get her out
now. But…"

She digs her nails in so deep that she draws blood.

"I wanted to say goodbye first." Her voice cracks on that
one word. *Bye.*

Ironically, that's a word I'm not used to hearing. Few people
take the time to tell me they're leaving to my face—even
Dante couldn't do much. Maybe this icy burn in my chest is
gratitude. Relief. I got my wish at least. I don't have to chase
after her.

She'll cut out while I'm still high on her. It's more than lust.
Breathing her in feels like a necessary evil. The way I need a
cigarette. The way Arno needs liquor. The way I've
developed a certain fondness for the damn color yellow. I
need to be used.

And I can't leave. I have Arno to babysit. Dante to chase. I
have a life tied to this damn city. Good old Espi still has to
do his part and play his supporting role.

He can't leave. Not until the fat lady sings and the fun and
games are all over. It's his fucking fate. I've told myself that
for so long. But maybe I'm the only fucking one who ever
really believed it.

"Where?"

She shakes her head. "I don't know. We just have to go tonight."

It's like I'm in her head, seeing what she can't admit out loud. Her soul. My name is written on it in gold—her new addiction. Her way to cope. She smokes me up like heroin, and I take her in hits and lines like fucking cocaine.

But the high's gotta wear off sometime. I bail on him now, and Arno would hate me. Dante wouldn't give a fucking shit.

She leaves? I'll wind up like Parish. The way she would have even had she not been a casualty of her brother's war. A speck on the sidelines. A forgotten side note.

"I'm coming with you." I never knew that those four words could be so fucking hard to say.

And whether it's the dimming lightbulb in the ceiling that casts a golden glow over her skin or my own imagination, my entire world is yellow.

It's not darkness or light. It's something in between. And, for some reason, it's easier to stomach than anything else.

CHAPTER TWENTY-NINE
CHLOE

I NEVER THOUGHT DAWN COULD BE BEAUTIFUL. NOT after my family was torn apart. Not after mornings ceased to be a lazy affair that consisted of eating warm cereal on my father's lap while he smoked a pipe and read from the paper.

I never thought the sunrise could be so welcome. That a day would come when I craved the sight of it. When I hoped to see many, many more. If only they could all be like this— reeking of smoke, death, and...*freedom.*

It's been hours since we left the city and he still hasn't told me why he came. A part of me really doesn't want to know. Maybe Arno did something to piss him off. Maybe his choice has nothing at all to do with me.

I don't care. For the first time in my life, I feel content to be an addict with a limited supply of her chosen narcotic. I'll take him any way I can. Standing beside him, crammed within the bow of a tiny fishing boat, is enough. I don't even know where we're going—Ivan wouldn't say. But, somehow, just moving is enough.

Breathing him in is enough.

I look over at him, but his face reveals nothing. It's just a mask of exhaustion. Regardless, his fingers tighten over my own, and in the smoldering ruins of my soul, which Piotr left behind…

I feel the stirring of something that might be hope.

AFTERWORD

If you or anyone you know is or has suffered from sexual abuse, please get help via the National Sexual Assualt Hotline: https://www.rainn.org/about-national-sexual-assault-telephone-hotline

A WORD FROM THE AUTHOR

Hey there!

Thank you so much for reading! If you enjoyed the story, please leave a review and recommend the book to any friend you think would love this twisted world. You'd have my eternal gratitude. Even a short sentence goes a long way!

Then, come join the rest of us dark romance lovers in my Facebook Group where you can get snippets, sneak peeks of upcoming books and even help vote on aspects of future novels.

Come to the dark side:
https://www.facebook.com/groups/lanasbeautifulmonsters/

WANT MORE STUFF TO READ?
Join my newsletter and get a **free book**! Plus, you get to stay updated with any new releases, random giveaways and exclusive sneak peeks!
https://www.lanaskybooks.com/newsletter

Other Novels: https://lanaskybooks.com/

ABOUT THE AUTHOR

Lana Sky is a reclusive writer in the United States who spends most of her time daydreaming about complex male characters and parenting her Cockapoo Joey. She writes dark, twisted romance across several genres. Her titles include everything from mafia romance to vampires.

facebook.com/AuthorLanaSky

twitter.com/lanasky101

amazon.com/author/lanasky

pinterest.com/lanasky101

goodreads.com/lanasky

instagram.com/lanasky101

bookbub.com/authors/lana-sky